Destined for Power

Women of Power Series

Kathleen Brooks

An original work of Kathleen Brooks.

Cover art by Calista Taylor

http://www.coversbycali.com

Acknowledgments

I have been blessed with some wonderful friends through writing. I want to thank Robyn Peterman, Heather Sunseri, Jennifer Probst, Ruth Cardello, Kris Calvert, Melody Anne, Cali McCay, JS Scott, Liliana Hart, Jana Deleon, Donna McDonald, JM Madden, Solease Barner, Laurel McKinley, Sandra Marton, Chrisite Craig, Lynn Raye Harris, and so many more wonderful ladies who are truly women of power.

But, the most important women of power are my mother and daughter. My mother taught me to be fearless and that there was nothing I couldn't do if I just tried. And as my daughter types *The End* to each of my stories, I hope she's learning to follow her dreams. For nothing can stop women when they reach for their dreams.

Prologue

Windsor Academy, seventeen years ago . . .

Mallory let go with a mixture of sadness and excitement. Her dark green graduation cap flew into the warm summer air. One hundred thirty-three caps filled the blue sky as cheers erupted from the students of Windsor Academy's graduating class.

Her best friend, Elle Simpson, wrapped her arms around Mallory and laughed joyously. Mallory smiled at her, but sadness filled her, knowing they would be away from each other after this one last summer. She and Elle had been inseparable for years. Mallory was closer to the Simpson family than to her own. Case in point, Mr. and Mrs. Simpson and their other children, Reid, Bree, and Allegra, stood by clapping as the graduates celebrated. On the other hand, Mallory's family was absent. She didn't even remember where they were this weekend.

Her father, Senator George Westin, was too busy campaigning for reelection to the United States Senate and her mother, as always, was by her husband's side. It had been two months since she'd seen her parents. Luckily, she had the Simpsons, or she would have been alone in a huge mansion with no one except a cook, two housekeepers, and a driver. One thing Mallory had learned from an early age—money didn't buy happiness.

No, but money bought you four years at the best private high school in Atlanta and four more years at a premier Ivy League college in the Northeast where she was expected to set up a political marriage. Her father didn't even let her pick her own school. Her happiness and feelings certainly didn't matter to money. And since money and power were the only thing her parents cared about, her happiness didn't matter to them either.

Mallory held her hands in the air as her cap came back down to earth. She caught the fabric-covered cardboard and brought it to her chest. Two more months of freedom, and it was time to stop living according to her parents' expectations. She'd rebelled some in high school, but there was no one around to notice. Now she was eighteen. Now she had access to a small portion of the trust fund set up by her grandmother. Now she could rebel enough that her parents in Washington, D.C., would notice.

Mallory felt for the pearls at her throat. The family attorney brought them by this morning with a note from her grandmother who had passed away more than six years ago. It was her note that was sparking the rebellion. Her grandmother expressed her love and hope that Mallory would find happiness in her life—no matter the cost.

Mallory looked over to where Elle was hugging her mother. Mallory's electric blue eyes connected with Reid's, and she felt a blush creep up over her face. It didn't feel right to have a crush on Elle's older brother, but she was helpless to stop it. They had been flirting since their first meeting. She knew he didn't take her seriously, but maybe now he would. After all, she was no longer a high school student. And legally, she was now an adult. It was time he started seeing her like one.

Reid was two years older than Mallory, was in college, and was sinfully handsome in a bad-boy way her parents would never approve of. He'd grown up poor, from the wrong side of the tracks, literally and figuratively, and had zero political ambition. What Reid did have were muscles in places the men she danced with at her coming-out party didn't even know existed. His chestnut hair was trimmed short along the sides of his head while the top was slightly longer with an I-don't-care mess to it. His smile made her heart speed up and had an edge to it that led her to believe he was more than just a sexy face. His face was covered in a sexy scruff that had her imagining it scraping against her delicate skin in a moment of passion, and his forest green eyes pierced her heart and soul. It was love.

Why love and not just lust? There was definitely lust involved, but it was the love that held her hostage. Love for the way he watched out for her and his sisters, the way he and his father seemed like best friends with a healthy dose of mutual respect, the way he hugged his mother, and the way he helped others who were not strong enough to help themselves. He stood up for kids who were bullied and asked the wallflowers to dance at prom. That's why she loved him.

"Come on, Mallory," Elle called as she held out her hand.

Mallory smiled and hurried to put her arm around her best friend. Would Elle care if she liked Reid? Mallory cringed a bit. *Like* wasn't the right word. She'd fallen for him with the wild abandon of young love. For years, she'd sat next to him at the dinner table, hoping he would shift so his leg would touch hers. For years, she'd wished upon every fallen star that Reid would realize she was a woman. For years, she'd desired . . .

"Mom has made all of our favorites for dinner," Elle said excitedly as she put her arm around Mallory's waist.

"Even the chocolate torte?" Mallory asked.

"Especially the chocolate torte." Reid winked. "We all know your secret desire . . ." Mallory felt her face heat up again. How did he know what she'd just been thinking? "… for chocolate."

"Oh, yes, chocolate." Mallory stumbled over her feet and Reid's hand shot out to take hold of her elbow. She looked up into his eyes and saw for the first time they were lingering on her lips and then moving downward.

"I can't believe you're throwing a graduation party for the whole class." Bree's comment interrupted Reid's perusal down her body. "I wish I could go."

Margaret, Elle's mother, shook her head. "Two years isn't that long to wait for your own graduation party. But, Mallory, are you sure you should be doing this? Did you ask your parents?"

Mallory shrugged. "As if I could get hold of them to ask. Besides, I'm having it out at the farm. We won't bother anyone out there."

"As long as you promise me you'll be safe, be aware, and call me if you need anything. I expect a phone call at midnight to check in. Got it?" Margaret stared at Mallory and Elle.

"Yes, ma'am," they both said before sharing a sly grin with each other.

Music poured from the outdoor speakers. The paddock closest to the large old plantation house was filled with people dancing. Some were holding beers, some were holding each other, but most were just letting loose after four years of working hard. Elle had her head thrown back, her red hair whipping to the music as she danced with a group of their friends. Mallory sat on the flagstone patio watching them as thoughts held her in place. She was serious as she contemplated her already-planned-out future.

Rebellion surged through her as she took a drink of cranberry juice and vodka she had just gotten from the locked house. She was smart. She controlled every aspect of this party. There were bathrooms in the barns. The horses were at the other end of the property. The house was off limits. There was food and plenty of water in the outdoor kitchen. The gates to the farm were locked. Keys to all the cars were in a bowl locked inside the house. It seemed to be working. Everyone was happy. Everyone except her. Even when she wanted to rebel, she couldn't. She was too practical, too logical, too reasonable, to completely let loose.

"What are you doing sitting here? Shouldn't you be dancing?" A deep voice behind her caused her to jump.

"Reid! What are you doing here?"

"I promised Mom I would make sure everything was going well. I just called to let her know it was well-in-hand." Reid took a seat next to her on the stone steps and reached for her cup before taking a tentative sip. "Vodka?"

Mallory nodded. She didn't know what to say. The whole side of his body was pressed up against hers. She felt her breathing hitch and a warmth pool in a very delicate place her nanny had describe as a "woman's pearl" Reid took a generous drink and then handed the cup back to her. When she took it, their fingers touched, and Mallory's eyes shot to his.

"Would you like a drink of your own?" Mallory asked.

"Sure. Let's go inside." Reid stood up and held out his hand. She placed hers in his, and he pulled her up.

Mallory closed her eyes as she stopped in front of the door and dug the key from the pocket of her jean miniskirt. Reid was not acting brotherly, right? Was this her chance? What happened if it didn't work out? Oh, nonsense, it would work out. They were so perfect together. She loved him and knew everything about him—his good points and his bad ones. They didn't matter. She loved them both, the good and the bad. He was her dream come true, and now he was paying attention to her. Mallory was breathless as she unlocked the door and walked inside. She heard the lock click behind her, and then he was there.

Reid's firm hands grasped her shoulders from behind. His lips nuzzled her neck as he pulled her against him. "This is crazy. I shouldn't be doing this. You're my sister's best friend."

"I know, but I want it too," she whispered as her heart pounded.

"Do you know how long I've wanted this? How hard it has been sitting next to you every night for dinner? And dear God, woman, were you trying to kill me when you slept over? Those tiny shorts . . ." Reid kissed her neck and Mallory let her head fall back against his shoulder.

"I wanted you to notice me. I thought you only saw me as a little kid."

"I never saw you as a little kid. I always saw you as a strong woman who was making the best of a bad situation. I just had to wait. Regardless of how I felt, I knew I had to wait for you to grow up. But now, I'm tired of waiting."

Mallory turned around in his arms and looked up at him. He brushed a lock of her blond hair from her face and cupped her cheek. "You're so beautiful," she heard him whisper before his head came toward hers. Their lips touched gently as they took their time getting used to the feel of each other. Reid waited patiently as Mallory brought her hands to his chest and leaned in closer.

She felt dizzy as she put her arms around Reid's neck and pressed her body against his. She opened her mouth to him, and soon the kiss turned to something more than gentle. It was filled with desperate longing.

Someone knocked on the door, and Mallory jumped back. Her fingers touched her lips as she looked dazedly at Reid. Had this really just happened? The knock sounded again. Reid turned and opened the door.

"Hey, where's the ice?" a guy from her class asked.

"Over by the refrigerator. It's the black thing. It's full of ice," Mallory muttered. Her classmate gave a smile and headed for the outdoor kitchen.

"Was that . . .?" Mallory stuttered.

"Completely amazing? Yes, it was. Mallory, what are we going to do?" Reid asked as he ran his hand over his head.

"I don't know. I'm only here for two more months. Oh, Reid, we could have been together this whole time if only one of us had said something."

Reid took Mallory in his arms and squeezed her tight. "It wouldn't have worked. It would have been unfair while you were still in high school and I was away. It would be selfish to make you wait. I needed you to experience life, dating, and not jeopardize your friendship with my sister. Elle, Mom . . . there wouldn't have been any sleepovers. And Elle would be wondering if you were there for her or me. Let's not focus on the past, but on the now."

"Should we tell Elle? Wait, what would we even tell her?" Mallory scrunched her nose as she thought. What were they exactly?

Reid let out a long breath. "I don't know what we are. But, I think it's time to see what's between us now that we're both adults."

"Well, I think we got kissing covered," Mallory teased.

"Let's see how we do with dancing." Reid shot her a sly smile and took her hand in his. "And it will give us a chance to gauge Elle's reaction and see how secretive we have to be."

Mallory let him lead her to the dance floor where she nervously waited to be called out by her best friend. Elle noticed them immediately. Her eyes narrowed, and she gave them a hesitant wave as she danced. Mallory didn't care about Elle's response as Reid pulled her closer. She swung her hips seductively to the music and felt Reid's chest vibrate with a groan. He slid his fingers up under the loose white peasant top she wore to caress her bare back.

Mallory gasped and looked around, but no one was paying attention. They were all celebrating and it was so dark it would be hard for others to see much detail.

"God, Mallory. We're like lightning together. It's a high I might become addicted to," Reid said low enough for only her to hear. He ground his hips against hers and she lost her ability to think. Her body felt on fire.

"Mallory! Come dance with us. You don't want to be stuck with my brother all night," Elle shouted as if the thought were revolting.

Reid's hand slid out from under her shirt, and he let her go after one last suggestive push of his hips. "Tonight's your night. Enjoy it. We have all summer. I'll sneak out of the house tomorrow. How about dinner and a movie?"

"Sure. Pick me up at eight." Mallory smiled at him. He stepped back, and she went to dance with her friends.

Mallory watched until he disappeared into the night. Tonight her dreams had finally come true.

Mallory slammed the door shut without breaking Reid's kiss. Her summer was almost over, and tonight had been magical. Reid had told her he loved her as they shared a horseback ride at her farm. Passion overtook them on the hot summer night.

"I think it's time," Mallory had said breathlessly as she and Reid lay in the grass with the horses eating nearby. The sound of the bubbling brook filled the brief silence after her pronouncement.

"Are you sure?"

"I love you, Reid. I have for so long. I want nothing more than you to be my first and only."

Reid had leapt up and quickly pulled on his shirt. "The first time we make love won't be on the hard ground. Come on, let's get home."

They had frantically raced across the fields together. Mallory had never been as happy as she had been this summer. She and Elle spent the afternoons together, but her nights belonged to Reid. They had talked, gone on dates, and of course made out at every possible moment. When she told him she was a virgin, he'd never pushed the issue. He had told her she was the only one who could decide when and to whom to give that gift. And tonight, she had decided.

The second the front door to the plantation slammed shut, Reid pulled her tight against him. He slid his arm down behind her knees and swept her up. Mallory wrapped her arms around his neck as he carried her up the stairs. Using his foot, he shut the bedroom door and walked across the room, looking down at her with love in his eyes. She knew she had made the right decision. They were destined for each other.

Reid gently set her down in the middle of her antique four-poster bed. Slowly he stripped off his clothes, rolled on a condom, and crawled into bed. He lay next to her as his fingers teased her buttons free. He gently pulled the clothes from her body, and Mallory could only moan as his fingers did oh so much to her.

"I love you now and forever," Reid pledged as he kissed her.

Her body heated, and when he thrust inside, the pain was so brief she hardly noticed. Instead she breathed him in. The sounds, the scents, and the love engulfed them. She lost herself in the new feel and soon the grips of an orgasm had her crying out.

She looked up at Reid as she breathed heavily. He had his forearms braced on each side of her head and slowly bent his head to kiss her. She felt his movements grow erratic before he ripped his lips from hers and tossed his head back.

"Mallory!" he rumbled as he came.

He blinked as if he were coming back down to earth and covered her face with kisses. "Come to Europe with me."

"What?" Mallory asked with a giggle.

"I'm in a study-abroad program. I found out today I was accepted. I leave in one week for Switzerland. Come with me. With your connections, you could easily get into the same school. We could be together in Europe for a whole year." Reid pushed her hair back from her face and kissed the tip of her nose.

"I'm sorry, young man, but my daughter isn't going anywhere with you."

Mallory's head shot up, almost hitting Reid. She felt all the blood drain from her face. "Daddy!"

"Just what in the hell do you think you are doing?" her father hissed. "Do you have any idea how badly you've messed up? Now get up and put yourself together. I have Ambrose downstairs waiting to meet you, and you're up here playing the common strumpet for this . . . this nobody!"

Mallory felt her mouth open to defend them, but she couldn't find any words. Anger and humiliation rendered her mute. Reid stood and didn't bother to hide himself. Instead, he made sure Mallory was protected. While her father was in good shape for a man his age, he was no match for Reid. Her father simply narrowed his eyes and put his hands in the pockets of his expensive three-piece suit.

"You think you can intimidate me, young man? I run this whole damn country. Some hooligan like you isn't going to cause me to blink an eye. Get dressed and get the hell out of here. And use the back door. That's the only door you're good enough for. As for you, young lady . . ."

"As for her, she's coming with me. We're going to go to Switzerland, and there's nothing you can do about it."

Her father laughed so coldly it gave Mallory chills. "Downstairs there is a young man from an impeccable family waiting to meet Mallory. He is wealthy, went to the best university, and has connections with more than the local jail, unlike you. They will date while she is at college, during which time he will work for me. Upon graduation, he will ask her to marry him. She will say yes and will become the First Lady of this great country by the time she's thirty-five. Now, tell me, what can you offer her?"

"Love. That's more than you've ever offered her." Reid turned and looked at her. He held out his hand. "Take my hand, Mallory. We can be married in Europe. You'll have a family who loves you and a husband who will work every day of his life to deserve you and to give you everything you've ever dreamed of."

Mallory stared at Reid's hand. The deep love he had for her shone brightly in his eyes. But then she looked at her father. His face was calm, only the lines around his mouth showing his displeasure.

"Mallory, you will get dressed right this instant. I'll forget this ever happened. And so will you. All Mr. Simpson here will give you is pain. Do you really think he'll be able to keep you in the lifestyle you are accustomed to? Do you think he'll manage to make anything of his life? He's just like his old man—a dreamer with no sense of reality."

Reid spun on her father. "How dare you! My father is the best man I know. If I'm half the man he is, then I'll be proud of my accomplishments. He's certainly not a silver-spooned bastard who thinks we should all kneel before his greatness. But he has dragged himself out of a tough life with the love and support of his family—something you know nothing about. Mallory, come on, we're leaving."

Mallory swallowed and wrapped the sheet around her. She would have her trust fund when she was thirty-five. She didn't need all the things she had grown accustomed to. All she needed was Reid. She stood up, and Reid shot her father a victorious smile. Her father stepped into the room and blocked her from reaching Reid. She had never confronted her father before. She had never needed to because he was never around. But she loved Reid. She'd die inside without him.

Her father bent his head and whispered into her ear, "If you leave, I will destroy him. He will be kicked out of college, and his father will be audited by the IRS and the SEC for starters. I'll have their mortgages and loans called in and his sisters blacklisted from every college in this country. I'll bring down the full power of every committee I'm on to send that family not only back across the railroad tracks to where they belong, but to jail as well. Do you understand me?"

Mallory swayed on her feet and felt a weight on her chest pressing until her heart broke. She gave a slight nod of her head before her eyes filled with tears.

"I'm sorry, Reid. I can't go with you. My duty is to my family."

Reid paused as he buttoned his jeans. "Mallory, you don't mean that. We love each other. We don't need anything else. I promise you, I will love you and take care of you. I'll make you happy," he pleaded to her.

Mallory died in that moment. It was as if her soul had left her body and was looking at this scene from above. She was numb, empty. "I'm sorry, Reid. I'm so sorry. I need you to leave."

"And never come back," her father whispered. "If he ever comes back into your life, I will annihilate him and his entire family. Do you understand me, Mallory? End this now."

"What is he saying to you?" Reid asked. "It doesn't matter. He's just manipulating you. Mallory, what can he do if we leave together? He'll cut you off. Fine. I can take care of you. Let me love you. Let me cherish you. I want to spend the rest of my life with you. Mallory, come with me now, please," Reid begged.

"I'm sorry, Reid. My father is right. It would never work with an upstart like you. You'll never amount to anything. This was just a fling to cross off my list. Every girl loves the bad boy, right? But, she doesn't marry him."

Mallory didn't move as she watched Reid's heart breaking. Her face was blank even though she wanted to rush to him, to tell him she was doing this to protect him. She wanted to beg him to wait for her—wait until she was thirty-five and came into possession of all the land and money her grandmother left her. Even if her father did what he threatened, she could protect his whole family with her inheritance. There was enough in her trust for all of them to live with her. However, thirty-five was a lifetime away.

"Do you mean that?" Reid asked, his voice suddenly so very small.

"Yes. I mean it. It was fun while it lasted, but you and I both know I was destined for things larger than being your wife. You've known the plans for me, and you know they can't include you."

Mallory implored him with her eyes to see the hidden meaning in her words, but Reid suddenly couldn't look at her. He slid his T-shirt on over his head and walked out of the room. He didn't look back.

"Reid," Mallory gasped as she fell to the floor at her father's feet. She couldn't breathe. She tried to gulp in the air as her world spun out of control. The sharp crack of her father's hand against her face made her blink the world back into focus—her father's angry face front and center.

"Stop being so dramatic. Get dressed and do your job. I'll meet you downstairs."

"I hate you," she stated with no feeling. Her emotions were gone. Her heart was frozen and her body numb.

"You'll see this is for the best. That boy will never amount to a hill of beans."

"And if he does, I'll love every minute of it. But I'll never love you. And I'll never marry some preppy mama's boy just because you want me to. No, I gave you this win to protect the Simpsons, but I'll never do anything for you again."

Chapter One

Keeneston, Kentucky, Current Day . . .

Mallory Westin, president of Westin Security, stepped from the private jet that had flown to Atlanta to pick her up. With every step she took, she fell deeper into the past she had tried to forget. The solitary figure in black who stood in the night waiting for her was the man who had made her who she was today. He had picked her up, dusted her off, and given her a way to forget Reid and her father.

He didn't move as she walked toward him. His slightly tanned Middle Eastern skin and black hair with a sprinkling of gray blended into his black suit as he stood in the shadows waiting. He didn't smile, but one of the world's most dangerous men didn't need to.

"Twice in one year," Mallory quipped. She'd seen him the previous summer while on a job in Hung Island, Georgia, eight years after they had last seen each other.

He simply raised an eyebrow in response.

"You know how to sweep a girl off her feet with your pretty words. Now, why did you summon me to Kentucky?" Mallory asked.

"I have come across some information I thought you would want."

"I gave up the cloak-and-dagger world a long time ago, Ahmed."

Ahmed Mueez didn't bat an eye. He knew she would give in. No one said no to the Prince of Rahmi's head of security and lived to tell about it. It didn't matter that he was retired, married, and father to a young girl now. From what she had heard, his wife was just as much a badass as he was. She felt sorry for the men who would come calling on his daughter as she grew up. Ahmed was beyond good-looking. He was "blessed by the devil," as her grandmother used to say. He was dark, mysterious, and sexy as hell. The price you would pay for a night with someone like him was more than her good Southern delicacies could bear to think of.

Mallory let out an exaggerated sigh. "Fine. Tell me more."

"Nabi, the man who replaced me as head of security, is an expert digger. He came across some information that affects you directly. There is a world summit in Europe tomorrow. The who's who of the international political and charitable scene will be there. It's the Prince of Stromia's pet project and whatever he wants, he gets. It's a summit on renewable energy followed by a huge charity gala for saving endangered species that night."

"It's been a decade since I've been in Stromia. The Playboy Prince was what, twenty-seven then? I've read he hasn't changed at all. But he gets lots of action by playing the charity card."

"So, you've been keeping up with the world news, have you? I thought you said you were out of the business." She heard a hint of amusement in her former mentor's voice.

"Just staying current in politics."

"Good. You'll need it. Mallory Westin, international

party girl, needs to reappear. I need you to get information on Prince Liam and everyone he deals with."

Mallory shook her head. "I left that life behind me."

"I'm not the only one asking. President Nelson is requesting this as a personal favor."

"The election is just a couple months away, and then she won't be president anymore. Why does it matter to her?"

"Because she doesn't want an assassination to ruin her legacy," Ahmed stated.

"Whose assassination?"

"We don't know. One of the presidential candidates."

"My father is running for president with Ambrose Childs as his VP. Is he in danger?" Mallory asked. Her body was frozen in place. She didn't want to care. But no matter how much she hated him, he was still her father.

"We don't know. It could be one of them, or it could be someone from Easton Graham's campaign. The governor and Senator Malcolm Orson are neck and neck in the polls with your father and Ambrose."

Mallory blinked. Her mind was running a mile a minute. "So, either my father and Ambrose are in danger of being killed, or someone was hired to kill Easton and maybe Orson as well?"

Ahmed nodded. "The information Nabi found points to this summit as the payoff to set the wheels in motion for the assassination."

"How does this affect Rahmi and bring you into it?"

"I'm not officially in it. President Nelson is going off the books with this. She knows Rahmi is of the same mindset as she is in their dealings with Stromia. To say Liam and King Dirar are enemies is an understatement. As you know, Liam is corrupt, reckless, and only concerned about furthering his own personal agenda. King Dirar has refused to meet with him and called him out at the United Nations for his misuse of power. It would be in Rahmi's national interest to see The Playboy Prince discredited and possibly prevented from taking the throne with proof of his illegal activities. His first cousin is a good man who is acknowledged as a better option for Stromia both nationally and internationally."

"You want a revolution?"

"Revolution, no. Diplomatic change of leadership, yes. Both President Nelson and King Dirar will support it. Handing off payment is scheduled during this summit. You need to be there in your old role. Liam will be happy to see you again."

Mallory took a deep breath. "Where is this summit?"

"At the Luxus in Stromia," Ahmed said before crossing his arms and waiting.

Mallory hesitated. "Reid's luxury hotel and casino?"

"Can you handle that?"

"Of course I can. The opening for his resort in Atlanta is next week. A charity event is planned to launch the official opening. I'm sure he'll be in Georgia prepping for it."

Mallory tried to calm herself as Ahmed reached into the nearby car and produced a thick folder. He handed it to her, and the familiar feeling of being on the job came rushing back. She flipped through the information and closed the file.

"Rekindle my fake romance with Liam and stop the assassination. It's nice to feel wanted again. Will I have backup?"

"Limited. The CIA director is filled in. Of course, he didn't want to reactivate you, but President Nelson didn't give him much choice. Bowie will be your handler."

Mallory rolled her eyes. "Ugh. Couldn't the CIA director give me someone who wasn't such a flirt?"

Ahmed shrugged. "It'll work for your cover. Heiress gone wild has worked before; it'll work again."

"No one will buy that. I'm thirty-four, for crying out loud. How about husband-hunting heiress?"

"That could work. Liam is a catch, and so is Bowie for that matter. He's known as a bad boy on the party scene so he would naturally be drawn to you. Now come up with the background on what you've been doing for the last eight years, and let me know." Ahmed handed her a cell phone. "It's encrypted. It has my number and Bowie's."

"Is that it?" Mallory asked.

"I've trained you well, Mallory. You'll be fine. If you feel you are in danger, I want you out. I don't give a damn about the CIA or the president. I want you out. Just walk away." Ahmed held out a small briefcase. "Weapons, emergency cash, and identities are inside."

"Let's hope espionage is like riding a bike," Mallory said sarcastically as she took the briefcase.

Chapter Two

Mallory closed the file and looked out the window of the private plane the CIA had provided. Designer luggage and a wardrobe that could only be described as nightclub chic were waiting in the cabin. She planned to go on a very public shopping spree to find some clothes better suited to her instead of a twenty-year-old.

She closed her eyes as the past came flooding back—the tears, the pain, and the complete vulnerability of a teenager with a broken heart. She remembered the first time she had been approached by the government. She had just turned nineteen and was partying her way through Europe on summer vacation. She was dancing with royals, flirting with billionaires, and floating through life. She did anything that might piss her father off and keep her memories of Reid buried.

When she had started her sophomore year at college, she had walked into her apartment after classes and found Bowie sitting in her living room. He was edible. Twenty-four years old with sexy brown eyes, dark blond hair, and the body of a pro athlete.

"Can I help you?" Mallory had asked with all the haughtiness that ran through her blood.

"You sure can, babe. Uncle Sam wants you. And after

having a look at you, I do too."

"And just who are you?"

"That's need-to-know and you don't need to know . . . yet." Bowie winked.

Mallory's face had tightened as she ground her teeth. "If my father sent you, you can tell him to fu—"

Bowie had laughed, interrupting her. "I'm not here for your father, but because of your father. The director of the CIA wants a meeting. Come with me."

"Screw you."

"I'd love to, but the CIA frowns on sex between coworkers."

"We're not coworkers," Mallory had protested as Bowie grabbed her arm and led her out of the apartment. A dark SUV was waiting in the alley behind her building. Bowie had opened the door, shoved her in, and then settled himself on the seat next to her.

"Miss Westin, I'm Director Grayson. Your country needs your help," the serious looking man in the front seat said as he turned to stare at her.

Mallory had rolled her eyes. "Don't give me that crap. I've sacrificed enough for my country at the hands of my father. I'm sure you know him."

"I do. But he's not to know of our little arrangement. In fact, no one is to know about our arrangement except the president and Mr. Bowie here."

"Okay, you have my attention. What do you want?" Mallory had asked.

"I want you to transfer to a college in Great Britain. You'll be with the old money of Europe—much older than yours. You should like it; being away from your father should be a plus. You'll study political science to please your father. That's how it will allow the president to make it happen. He will announce, along with the British prime minister, there will be an exchange program of sorts. You to Oxford and the prime minister's son to Yale to study each other's political culture."

"I'm sure it has nothing to do with the fact the prime minister's son has a drug problem he wants to keep out of the newspapers this close to elections."

The director had just smiled. "Smart and pretty. You'll be our best asset. We want you to continue to party. Gather information on all things political that could be used for leverage."

"Blackmail, you mean."

"For power. Everything always comes down to power. The one with the most knowledge holds the most power as long as they are prepared to use it. The president is prepared to use it if it will bring more peace to the world."

"Bullshit. He'll use it to get his way, just like every other person in Washington. You included." Mallory had been disgusted.

"As if you don't hold and wield power, Miss Westin. You hide your brains and only show them to squash a man who dares to compete with you. You flaunt yourself and your family's name all over the world to hurt your father—to take his power. You're destined for great things with cunning like that."

"It's not cunning. It's revenge."

"Whatever makes you feel better, Miss Westin. I'm offering you the ultimate payback. Being the bad girl to upset your father while in reality doing a duty to your government. Not too many people get a free pass from us. You do. We will bail you out of jail, buy your clothes, get you invitations to every concert or party you want to attend. All you have to do is target the people we tell you to and feed us information. Do we have a deal?"

"I don't have to hurt anyone, do I?"

"Only your father with every article in the gossip columns."

Mallory had held out her hand. "Deal."

Mallory had gone to parties her whole sophomore year and had never gotten an assignment. She had fed all the gossip back to the director and heard nothing in return except to keep at it. Then one morning Bowie had dropped off a packet at her apartment. She was to target a prince of some small country in order to find out what his American interests were. If favorable, the US would move forward with a trade treaty between the two countries.

Mallory had devoured the package. The prince was handsome and a little older than her twenty years . . . okay, a lot older. He was in his late thirties. It didn't bother her, though. He was too good-looking for her to care. His wife was not with him, so that made it easier. It was amazing what men of power did when their wives weren't around. Plus it looked like he was a nice man. Something most of the people she was "friends" with couldn't claim. They were to meet that night in London.

She didn't even bother going to her classes that day. She was a third-year student and a darling of the school. She could get away with it. Instead she found the perfect dress. It was sexy without being revealing, something she was sure the prince would appreciate. She styled her long blond hair into perfect waves and applied natural makeup. She topped off the look with the pearls her grandmother had left her. She had managed to age herself several years. She was the walking definition of sexy sophistication.

Mallory had arrived at the party in a limousine. She had

posed for pictures and passed on all the drinks. She circled the room, pretending it was one of the many political fund-raisers she'd had to go to when she was young. She fell into the role so easily it scared her. She batted her eyes as the old men leered, and she chuckled at their stupid jokes.

The room started buzzing as the prince arrived. She was standing with an old man whose company owned oil refineries. When he cursed, she blushed innocently and lowered her lashes demurely.

"Sorry, my gem," he said in English heavy with his Russian accent. "I can't stand that family. Our countries are rivals. But, they will get what they deserve tonight. Just as I will." He had looked her over, and Mallory had felt her skin crawl. His hand brushed against her breast as he reached for another drink.

Mallory had simpered, batted her lashes, and then excused herself as quickly as she could by claiming to see an old family friend. She had hurried to the bathroom to hide when she collided with a man in a dark suit. She guessed he was in his early thirties. He was built like a man who worshiped the weight room. His shoulders were so broad, it was hard to see around them. She bounced off a chest made of warm steel.

"Oh! I'm so sorry. I was, um, in a hurry and not watching where I was going," she had said with a quick look behind her to make sure the Russian wasn't following her.

The man followed her eyes and gave a quick nod of understanding. "Let me be of assistance then." He had held out his arm for her to take. "Would you care to dance?"

"I'd love to." Mallory had smiled. She felt her mask of polite stupidity fall back into place. "I'm Mallory Westin from America."

"Ahmed of Rahmi."

"I've never been to Rahmi. What's it like?"

Mallory had thanked her lucky stars she had found someone from the small country she was supposed to gather information on. She asked questions as they danced. He wasn't the prince, but he knew his country's political tendencies. He answered them freely, and she found herself suddenly feeling bad for gaining his trust. This whole conversation would be relayed to Bowie for them to pick apart.

"One of your princes is moving to Kentucky? We'll practically be neighbors." Mallory had giggled inanely. When she looked up, she saw the Russian look at his watch.

"Yes, Rahmi is looking forward to its treaty with America. Prince Mohtadi, the man over there with the Princess of Denmark, is the one moving. His brother Dirar, the man standing by the podium, is the heir to Rahmi. He and his father, the king, are both supporters of the treaty."

Mallory stared at her target. She was supposed to get close to Prince Dirar, but Ahmed was giving her plenty of information.

"Do you know Prince Dirar? I'd love to meet him."

"I am sure he would be charmed. But, the prince does not meet with spies."

Mallory faltered but Ahmed covered for her as he twirled her around the floor.

"Spy?" she had giggled.

"No need to worry, Miss Westin. You are serving a great purpose tonight. I am being truthful in Rahmi's desire to move forward with the treaty, and you have succeeded in your first mission. It is in Rahmi's best interest for this treaty to go through. By conveying our previous conversation to the CIA, it will benefit us all. Now my duty is done. I bid you goodbye and a word of advice, Miss Westin. Get out of the spy game. You are not good at it."

Mallory had stood sputtering, but Ahmed had just kissed her hand and strode from the floor. She watched as he leaned in and spoke to Prince Dirar who in turn looked up at her and gave her a barely perceivable nod of the head. No, she couldn't fail like this. She had to make sure they wouldn't say anything. If she lost her ability to be an asset for the CIA, she would have to go back home. That was the last thing she wanted to do.

Ahmed and the two princes of Rahmi disappeared behind a door. She pushed her way through the crowd in time to see another man slip through the same door. Keeping her eyes on the door, she ignored the call to listen to the speech. She ignored the surge of people crowding forward to listen and continued to maneuver her way to the door.

She had run down the hall as she heard clapping, signaling that the speech was over. Her heels sank into the carpet as she picked up her floor-length gown and ran faster through the empty hallway. Music started again, and she could only hear faint strains of the waltz when she pushed open a door to a storage area. She had jumped and covered her mouth with her hand when she saw the man who had entered the door before her, screwing a silencer onto the end of a pistol. He stood across the room in an open window overlooking the alley behind the building. She looked out the open window and saw her target walking toward a limo. The man had aimed his weapon, and Mallory jumped into action without thought.

She had grabbed a stone bust of the Queen of England sitting on a pedestal and crept forward. "Ahmed!" she had shouted as she threw the bust at the armed man. The bust had sailed through the air and landed at the feet of the man with the gun. Tires squealed outside and the man cursed. Oh Lord, she'd failed. The statue she intended to knock the guy out with sat upside down on the floor staring at her. The gunman had swung and fired at her. Pain tore through her shoulder as the impact sent her tumbling to the ground. Her head bounced off the carpet, and she wondered if her last vision before dying would be of the little smirk on the queen's bust.

Mallory had heard a snap, and then Ahmed was standing over her. "You are safe. That was a very foolish thing to do, Miss Westin. But I thank you for saving my princes."

"Am I dying?"

"No, my dear." He had bent over and scooped her effortlessly into his arms.

"What are you doing? I'm bleeding all over that nice tux of yours."

"I am taking you to a doctor. And I have a closet full of these tuxes."

Mallory had then gotten lightheaded. The world was spinning as she tried to blink it back into focus. "How did you know I was a spy?"

"Because I'm a better one."

"Help me, please. I can't go back to America yet. If I can't do this job, I'll definitely be sent home."

Ahmed had been silent. Mallory was quickly losing touch with her surroundings. He had patted her cheeks, and her eyes had popped back open. "I will do it, but no one must know."

"Deal. I'm going to pass out now, okay?" Mallory had asked as her eyelids fluttered closed.

"Okay, my dear. I will take care of you."

Chapter Three

Mallory jerked awake as the plane landed on the runway in Stromia. With the dream of Ahmed teaching her his secrets still fresh in her mind, she brushed her hair and slid on her sunglasses. If her mentor needed her, then she would do this for him. It wasn't the most dangerous of her missions, but it was one she hadn't prepared for. And winging it was never a good idea.

The plane door opened, and Mallory stepped back into her former life. The cool mask of boredom fell into place as she walked straight from the plane to the limo. She directed the driver to the appointment-only clothing boutique she'd favored when she was part of the game.

Driving through the city was surreal. She thought she had left this part of her life behind forever. When the government had found out she was getting better at her job, they had started assigning more dangerous missions. She had snuck into estates and stolen information from the computers of kings and dictators. She had kept her cover in place as she shot her way out of hostile territory. She had been shot, stabbed, and beaten up in the name of national security. She had flirted with, drugged, blackmailed, and killed people all across the world. She had prevented terrorist attacks, saved the life of the president twice, and provided information that led to peace treaties. Then, one day, she'd had enough. Mallory had walked away from it all by blackmailing the CIA director. It was no wonder he wasn't thrilled with her being back on the job.

Mallory wasn't even sure she would have agreed to this mission if it hadn't been a favor for Ahmed. She sure as hell would have thought twice about doing it for her father—the father who had ruined her chance at true love; the father who had tried to marry her off to his protégé for political gain. Neither man had taken her rejection well. She still remembered the look on Ambrose's face when she turned him down. It was quickly followed by her father's lecture on family obligations. She ignored them and headed back to Europe. Only her friendship with Elle brought her back to Atlanta regularly.

And now she was going to be in the hotel owned by the man she loved who also despised her. He despised her so much he'd forbidden her to step foot on his Atlanta property. On top of that, this would be her first time in the room with her father and Ambrose since the failed marriage proposal, making this a barrel of fun.

The car came to a stop, and the driver opened the door. This time around she was the reformed party girl, looking for a husband. Sexy, yes. Nightclub, no. Silk instead of leather. It was a shame; she did love her leather pants.

Mallory rang the bell and waited for the disgruntled clerk to open the door. "I'm sorry, but we are closed. Appointments only."

"I'm Mallory Westin, and I don't do appointments," Mallory said as she walked into the shop. The owner hurried from the back only to stop and clap her hands in excitement.

"Welcome back, Miss Westin. What can I do for you?"

"Dress me to find a rich husband."

The older woman's eyes sparkled as dollar signs danced before them. "I'd be happy to. Cheri, bring out the champagne. It's time to celebrate Miss Westin's upcoming wedding."

Reid Simpson stood in the dark room with his arms crossed over his chest. He was tired. He had too much to do overseeing the opening of his new resort, but instead he was stuck babysitting a bunch of whiny diplomats.

"There's the French president. We caught his bodyguard in the stairwell with one of the poker dealers," Luke, Luxus's head of security, told him as he pulled up the footage on one of the fifty monitors in the room. "Don't they realize we have cameras everywhere?"

Reid just clenched his teeth. "No, they don't. They think they're above reproach. Almost two thousand cameras in this place, and they think not a single one will record them. Pull up the facial recognition, and track his steps since he entered the hotel three days ago. I want to see every person this guard has talked to."

With a couple of clicks of his computer, Luke pulled up the footage. Reid watched in chronological order as the guard came in with the president and stood on duty. Three hours later, he was released from his post and went to the casino. He started at the slots, played a little roulette, and watched the poker tables. As soon as the one with the girl opened up, he sat down. He played normally. When he left, he placed a chip on the table as a tip. A small piece of paper sat under it.

"There. They're setting up a meeting. Keep watching

and give me the full report before you call them both into the interrogation room," Reid instructed as he looked down at a text from the marketing suite.

"Should I notify the president?"

"No. As much as he likes to think he has power here, he doesn't. I'll notify him of our decision once I have all the facts. I have to go to a marketing meeting. Let me know what you find after you run the relationship awareness software. Let's see if he has any previous ties with this girl."

"Yes, boss," Luke said as he went back to work on his computer. With the input of the guard's name and information used to register with the hotel, their system allowed Reid to see every person the guard had shared an apartment with, every plane ticket or car rental he'd made, even the name of his college roommate. Everyone thought casinos were places to let go and their secrets would stay put. In reality, there were no secrets at casinos. Everything was recorded, documented, and preserved. What happened in a casino might stay there, but only as long as you didn't break the law or piss off the casino's owner.

Reid walked through the hidden corridors and up to the marketing suite. Using the iris scanner, he opened the door. The suite overlooked the casino floor through hidden windows. From the floor, it looked like artwork hanging on the walls. But it was actually a two-way mirror hidden behind specialized paint.

In this room, every bet, win, and loss was being tracked. A mock layout of every table covered an entire wall. Lights representing the chips were lit up at each table. In every casino Reid owned, radio frequency identification chips were embedded in every single marker. They were flashing on the screen now. They could track how much was being bet at each table, who was betting big, and which baccarat spot was hot.

The people in the marketing suite used this information to pick out high rollers for special treatment or people who were losing big for perks to keep them at the tables. They would identify a person, run him through the software, and find perks he or she enjoyed. If the gamblers were hot and they wanted them away from the table, they would offer tickets to a sold-out show, a massage by four of the hotels loveliest masseuses . . . whatever the system showed as that player's weak spot.

If the player was losing big, they offered free drinks, a free room, and an extended line of credit after a bank check of assets. Reid was a little different from some of his contemporaries. He wouldn't let an average Joe lose all his money. He'd comp his room, give him free tickets to the shows, and get him away from the table. But people of means were something else entirely. He saw Senator Westin in every single one of them and would happily take advantage of their arrogance.

"What do you have for me?" Reid asked as he stopped by Sophia's desk. The beautiful woman, with a sharp eye and a smooth smile, was his head of marketing.

"The US delegation has arrived. Senators Westin and Childs are asking for permission to wire money into our account. Prince Liam has reserved the high rollers' suite for a diplomatic poker game after the ball. Supposedly part of the money will go to charity, but it's $100,000 per player just to sit at the table. The senators are asking for credit until the money is wired."

"No. They can get cash from one of the other banks in town."

Sophia raised a perfectly sculpted eyebrow. "We

always approve the wires and the banks have verified they have the cash to support a very large casino credit."

"Not for those two we don't. Don't worry, Sophia, I'll be more than happy to tell them we denied their request." Reid grinned a cold grin. His day had just improved.

Reid smiled for the first time all day as he approached the two senators. They were in deep discussion with one another and didn't see him coming. Reid knew the instant Senator Westin recognized him. The senator's jaw clenched and that only served to make Reid happier.

"What are you doing here, boy?" Senator Westin snapped.

Reid didn't let the barb bother him. He just smiled wider. "I wanted to welcome you personally to Luxus. As owner of this casino, it's with great pleasure I get to inform you that your application for credit has been denied. If you'd like to receive any money, there is a bank across the street you may use. All courtesies normally afforded to our guests are off limits to both of you. I hope you enjoy your stay at Luxus."

"Owner?" Ambrose snorted.

Reid's smile slipped, and he narrowed his eyes. "That's right. I own this hotel. It's one of many I own."

"You mean your sister owns," Senator Westin said snidely. "You know, the one your father appointed to run Simpson Global because you were too immature and unqualified to manage."

Reid put a smile back on his face, but it must have been predatory since the girl at the credit application desk sucked in an audible breath. "See, I'm having a hard time thinking of how to phrase this since family is a concept you don't understand. I'm proud of each of my sisters. My father made the right choice, and it's a choice that doesn't concern you. My passion is money, and by last count I have more in my *small* part of Simpson Global than your whole family has. So, for someone who will never amount to a hill of beans, not only have I accomplished more than you, I also have something you will never have . . . a family who loves me. Credit denied. Good day."

Reid didn't bother to look back as he strode from the casino floor. He hadn't come face to face with the senator since the night Mallory had rejected him. Proving him wrong and showing him he had become wealthy didn't ease the sharp pain in his heart as he had hoped it would. He had worked all those years to be a man the senator could only wish for Mallory. As he walked away, he still felt empty. Revenge had felt good, but it hadn't fixed everything—his heart was still broken.

Chapter Four

By the time Mallory was stocked with clothes for the summit and ball, darkness had fallen. Her limo slid to a smooth stop in front of the Luxus. A liveried man opened her door and held out his hand. She accepted it and stood up. Her skintight, knee-length red sheath clung to her curves as she walked on five-inch heels into the lobby.

She approached the check-in and set her watch. She wondered how long it would take for someone to approach her to kick her out. She was sure Reid had her flagged at each of his properties.

"Mallory Westin. I'm checking into the Grande Suite."

"Of course, Ms. Westin. Welcome to Luxus. What can we do to make your stay perfect? Do you need tickets to tonight's show?" the woman behind the desk asked.

Surprised she wasn't being barred, Mallory smiled nicely and leaned forward conspiratorially. "Actually, I'm here to surprise an old friend of mine. Is Liam . . . oh, I mean, the prince, hosting any parties tonight? I'd hate to wait until tomorrow to see him."

The woman smiled. The Playboy Prince was famous for his paramours. "Not tonight, I'm sorry. You're an American and the embassy is hosting a party at their place. I can try to get you an invitation if you'd like."

Mallory pouted. "Don't worry about it. I see those stuffed shirts all the time. I'll just send a message to Liam and see him tomorrow. Thank you."

Mallory took her key and headed to her suite. Her luggage was already on its way and some unseen person would be quickly unpacking it for her. By the time she arrived in her suite, her clothes would be in the closet and a bottle of wine would be open and waiting for her.

Ambrose and her father would be at the embassy tonight. She wouldn't have to worry about seeing them there. She needed to get a feel for the party scene if she was to prepare for tomorrow night. Mallory knew just the person to call to find out. As she rode up the elevator, she called Tilley Vanderfield. The young party girl was in every tabloid imaginable for her wild ways.

"Tilley, darling, it's Mallory Westin."

"Oh my! Mallory. It's been forever."

Mallory almost laughed. Yes, a couple of months would seem like forever to her. It had to Mallory when she was twenty-one. "St. Barts did seem like forever ago. I'm in Stromia. Are you here, darling?"

"That's totes fab! I'm here. I'm going out with the girls to Montlark. Meet us there at midnight. We should be done with dinner by then. Hey, come to the embassy with us. Lots of hotties there."

"Oh, I'm so sorry. But I have plans for dinner. I'd love to see you at Montlark, though. Save a spot for me and we'll split a bottle of champagne while you fill me in on what I've missed since St. Barts. You have to give me all the deats on the men. Don't tell anyone, but I've decided it's time to marry."

"*O-M-G*! Are you for real?"

"Totes." Mallory rolled her eyes as the elevator door

opened. She was too old for this. "I get my trust fund this year, and I just simply have too much money to spend on my own. A husband would be amusing."

"Oh! Can I tell the girls? We can all give you the inside scoop on everyone in town."

"Sure, but pinkie promise not to tell anyone else, okay?" Mallory tried not to gag as she opened the door to the suite. Was she really this vapid when she was young? She probably was until Ahmed started training her. Seeing and doing the things she did quickly erased any innocence she had left.

"Of course. See you tonight. We're going to have so much fun!"

"Toodles, Tilley." Mallory hung up the phone and tossed back the glass of wine waiting for her on the mahogany table. She walked through the living area, past a sleek couch and two chairs, to a desk next to the wall of windows. Picking up the phone, she ordered room service before kicking off her heels and standing at the bank of windows, overlooking the beautiful ancient downtown. For a split second she felt old. It had been a lifetime since she was last here. The memories of the cobblestone streets, the tiny shops, and sitting on the sidewalk sipping cappuccinos seemed just like yesterday.

There was a knock on the door only a split second before it opened. Mallory didn't bother turning around. She knew exactly who it was. She just wondered what took him so long. She'd already finished her first glass of wine.

"Hello, Bowie." Mallory watched in the reflection of the glass as her old handler walked over to the table and poured more wine. Old was just a term for how long they'd known each other. Bowie was anything but old. He hadn't changed much in the years since she left the CIA. He was still drop-dead gorgeous and had a swagger that suggested he knew it.

"Hey, babe. Long time."

"Dinner is on the way up, and I'm already a glass of wine ahead of you. What, are you slowing down in your old age?"

"Ouch. I didn't know thirty-eight was old. You certainly have only gotten better with age."

Mallory turned around and found him enjoying the view of her in the dress. "Thank you. You too."

"You know, we're not really working together anymore," Bowie winked. This had been their relationship since she was nineteen. Outrageous flirting but no follow-through.

"You're right. Let's get naked and have wild sex. How do you feel about whips? I've been dying to try them out on someone," Mallory asked casually as she poured another glass of wine. The shocked look on his face lasted only a blink of a gnat's eye, but it was enough to make her smile.

"That was good. You had me for a second. So, really, how have you been?"

"As if you haven't been keeping tabs on me."

Bowie didn't look embarrassed. "Once a spy . . . Sorry you broke up with that Secret Service agent. He seemed like a nice guy. It was nice of you to hook him up with that girl from the FBI. They're a cute couple."

"Yeah, they are. I think he's going to propose. What about you, Bowie?"

"You know the game. I have my role to play just like you do. Speaking of which, what's on the agenda? I'm sure you already have a plan."

Mallory nodded but didn't explain further as room service knocked on the door and brought in the romantic dinner for two she had ordered. The waiter lit the candles, uncovered the plates, and quietly exited the room.

"Candles?"

"A bride should have some romance, don't you think?"

"Bride? Who are you marrying?"

"You."

Bowie choked on his oyster. "Excuse me. I thought your cover was of a wild child."

"I changed it. I'm spreading the word that I'm looking for a husband to help me spend my trust fund."

"And I'm your husband?"

"No, you're the man I'm going to use to make Liam remember his interest in me," Mallory said before taking a bite of her steak.

"Ah, jealousy is a wonderful thing."

"Exactly. I'm meeting with Tilley and her friends tonight at Montlark. They're going to help me find a husband. I need you to show up around one and fuel some rumors. They need to be outrageous enough that Liam hears about them."

"Will he really care that much?"

"He did propose to me, Bowie. I turned him down because I wasn't ready to get married. He needs respectability, and the daughter of the highest-ranking senator can give him that. He'll be sniffing around in no time."

Bowie raised his glass. "Together again."

"For one last time." Mallory clinked her glass to his and drank the wine. One last time and then she'd finally move on with her life. She'd move away from Georgia and just maybe she could find someone to love beside Reid.

"O-M-G! How did I forget Bowie?" Tilley gasped as she saw him walk into the nightclub with a girl on each arm. "He'd be so much fun to spend your money with."

The party girl was dressed in a skirt that didn't hide much and a see-through shirt that let everyone there know she wasn't wearing a bra. Her dyed blond hair was pulled back into a sleek ponytail with extensions making it fall almost to her bottom. Her friends all looked the same in their club gear, and Mallory was thankful for the CIA's twenty-something attire.

Mallory hadn't been this undressed in public for a long time. A black lace bustier matched her lace miniskirt and was paired with silver stilettos. Her normally long legs seemed to go on for miles. Her waist was cinched in and her breasts thrust forward. She was sure Bowie was going to love it. She might have too if she weren't so worried her breasts would fall out with a deep breath.

"Hmm. He is sexy. But I wanted to be a duchess or something. Wouldn't that be fun?"

"Oh, I know!" Tilley squealed with excitement. "What about a princess?"

"Like there are any good princes available," Mallory said sarcastically.

"Prince Liam is. He just broke up with that porn star."

"Really?" Mallory acted shocked. "Hmm, Bowie or Liam it is. May the best man win." She winked at the girls as they giggled.

"Mallory Westin? Where have you been? Not in my bed where you belong, that's for sure," a deep voice said from behind her. She fought the urge to roll her eyes. The girls at the table all giggled and fanned themselves.

Mallory took her time turning around. "Bowie! If only I'd been in your bed, I wouldn't be so bored now."

"Let's see what we can do to rectify that. Come dance with me. Excuse me, ladies, I have a woman to seduce." Bowie winked to the girls around the VIP table.

Already they had their phones out and the first time Bowie's hand slid down to squeeze her bottom as they danced, she heard the social media world explode. Pictures of her and Bowie would be all over the tabloids by morning, and Liam would know she was back in town.

His hands were on her the second the elevator doors closed. His lips were hard on hers, and she ran her hands roughly through his hair. He shoved her against the wall and devoured her until the doors to the elevator opened. They stumbled out and kissed their way to her room.

"Heaven help me, Mallory, are you sure we can't continue?" Bowie said out of breath as soon as the door to her room closed.

"Sorry, Bowie. As much fun as it would be, we both know it's not a good idea. Can you make sure that video footage gets leaked?"

"Yeah. I'm friends with one of the guys in security. He'll release it for me. Do you think it will work?"

Mallory nodded. "I need to make Liam think I'm not here for him. If he thinks he's won me, he's more likely to trust me and not doubt why I'm suddenly back after all these years."

Bowie walked over to the bedroom and a second later came back with a pillow and blanket. "Sounds like a plan. I have a feeling I'll get a lot of action after you break my heart and choose Liam. Maybe this will be good for me."

"And there's the reason you're sleeping on the couch

tonight. Goodnight, Bowie."

"Goodnight, Mal."

Mallory closed the door and let out a deep breath. So far, so good. By the next night, she would have reentered international society with a splash. She just hoped Reid didn't see it. It shouldn't matter to her; after all, she'd seen him with models in the papers. He had moved on. She needed to as well. After this assignment, she would. Her phone rang, and she dug it out of her cleavage.

"Hi, Elle. What's up?" she asked her best friend.

"You're getting married?" Elle accused.

"Wow, word travels fast."

"So the tabloids are right; you're actually getting married?"

"Maybe. I thought it was time to start looking to settle down." It hurt Mallory to lie, but she had to keep her cover. She couldn't risk Elle saying anything to anyone.

"What about love? And this guy at the club, do you even know him?" Mallory tried not to cry at the worry in her friend's voice. Elle had loved her unconditionally, even when it appeared she'd gone buck-wild during college and afterward.

"Bowie? I've known him since I was nineteen," Mallory answered truthfully.

"Well, that's good. But are you really going to marry him?"

"Oh, I don't know."

Mallory pulled up one of the gossip sites and cringed at the picture. It was from the club and her breasts were pressed against Bowie's chest, and his hands were pulling her bottom against him while he kissed her. The headline read *Wild Heiress Ready to Settle Down?*

"As long as you're happy, I'm happy for you," Elle said

with forced support.

"Thanks, Elle. I just want what you and Drake have," Mallory said truthfully. Her best friend had married her true love, but Mallory knew she'd never have that. Her true love rightfully hated her. She doubted he'd believe she'd said all those things to protect him.

Mallory had written a letter as soon as Reid had fled her bedroom that night. The next day she had found her own lawyer and finance expert. She began the separation of her life from her parents. She had handed her lawyer the letter addressed to Reid with the instructions to deliver it on her thirty-fifth birthday. Next month, he'd know the truth if he read the letter though he'd probably just burn it before opening it.

"If you need anything, Reid is there, and I'm sure he can help you."

Mallory was yanked from her thoughts. "What? Reid's here in Stromia?"

"Yes. He's there until that summit thing is done. I'll message him and let him know you're there."

"No!"

"Why not?" Elle asked suspiciously.

"He probably already knows. And I don't need anything. I promise. He's going to be so busy with this summit. I don't want to bother him." Mallory's heart pounded wildly. Then it plummeted as she realized in the next hour images of her making out with Bowie in the elevator would be released. Reid would see them and know she was in his hotel with another man . . . and with her father here. Could this get worse?

"Okay. If you need anything at all, you know you just have to call. We're sisters, right?"

"Right," Mallory struggled to say confidently.

"No matter who you marry, we'll love him because you do. Gosh, it's almost morning there. I'll let you get some sleep. Love you."

"Love you too." Mallory hung up the phone and hurried to the bathroom. Sitting on the floor of the massive shower, she cried as the hot water washed away the night.

Chapter Five

Reid slammed the newspaper into the trashcan. He shoved his chair back and paced his office on the top floor of the hotel. This morning the hotel was quiet. The summit was going on at the government building two blocks away. He had meant to relax and read the paper, but when he turned to the lifestyle section, an image of Mallory with another man filled the page. Her hands were in his hair. His hands were on her ass.

What the hell was she doing here? He pulled up a gossip site and cursed again at exclusive video footage of her making out with the guy in *his* elevator. How dare she? Reid seethed as he felt the betrayal from all those years ago flood him all over again. He closed the screen and pulled up the hotel database to do a quick search. He found her room number and saw nothing but red as he stormed from his office.

Why would Mallory break his heart all over again? Wasn't it enough to do it once? She had to come to his hotel to have sex with another man for the whole world to see? To get married . . . he closed his eyes, and the pain washed over him. The thought of her with someone else was too much to bear. As soon as the elevator doors slid open, he strode down the hall. Not bothering to knock, he slid the master key into the door and shoved it open.

"How dare you," he ground out as the door slammed against the wall.

Mallory looked up from her breakfast without a hint of the surprise he expected to see. "Did Elle call you?"

"No. I saw the news. Get out of my hotel," Reid said with such coldness he saw her flinch.

"I thought you were in Atlanta."

"It doesn't matter where I am. You are not welcome at any of my properties, especially when you act like . . . what was it your father called you . . . a strumpet?" He saw Mallory's face pale momentarily before that damn hard mask fell back in place.

"Hey, man. That's harsh."

Reid looked up to where the man from the video was standing with nothing on but a towel wrapped low around his waist. "Bowie, is it? You and your *bride* can both leave. And you're not to step foot back into this hotel. Do you understand me?"

"Sorry, but we can't do that. We will leave first thing tomorrow, though. Tonight we will be at the charity ball."

Reid snarled, but Bowie didn't back down. "This is my hotel . . ."

"And I'm a guest of the prince who, I believe, gives you permission to operate your casino in his country. You prevent us from attending, and I'll have your license pulled."

"I don't take too kindly to threats," Reid said coldly as he stepped forward.

"Stop," Mallory said quietly. "Bowie, please go get dressed. I need to talk to Reid privately."

Bowie gave a grunt of understanding and turned back toward the bathroom. "I don't want to hear it, Mallory," Reid snapped.

"Please. You trusted me a long time ago. I'm asking you to do so now." Mallory held up her hand as Reid opened his mouth. "Please let me finish, Reid. I love your family, and I swear on their love and friendship I'm not here to hurt you. I didn't even know you were here. I will leave tomorrow, but there are things going on that you don't know about. I have to be here tonight. Then, I promise I will be out of your life forever. I will leave Atlanta by the end of the month, and you will never have to see me again."

Reid clenched his jaw. He hated her. He loved her. He wanted her gone. He wanted her in his arms. "No more dinners at my mom's?"

"Never again. I'm going to relocate to St. Barts. I'll host all dinner parties there."

With a nod of his head, he turned on his foot and walked out. He didn't see the blanket and pillow on the couch as he slammed the door. The pain of knowing after tonight he'd never see her again blinded him.

Mallory slid her arm through Bowie's tuxedo-clad arm and smiled. They entered the ballroom to a flourish of gossip. Old friends from the party circuit surrounded them within seconds of entering the room. She kept her smile plastered on and shot a quick glance around the large ballroom. It took less than a second to spot him. Reid was standing near the door to the kitchen. Seeing him dressed in a white tux jacket with black slacks and bowtie was enough to cause her smile to falter. He was breathtaking. After all these years she still remembered every muscle, every dimple of the body so elegantly highlighted by his formal attire.

Bowie patted her hand absently as he talked to some of

the people surrounding them. It was the signal she'd been waiting for. It meant Liam was near. The fun was about to begin.

"I'm going to the bar. I see a tasty morsel over there," Bowie laughed. Some of the people in their group laughed along with him, but then some looked confused.

Mallory shrugged as if she didn't care and didn't watch Bowie walk away. Tilley looked heartbroken. Her fake lashes almost fell off as her eyes widened. "But . . . but, aren't you two getting married?"

Mallory waited until she felt Liam behind her. "Bowie? I don't know. I mean, we've known each other forever, but I don't think he's the marrying kind. I'm looking for someone to sweep me off my feet. Someone I feel is up to the challenge of keeping me . . . or keeping up with me," Mallory laughed.

Before she knew it, she was grabbed from behind and whisked up into a set of lean, muscular arms. "Look no further; your prince has arrived."

"Liam!" Mallory swatted his shoulder and laughed. "It's so good to see you again."

"You're even more beautiful than when I last saw you. Now, excuse me, ladies, this prince has some wooing to do."

Mallory waved to Tilley as Liam carried her out of the ballroom and into the hotel library. The room was paneled in dark wood and lit only by low lights that night. The deep red carpets and rich leather couches made the room feel cozy despite its enormous size. "Really, Liam, you can put me down now."

"Never." Liam took a seat on one of the couches but kept her in his lap. "Are you really back? Are you really wanting to get married?"

"I'm really back. And yes, all those years ago I wasn't ready to settle down. I've spent time growing as a person. I'm ready to sit back and enjoy life again. But, I'm not like Tilley anymore. I'm a woman, Liam. One who wants devotion and companionship as I spend all the money I get next month."

"Your rejection hurt, Mallory. I'm willing to overlook it if you promise me you're not marrying Bowie. Don't get me wrong. I like the guy, but you've always been mine, and I always get what I want—eventually. I can make you a queen and give you riches your trust fund can only dream of."

"You certainly know how to sweep a girl off her feet, too," Mallory teased. Then she grew serious. "Your parents will never allow you to marry me. You know that. I know that. A prince is not going to marry an American heiress. He's going to marry another royal."

"My father will be dead soon, and then I will be king. Things are going to change. I will have so much power I can do, or marry, whoever I want. And if they try to stop me, they'll find out how strong I am becoming in my own right. Stromia is not a weak, defenseless country anymore. We will have weapons . . ." Liam stopped and then smiled. "We also have jewels for me to shower you with. Imagine being naked with only a sapphire the size of your fist around your neck and a diamond tiara on your head as I make love to you."

Mallory smiled slowly. She wouldn't say anything about the weapons, but Liam had always had a weakness for trying to impress. This was what she came for. The CIA was right to worry. "You have one night, Liam. One night to prove I should pick you."

"Then we don't have a moment to lose. Let's dance, my

princess."

"From a queen to a princess so fast," Mallory tsk-tsked. "What will I be by midnight, a pumpkin?"

"You'll be mine."

Mallory fought the urge to roll her eyes as he led her back into the ballroom and onto the dance floor.

Reid tossed back another drink and watched Mallory dance with a prince who was no better than a slug. He would treat her well enough until he had her on his mantel, and then he'd start working on his next trophy. He was sure her father was happy about it, though.

Senator Westin and that prick Ambrose Childs had entered the ballroom ten minutes earlier. Her father stood watching Mallory with a slight smile on his face. Too bad for Ambrose, Mallory had found someone even better than a vice president.

The dance came to an end, and Reid watched Bowie lead a simpering blond aristocrat off the dance floor and over to the bar. Reid felt his blood boil as he watched Bowie slide his hand around her waist and lean in toward her. He smiled down at her and whispered something in her ear; she turned pink as she giggled.

Before he knew it, Reid grabbed Bowie by the back of his neck and steered him into the kitchen. "You share her bed and then have the audacity to try to pick up someone else while you are at the event with Mallory?"

Bowie held up his hands. "Hey, man. It's not like that. It's an open relationship. Besides, she's out dancing with Liam, and we all know what he wants. Not that I can say I blame him. Mallory is . . ."

Reid didn't let him finish. His fist cracked Bowie's flapping jaw. "Mallory is a woman who deserves respect, not some tawdry bit to be passed around and joked about with your buddies." Reid dropped his hold on Bowie and slammed his hands into the black swinging kitchen door.

"If you love her so much, you should have fought for her when you had your chance. Don't hate me for being able to finish what you were too cowardly to start."

Reid had his hand around Bowie's throat so fast, Bowie blinked in surprise. "What do you know about it? What did Mallory tell you?"

"Nothing, just that you two were once a thing," Bowie choked through his smug smile.

"Then don't call me a coward when you don't know a thing about it." Reid let go of him and let him scamper from the room. He took a deep breath and headed up the staff elevator to the control room. He couldn't stand to be near her. His heart ached in recognition of the soul mate he'd never have. It's why he'd had to stay away from his own family for so long. He couldn't sit next to the woman he loved at dinner every week. It just hurt too much.

Leaning forward, he scanned his iris and entered the dark room filled with monitors. "Do we have anything interesting?"

"Besides you beating the douche in the kitchen? Not yet, but the night's still young. We have video on the high stakes game Prince Liam has set up. We have security posted outside the room. It's been swept by the Secret Service, the French contingent, the prince's guards, and our own. Catering and the bar are being set up now and will clear as soon as everyone is ready to sit down and play," Luke said from behind the main control center.

"Who's the dealer?"

"One of the prince's guards. He insisted, and everyone has agreed to it. They don't want any ears on this game."

An uneasy feeling rolled through him. He knew high rollers liked to keep things secretive, but they never brought their own dealer. If it were more confidential, Luke or Reid himself would deal. The guests made them sign confidentiality agreements and then freely talked. The secrets Reid knew . . . but it's what made his casinos the place to be for whales. They felt secure here, and that was worth it.

"I don't like this. Keep all cameras up on the screens. I'll be back up at midnight to monitor it personally. What do the players all have in common?" Reid wondered aloud.

Luke shrugged his skinny shoulders. "We've seen stranger things before."

"True. I'll see you in a couple of hours." Reid headed to his office and pulled up his computer. They may have seen stranger things; the Motorcycle Grandmas for Yeti Rescue was one of them. But his gut told him this was something more.

He looked at the list of people participating in the poker game. There had to be a connection, a link somewhere. The prince, the senator, and Ambrose had a connection—Mallory Westin. As for the others, he had some digging to do.

Chapter Six

Mallory twirled around in her red ball gown. Her hair reflected the romantic glow from the low lights, her makeup was flawless, and her laugh seductive. She had Liam right where she wanted him. Every move was predetermined. Every look and every hand placement was meant to encourage his trust.

The dance came to an end, and Liam looked at his diamond-encrusted watch again. What was she doing wrong? Every so often she caught him looking distracted. "Am I boring you?"

"What?" Liam looked up quickly. "Never. It's just that I have to go. I have a meeting in five minutes."

Mallory raised an eyebrow. "Then your evening's up. Sorry, but I didn't have enough time to make a decision," she said coldly as she looked over Liam's shoulder. She found Bowie and smiled. Bowie took the hint and headed straight for her.

"There's my girl. Let's get out of here," he said as he put his arm around her waist. "You don't mind, do you, Prince?"

Mallory held her breath. It was now or never. "Why should he mind? He's leaving me."

"His loss is my gain," Bowie chuckled.

"Not tonight. I'm sorry, Bowie, but Miss Westin will be

joining me all night. After all, I only have tonight to make a favorable impression." Liam's eyes twinkled, but his jaw was tight as he held out his hand for Mallory.

Mallory looked between the two men and rewarded Liam with a dazzling smile. "That's right. And a man who puts his lady first, even if he has to do business, is one I'd like to spend more time with."

Liam shot Bowie a haughty smile as Bowie frowned. "Shall we?"

"We shall." Mallory walked quietly with Liam to the elevators. "Where are we going?"

"To a private room. I'm meeting with some people over a game of poker. You will know most of them, your father included. Should we announce our engagement?"

Mallory covered her surprise with a giggle. Her father was going to be there? And wherever her father went, Ambrose went too. This was not a complication she foresaw. "I don't think so. It'll irritate him more to not know. Besides, your night isn't up yet. You don't know if I'll accept."

Liam cracked a smile. "That's right, I'm not the only one with daddy issues. Very well. You can be my good luck charm."

Mallory closed her eyes briefly before the door to the private room opened. She pulled her shoulders back and plastered the smile that Southern women had practiced for generations when they had to meet with people they didn't like. One that said *I'm a better person for doing this, but I'll knock you down a peg . . . or ten, if you push me*. Her grandmother would be proud.

She saw Ambrose first, at the bar. He was talking to Governor Graham. His eyes widened in surprise before narrowing into a look of hatred. Ambrose Childs wasn't told no often. But she had told him, and he clearly hadn't forgotten.

The wooden bar in one corner was polished to a high sheen. The entire back wall was filled with windows overlooking the historic city. Eight rich brown leather chairs sat around a green felt table. Identical stacks of poker chips were in front of each chair.

"Mallory, it's good to see you again. I was trying to get your attention while you danced to say hello." Mallory turned to see her father. It was always painful for her to see him. He'd aged since she'd talked to him last. Not that he was old, but he had gotten *older*. Gray hair and wrinkles had appeared. She fought the childhood urge to run and give him a hug. Instead, there was nothing but heartbreak between them.

"Hello, Father. How is Mother? Is she here or did you bring your mistress?" Mallory asked coldly.

"Brandy is not my mistress. She's just my assistant. Your mother is well. She was disappointed you were away from town during Christmas. She was hoping you would come home to celebrate. Home, with your family," he said quietly.

Mallory smirked. "Father, we haven't had a family since I was old enough for you to leave at home. Right around eleven, when I was no longer cute enough for campaign ads."

"Senator, would you like a drink? I have had the finest bourbons and vodkas brought up here for our game," Liam cut in.

"No, thank you. It is good to just see you again. I would like to talk to you before I leave tomorrow."

Mallory smiled noncommittally and headed for the bar.

One awkward situation down, one more straight ahead.

"You said no guests, Prince," Ambrose snarled as he downed another drink.

"Mallory is not a guest; she's my intended. Good luck at the game, Mr. Childs."

Ambrose slammed his glass on the counter and headed for her father. She nodded at Easton Graham, a current governor and her father's political opponent, and allowed Liam to introduce her to two other men.

"This is Mr. Jonak and Mr. Black." Liam introduced her to the men whom seemed to be around her own age.

Mallory tried not to act surprised, but it was hard. These men were clearly Eastern European goons. Their suits were too expensive and their tattoos were mafia symbols. Mallory smiled dumbly at them. She needed to get pictures of them to pass to the CIA. They had to have a connection to the group Liam was in bed with.

"It's nice to meet y'all." Instantly she saw the men relax as they heard her sweet Southern drawl. It was her secret weapon. She even threw in a giggle and an eyelash bat. Some men were so very stupid.

"Ma'am," one said, bowing his head. Definitely Eastern European.

Mallory smiled inanely and looked toward the bar. "I'm going to get myself a drink. Would any of y'all like something?"

Mr. Black shook his head and murmured to the others. Mallory tried to listen but only caught snippets. It wasn't English, but it wasn't Russian either. Mallory poured her drink and ambled back to Liam's side. They were in an animated conversation and didn't notice her sipping her drink while looking absently around the room. She took out her phone and slid it to her side before pressing the button and taking a burst of photographs.

Some of the words she understood. Mallory spoke Italian, French, Russian, and Arabic. She recognized their language as Slavic, though she didn't know which region. She didn't show a reaction when she heard the term for a million Euros. They all agreed, and she heard something about the job being done in America before the end of next month.

"I told you before, after you have your money, I'd give you the target," Liam said in Russian.

Mr. Jonak shot him an intimidating glare and nodded to her. Mallory smiled innocently and then started looking around the room again.

"Don't worry about her. She doesn't speak Russian and since you can't speak my language and I can't speak yours, we'll speak the language of our past." Mallory opened her purse and dug out her lip gloss as if she were bored. Liam and his assumptions always got him in trouble.

The men grunted and went back to their discussion. Money was mentioned again along with some event.

"Is your person reliable? The job will get done neatly, lots of press?" Liam asked. Mr. Black nodded in response. "Good. You'll have your money by the end of the night if you play your hand right."

Mallory took another sip of her drink and then smiled at the men as they looked at her. Liam patted her back and leaned down. "Sorry to speak Russian in front of you. They just don't know that much English. It was business anyway."

Mallory shrugged her shoulder. "No problem. What business do you do with them?"

"They provide services for Stromia. Now, give me a kiss for good luck."

Mallory kissed his cheek and followed him to the table. She stood behind him as he welcomed the group. "Thank you all for coming tonight. It is with great pleasure I welcome the President of France and the future President of the United States." He waited while his guests chuckled. "It's important to save the world's endangered species, and the only way to accomplish that is to work together. I hope for a long friendship between Stromia, France, and the United States."

The men clapped and then took their seats. Mallory found a seat against the wall and watched the game. Something had to happen; she just didn't know what.

Reid watched the screens in the darkness of the surveillance room. Cards were dealt; money was won and lost. He pulled up another screen on his tablet that showed where all the chips were. Liam was losing badly. But every chip went to Mr. Black of Blackriver Industries and Mr. Jonak of Jonak Transport. The report on Reid's desk showed them as shady business owners. Blackriver dealt in metals while Jonak owned container ships that sailed around the world.

There was never any proof to charge them with crimes, but many a dockworker suddenly had extra cash in their pockets, and Interpol's investigations crumbled as the dead bodies of witnesses piled up. They were friends and enemies of every country. Their fingers were in every pie, and no one was brave enough to tell them to get out. Instead, they just handed them the whole pie.

"Boss, I got something." Luke hurried over and handed Reid a printout. "Jonak and Black are related. They're cousins. And Black isn't his real last name. It's Cern. It's

Slovakian for black."

Reid looked as the research ran through their system. Black and Jonak had lived together during college. Luke had taken the search back a generation and found their fathers had lived next door to each other and still did. "Cousins?"

"Not first cousins; if that were the case their parents would be siblings. But both Jonak and Black, junior and senior, are only children." Luke held up his finger to stop Reid from asking a question. "But each father has the same middle name, and that name was passed down to both Black and Jonak. I dug around and that name is the maiden name of two sisters from the 1930s. One married a man by the name of Cern, the other Jonak."

"So, the grandmothers of those two playing cards were sisters. And having no siblings, cousins turned into brothers . . . or the closest thing to brothers. Do you think they're working in tandem at some con?" Reid asked as he zoomed in on them.

"I don't know, but it's strange they are here with politicians."

"Who knows what Liam has planned? He's the one who invited them. But keep an eye on everything they do. I want to know every time one blinks."

Mallory got up and headed to the bar. She needed something to keep her focused. The game had been going on for hours. The President of France and Ambrose were on their last chips. Graham and Orson weren't too far behind them. Mr. Black and Mr. Jonak each had a huge stack in front of them while Liam and her father were holding steady in the middle.

From what she could tell, Liam was purposely losing, but only to Black or Jonak. If they had folded, then the hand came down to him and her father. The start of the game had been the most interesting when all the players put $100,000 in cash on the table. The guard ran it through counters and the play began. Since then it had been pretty dull.

Ambrose cursed and threw down his hand. He was out. He slid his chair back and headed for the bar. Mallory tried not to run the opposite direction when he stopped next to her to pour a tall glass of bourbon.

"I hope you're happy," Ambrose said quietly as he tossed back his drink.

"I am, thank you," Mallory lied. She hadn't been happy since her time with Reid.

"Do you know you could cost your father the election with your selfishness. If you had just married me years ago, it would be me running for president, and you'd be First Lady."

"So, I didn't cost my father the election. I cost you the election. Come on, Ambrose, did you really want to marry me?"

"I want it all, and I'll get it—with or without you. Mr. President, the cards weren't in our favor tonight. Please, have a drink with me." Ambrose turned, effectively cutting her off as he started politicking with the President of France. Mallory made another turn about the room and saw Governor Graham fall. He shook everyone's hands and headed to the bar. Thirty minutes later, Orson similarly stood and shook hands before joining his running mate for a drink.

Mallory clutched her drink. She still didn't have proof of the identity of the target to take back to the CIA and certainly no way to stop an assassin.

Reid's eyes were growing blurry. He hadn't taken his eyes off the screen in the last thirty minutes. Senator Westin stood on camera and shook the remaining players' hands. Liam bet big and Reid sat up. He bet half his stack on the first cards.

"What's he doing?" Luke asked.

"I don't know. Look, Black bet a quarter of his money."

They watched the flop card turn over. The cards on the table weren't very enticing—a three of diamonds, a jack of spades, a seven of hearts, and a two of hearts. Liam upped his bet and so did Black. Jonak matched but didn't raise. The turn was flipped again. It was the ace of clubs.

"He's going all in," Luke said in wonder as Liam pushed all his chips in.

"He must think he has a run," Reid mumbled.

"A run where?"

They watched the river card turn. A four of spades. Liam slammed his cards face down and shook his head. Jonak smiled and raked in his winnings after Black turned over a pair of fours. Jonak had won on a pair of fives.

Liam stood, smiled, and shook hands with them. Reid watched as Liam turned and kissed Mallory before heading to the bar. Jonak quickly took Black and the game was over. It all seemed so strange.

"Get me the footage from the whole game. I want to watch it again when I'm awake."

"Dario, make Mr. Simpson a copy of the high rollers' game, please," Luke called to his assistant across the room.

Reid watched Liam lead Mallory from the room. They

popped up on another monitor as they walked down the hallway. Liam hands were all over her. "I'm flying home tonight."

"I thought you were supposed to fly home in two days," Luke said, surprised.

"There's too much to be done in Atlanta. If I sneak away now, I may have a shot of getting it done before anyone discovers where I am. So, don't mention it, okay?" Reid looked around at the other security guards in the room. They weren't paying any attention.

"Sure. Do you think they were laundering money?"

"I do. Liam's last hand was too strange. And if he owed Jonak money, what better way to get it to him? Bring in dirty money, win it in a high-stakes poker game, and then you suddenly have clean gambling winnings. Look into it for me, and let me know as soon as you have something."

Dario walked across the room and handed him the flash drive before Reid left. He pulled out his cell phone and dialed as he headed for his rooms. "Troy, I need to get home," he said to his family's personal pilot.

"I can be there tomorrow."

"No, it needs to be now." Reid couldn't stay in the same city with Mallory, not while knowing what she was doing at this very moment.

"I can't. I'm flying to pick Elle up from her meeting in Seattle."

"Never mind. I'll find another way home. The cargo I want carried back to the new resort will be waiting for you at the hangar. Just pick it up on schedule." Reid hung up and scrolled through his phone. He found a commercial flight that left in an hour. He was going home and never thinking of Mallory Westin again.

Mallory let Liam put his arm around her as they left the hotel. Her bags were packed, and she'd already checked out of the hotel. Bowie had taken them to the CIA's plane and was to meet her there.

"Come on, my darling," Liam begged as she wiggled out of his arms. "Let's make love in the limousine. Andre won't care. I think he likes it, actually," he said about his driver.

"If I'm going to do that, at least make me a drink first," Mallory giggled as she put up the privacy screen. She opened her purse and twisted open her lipstick. Liam handed her a glass and when he turned to make his, she poured the liquid hidden in the lipstick container into the glass.

"I thought you were thirsty?" Liam asked when she put her drink down next to his.

"I am. I'm sorry you lost your card game."

"Who cares about a card game when I have you?" Liam kissed her, and she kissed him back.

"I'll toast to that." She reached over and picked up a glass and waited for Liam to pick up the other one. "To me making my decision."

"Cheers," Liam said before drinking it down. "Now come here."

Mallory counted to three. He had only managed to get his bowtie undone when he suddenly slumped back in his seat. She lowered the screen. "Andre, the prince has had too much to drink. He's out cold. Would you mind dropping me off at the airport?"

"Yes, miss."

Mallory sat back and enjoyed her last look at the beautiful old town. When the limo pulled to a stop, she reached into her purse and pulled out a letter. "Could you give this to Liam when he wakes up?"

"Yes, miss."

Mallory thanked him and headed for the private airfield. If she wanted to stop the assassination, she needed to be back in the United States.

In the early morning light, Dario waited in the alley behind an old warehouse. He nervously clasped the flash drive he had stolen in his hand. The sound of shoes echoing off the old cobblestone street caught his attention. He turned to find two people approaching.

"Mr. Black, I'm sorry. I didn't know who to tell."

"This better be important," Mr. Black snarled.

"It is. My boss, Luke, asked me to make a copy of the security footage from the game for Mr. Simpson. They gathered all kinds of information on everyone who played last night."

"Good work, Dario. Is this the copy?"

"It's the exact copy I gave Mr. Simpson. I erased the mainframe, though. But, Mr. Black, they will know it is me. I had to use my employee login to erase the data. I have to get out of here. Mr. Simpson will find out before he leaves tomorrow, and I know I'll disappear."

"We'll take care of you." Mr. Black turned to his partner and gave a simple nod before walking away. The muffled gunshot was barely audible.

"Do you want me to take care of Mr. Simpson along with the candidate you gave me?"

"Yes. Do it on American soil. I don't want a connection to Stromia. And make sure you destroy both him and the flash drive."

"Consider it done."

Chapter Seven

"It has to be then," Bowie argued as he and Mallory looked at the papers laid out on the desk the next day. They had arrived in Atlanta the day after the ball and since then had been researching every political campaign stop the candidates were scheduled to make.

"They are with each other at the next event, but how are we to know if the assassination will take place when both candidates are together?" Mallory asked as she looked at their schedules.

"Because then they will both be in the spotlight. Think about it. Pictures all over the world of a dead candidate in the arms of his opponent who is frantically trying to save him. It would be election gold. The only timeline we have is what you overheard. It's going to be by the end of the month. This is the only event that fits that description."

"I don't know; you're assuming the person who hired the assassination would be there at the time," Mallory said as she looked over the paperwork. "I mean, this event my father is going to be at in two weeks will be huge. Thousands of people."

"You heard Liam demand it be public with lots of press. That has to mean the person behind it all wants to be seen there too. If he tries to save the injured man, or men, he'd be hailed a hero. How would you do it? How would you kill them publicly?"

Mallory let out a long breath. Bowie was right. She would do it at this event. It was a charity event for wounded soldiers. The press was already going to be there. Security wouldn't be as tight as if it were a debate, making it easier to smuggle weapons in. "I'd do it at the event. I would do it when the candidate makes his speech."

"How?"

Mallory looked at the blueprints of the resort. "There." She pointed to the maze of air ducts in the ballroom. The room was set up like a chessboard above the ceiling with ductwork running the length and the width of the room and intersecting at various points. "If the pictures of the ballroom are accurate, there's a huge return vent right there that looks out over the ballroom instead of facing downward. All you have to do is take some pliers to make room for the muzzle of a rifle. The industrial air ducts are large enough to crawl through. No one would see me. Escape would be simple if you had the layout of the maze of ducts. Take the right turns and you're at the restrooms. Drop back down and run out with the other guests."

"Hmm. I would go for a more direct approach. I would plant three small bombs under the stage. One at the podium and one under each side. Then I could detonate according to where my target was standing."

"We can stop both, but I have a bigger problem. This is Reid's new resort. If he sees us . . ."

Bowie just smiled. "He won't. You'll look fabulous as a brunette."

"Goodie, our little bag of tricks. I'll scope out the resort now. Reid isn't supposed to get back until later this afternoon according to the flight plan Troy filed. I'll spend the day there, getting a feel for the place, and be gone before Reid arrives."

Mallory walked the ballroom under the pretense of wanting to rent it for a wedding reception. The wig felt heavy on her head; she wasn't used to her hair swooping down and covering half her face.

"We can fit twelve hundred people in the ballroom, or we can put up room dividers to fit the size of your party. We have three dividers; the smallest room we offer seats four hundred," the event planner explained.

"Can I see where the room dividers are to get a better idea? We are expecting a large crowd, so I don't know if I would need a single room or if I would need to open one of the dividers," Mallory explained as she looked around and took pictures.

"Of course, Miss Andrews."

"When you host these big events, where do you put the stage and dance floor?"

"We have a pre-built platform we put right there and the dance floor is at the discretion of the host, but normally it goes right in front of the stage."

Mallory nodded and took some notes. "That would be perfect for throwing the bouquet."

"Yes, your reception will be lovely if you choose to hold it here."

"I'm sure it will."

"Now, a very popular plan for brides is to rent one of our suites to dress in. Would you care to see one?"

Mallory smiled. "What a wonderful idea."

"I'm sorry to interrupt, but we have an issue with the charity event. They need to talk to you about lighting," a young woman in a hotel uniform said as she joined them at the front desk.

"Can you just give me a key? I want to look around as well. See where we can take pictures and such." The event planner hesitated, but a pissed-off electrician stood impatiently nearby. "And if I like the suite, I can book the whole floor for the wedding party so no one has to drive home."

The prospect of a whole floor of suites being booked did the job. "Lisa, give Miss Andrews a card for the Star Suite. I'll meet you back here in thirty minutes?"

"Perfect."

Mallory took the room key and meandered around the lobby and the restrooms outside of the ballroom, locating every closet and storage room. Knowing the event planner would be able to tell if she used her key, she took the elevator up to the fourth floor. Might as well see what Reid had been busy working on for the past year.

Reid grabbed some papers from his office and ran up the stairs. So far he'd been undetected by most of his staff, probably because he was in jeans, a T-shirt, and baseball cap as opposed to his normal suit and tie. He had a little more work he wanted to get done in his room before he tackled the long list of questions he was sure they had for him.

He opened the door to the fourth floor and froze when he saw a woman walking away from the elevator. She was dressed conservatively in an orange sheath dress that hugged the curves of her bottom so well he couldn't stop staring. Her brunette hair was chin length and accentuated her long neck. Who knew necks could be so sensual?

Reid followed her as she placed a key into the suite next to his and walked in. Oh good. How was he going to concentrate knowing she was right next door? He hadn't seen legs like that since Mallory . . . no, he wasn't going to think of her. She was gone, out of his life forever.

Reid entered the suite he'd been staying in the past couple of months while the hotel prepared for the grand opening. The soft opening had been a huge success, and he knew the official grand opening would be too.

He tossed the papers on the desk and sat down on the couch. Work was going to have to wait. His mind was still on the mystery woman he saw from behind. He wondered what her face looked like, if she was single, if she was his answer to forgetting Mallory.

Mallory stood and looked out the windows of the suite. She had to hand it to Reid. He had done a remarkable job with the resort—with all of his resorts. He had done exactly what he had told her father he'd do. He'd made something of himself. She was so proud of him. Mallory set down the tablet Elle's husband, Drake, created. It controlled everything in the room with a simple touch of the screen. Mallory needed to ask him to put the same system in her house.

She looked at her watch. She'd been in here for five minutes. That would be enough time to convince the event planner she had looked around. Reid's plane was due to arrive any minute. Before she turned from the windows overlooking the lake and the woods, she saw it coming in for a landing on the private airstrip.

Mallory turned to hurry from the room when the earth shook. She spun back to the windows as a fireball erupted in the back of the property over the thick tree line. Mallory felt her world stop. Reid. Oh my God, Reid! Mallory ran from the room and shoved the man coming out of his room out of her way as she raced for the stairs.

She took the stairs two at a time and leapt over the last half-flight to get to the exit. Vaguely she heard someone behind her but didn't have time to look. Her thoughts were only on getting to Reid.

Reid slammed against the wall as the brunette shoved past him. He was already on the phone calling 9-1-1 and organizing the hotel's emergency response protocol. He had never felt such fear as when he saw that explosion. He'd looked at his watch and realized it was Troy arriving with his cargo. He felt himself disconnect from the world.

That was why the woman was able to catch him by surprise and push him out of the way. He raced after her, desperately trying to get to the golf cart he kept out back. The thought of Troy dead was too much to contemplate as he chased the woman down the stairs.

Mallory shoved the emergency door open, not caring when it set off the fire alarm. She saw a fleet of golf carts to her right, but they would be too slow. She looked to her left and saw the stables. She ran as fast as she could and flung open the first stall in the barn. A huge stallion stood tossing his head.

"Come on, buddy; I don't have time to fight over who is in charge." Mallory hiked her skirt up her thighs, grabbed a hunk of mane, and vaulted onto his back.

The stallion fought her for a second, but then saw the open stall door and bolted. Mallory leaned down as they cleared the stall and squeezed her knees. The stallion took off at lightning speed. She passed a man on a golf cart as she flew over the countryside.

She leaned forward and held on tight as she urged the

horse faster. Her wig flew off after she jumped a hedgerow. She could see the fire now through the trees. Black smoke billowed from the airfield ahead of her. The stallion slowed, but she dug her knees into his side to urge him forward through the woods. The stallion was lathered in sweat as she pushed him harder. He reared when they broke through the woods and approached the airfield. Mallory refused to give in to his demands and pushed him toward the crash. As soon as his hooves hit the runway, Mallory leapt from him. Sensing the fire and her panic, the horse retreated toward the stables instantly.

Mallory almost fell to her knees as she took in the full scene. The back half of the plane was almost completely separated from the cockpit. The gas had exploded and the fuselage was engulfed in an inferno. There was no way Reid had made it. He'd never know how much she loved him—how sorry she was for being weak in response to her father's threats.

What had happened? She had to know. The pilot! Mallory stumbled forward with a new purpose. The nose of the plane was lying on its side with the windshield facing her. The nose was smashed and the cockpit torn to pieces.

"Troy!" Mallory screamed in horror as she saw the Simpson family pilot dangling upside down from his harness.

The heat was almost unbearable as she raced forward. Her eyes dried out instantly, and her lungs felt as if they had seized. She coughed uncontrollably as her body tried to expel the soot. Mallory grabbed her dress and raised the collar so it covered her mouth and nose, hoping to find some relief.

The windshield was partially torn from the plane as she struggled to fight the heat of the fire. Using her sandal-covered foot, she kicked at the loose material enough to be able to wedge her upper body into the cockpit. Troy hung upside down in his harness. Blood was everywhere. Part of his clothing had been ripped from his body.

Mallory reached up and grabbed his dangling hand. She pressed her fingers to his wrist and waited.

"Oh my God! Troy, I'm here! Hang on," she yelled as she ignored her burning skin and leaned farther into the cockpit.

Reid cursed the golf cart as he bounced along the terrain. Sure, it was more of an all-terrain vehicle, but at fifteen miles per hour he now wished he'd taken a horse like the woman had. She must be a doctor to run headlong into danger like that. His prize stallion had already passed him, running back to the stables. As he crested a hill, what he saw stole his breath.

The plane was just gone. Everything but the cockpit had been reduced to ash as fire ravaged it. He squinted and saw two legs attached to an orange bottom sticking out of the cockpit window. Part of the window had been torn away. Troy!

He raced onto the tarmac and slid to a stop as the heat of the fire knocked him back. An explosion sounded, and he jumped away. It must have been the oxygen tanks. Pushing through the heat, he felt his body fight against it. His mind told him to run, to seek safety, but he fought it and surged to the cockpit.

Reid heard sirens and looked back to see the resort's emergency personnel racing down the runway. He couldn't wait. He had to get the woman and Troy away from the plane. "Is he alive?" Reid shouted.

"Oh my God, Reid! You're alive. Help me. Troy's alive.

I need a knife to cut the seatbelt. It's too hot to unhook," the woman yelled, without turning around.

Reid turned to the cart he'd driven and found a pair of pruning shears for her. How did she know him? She must be one of the new women in hospitality to think he was on the plane. He ran back to the cockpit to take over. "I've got something."

"Give them to me. Watch out, the metal surrounding the window is hot."

Reid kicked the windshield to loosen it some more. He pushed it aside with his hip and felt the heat through his jeans. He shouldered through the opening, rubbing against the woman as he slid into the cockpit. She turned her blond head and Reid froze.

"Mallory?"

"Give me the knife. Reid, give me the knife. We have to get Troy out of here!" Her point was made when another small explosion went off in the back of the wreckage.

Blindly, he handed her the shears and looked up at Troy. "You're safe now, Troy. We've got you." He reached for the seatbelt, but the heat of the metal burned his hand.

He placed his hands on Troy's shoulders, bracing him as Mallory cut through the harness. Blood covered his hands and trickled down his arms. There was no way Troy was going to live. But he'd be damned if he'd let him die in this fire.

"Hurry up!"

"I'm almost done," Mallory muttered as she cut through the belt.

Suddenly Troy was free and falling down. Reid and Mallory grabbed him as he fell. "There's so much blood—" Reid said as he wrapped his arms around Troy's body.

"Don't think about it. Just think about getting him out.

I'll push open the window, and you pull with everything you've got. Okay?" Mallory had seen terrorist attacks, but she had been able to separate herself from them. Not this time. Not when she knew it was Troy and Reid in the path of danger.

"You'll burn yourself," Reid told her as he adjusted his grip on Troy. He fought the urge to leave Troy and get Mallory to safety.

"It's okay, I can take it. Whatever happens, just get him out. I wouldn't be able to carry him. It has to be you."

Mallory slid from the cockpit before Reid could argue. Blood covered her face, arms, and upper body from working to free Troy. She brushed past Reid and wedged herself between the cockpit and the loose windshield. She felt the hot metal from the plane burning into her stomach and the hot metal from the windshield against her lower back and thighs.

Taking a deep breath, she focused on Troy and pushed with her back against the windshield. The pain on her stomach lessened as she separated the window from the plane. "Go!" The hot metal singed the material on her dress. She felt as if she were being pinned against hot irons. She watched Reid as he pulled Troy from the cockpit. He wedged himself past her, and then Troy's body was hefted from the cockpit. Mallory cried out in pain as the burning intensified.

"Clear!" She heard Reid a second before he was there pulling her to safety.

She fell into his arms as tears burst forward. "You're alive . . . I was so scared I had lost you . . . I . . ." Reid pressed his lips to hers, cutting off anything else she was going to say.

Reid grabbed the back of her head and brought their lips together in a frantic kiss. He had to be sure she was really here. He couldn't believe she'd dived head first into danger. He wanted to wring her neck, but he kissed her instead. He was supposed to be dead. If she hadn't hurt him so much and made him leave Stromia early, he would be dead right now.

He put all of the fear, the guilt, and the hurt into the kiss. It lasted less than three seconds, but he felt her desperation for him, felt her love just as he had when he had kissed her for the first time all those years ago. But now wasn't the time. It never would be. He was glad she was alive, but he'd never let Mallory hurt him again.

They pulled apart at the same time. Mallory crawled over to Troy and ripped open the rest of his shirt. There was a bad burn mark where the metal of his seatbelt had been and where his clothes had been burned off of his lower legs. Lacerations covered the left side of his face—some down to the bone. A piece of metal was embedded in his thigh.

"He's not going to make it, Reid. We can't wait for an ambulance. He's losing too much blood. And I think his lung is punctured. He's having trouble breathing," Mallory said as she put her ear to his chest. Reid knew it too. Troy looked a hair's breadth from death.

The first rescue crew arrived with fire extinguishers and first aid kits. Reid grabbed the kit and ripped open the gauze. He wrapped it around Troy's leg, but the blood quickly soaked through it.

"Come on. We have to get him into the back of the truck."

Reid nodded and helped Mallory lift him. An employee opened the back door for them and helped get Troy's broken body into the backseat.

"I'll drive," Mallory said as she tossed him a sweatshirt from the front seat. "Use this to see if you can stop some of the bleeding. Don't worry about hurting him; just press as hard as you can. Sit on him if you have to."

"Drive fast," he yelled as she stepped on the gas.

"Hang on."

Chapter Eight

Mallory cut through the fields and tore through the resort's manicured lawn. Dirt flew as guests and hotel employees jumped out of the way screaming. Mallory made the turn onto the main road on two tires.

"Sorry about your lawn," Mallory said as she floored the truck.

"I don't give a shit about my lawn. Drive faster. I can't slow the bleeding," Reid yelled from the backseat. Mallory took a glance in the rearview mirror and saw Reid kneeling on the floorboard as he pinned Troy to the seat.

Her heart beat loudly as she fought the panic. She took a deep breath to steady herself and focused on the road. She pushed all the questions from the front of her mind and kept her eyes on the road.

Pulling the car into the opposite lane, Mallory flew past an eighteen-wheeler. At the last minute she swerved back into her lane, narrowly missing a sports car. The drivers caught each other's eyes and the sports car slammed on its brakes and U-turned.

"Elle is right behind us. I think she almost lost Shirley out the window when she spun the car around," Mallory told them as she watched the white head of Elle's office manager of an undeterminable old age pull back inside the car.

"Damn, they would think I was on the plane. I didn't tell anyone I was coming home early except Troy."

"So, that's how you're alive. Reid, I was so afraid . . ." She felt her voice break and her vision went blurry. Going 110 miles per hour on a small country road, she couldn't afford to cry right now. She blinked the tears away and kept her mouth shut. Soon the sports car was right on her tail as she got off the country road and onto the interstate.

"I think we have a lot to talk about, Mallory. But now's not the time."

Reid pressed his ear to Troy's chest and frowned. He couldn't hear anything. "I'm losing him!"

He was flung onto Troy as Mallory exited the interstate and turned toward the hospital. Reid pinched Troy's nose, pressed his mouth to his, and blew. He felt Troy's chest rise and continued with CPR. The truck bounced and Reid lost his grip. He became airborne and landed half on Troy. Frantically scrambling to continue CPR, he barely noticed they were driving on a sidewalk.

There were the sounds of the truck plowing through something and the horn blasting. "Stopping," Mallory shouted a second before she slammed on the brakes.

Reid wrapped Troy in a bear hug and flexed with all he had to keep Troy from flying forward. The doors to the back were flung open and doctors rushed forward.

"Plane accident. He was stuck in the cockpit. Burns to his legs, collapsed lung . . ." Reid heard Mallory calling to the doctors as he helped get Troy out of the back and onto a stretcher.

"Troy," Elle cried as she and his sisters piled out of her tiny sports car with Shirley, who was moving surprisingly fast for someone so old.

"Reid, are you hurt?" Bree screamed as she ran for him.

"It's not me. I wasn't on the plane. I flew home early. I don't know if he's going to make it." Reid opened his arms and his sisters flew into them. Elle, Bree, and Allegra clung to him as tears mixed with the relief of knowing their brother was safe.

"You had us worried, boy. You should have told us you came home early. Do you know how hard it was to call your mother with the news of the plane crash?" Tears rolled down Shirley's wrinkled face. He'd never seen her look so old.

"Mom," Allegra gasped as she pulled out her cell phone. "I'll let her know. Finn said he'd go pick her up. She was too upset to drive."

Allegra took a couple steps away to make the call. Elle looked up at him, tears filling her green eyes that looked a lot like his. "How bad is it?"

"Bad. We don't know what happened. I was at the hotel and heard the explosion. Mallory actually got to the plane first. Rode a horse bareback to get there. When I arrived, she was halfway in the cockpit trying to free Troy. We worked together to get him out, but he stopped breathing on the way here. I did CPR, but . . ." Reid looked around at the suddenly quiet entrance to the emergency room. He noticed the shrubs that had been plowed down by the truck and the tire tracks across the front of the hospital. "Where's Mallory?"

"She went inside with the doctors and Troy," Shirley told him. "Come on, let's get you cleaned up before your mother gets here."

Reid looked down at himself for the first time. Blood was everywhere. His mother would pass out. "Let's see if we can get an update and maybe a nurse can get me some scrubs."

They walked into the lobby, and the nurse flagged him down. "They took your friend into surgery. A doctor will be out as soon as he knows anything. Miss Westin ordered us to look you over too. Please come with me."

Reid and his sisters followed the nurse back to the ER. Shirley waited in the lobby for Margaret to arrive with Finn and would reassure his mother he was safe. He looked for Mallory, but didn't see her. He needed to know what was going on. Why was she at his hotel and why was she in a disguise? And more importantly, they needed to talk about their kiss.

"Where's Mallory Westin?" Elle asked the nurse. "She's my best friend, and I want to make sure she's not injured."

"She's with a doctor. There were some burns that needed to be treated. I'll come and get you once she's able to have company."

"I'll tell you, it was the shock of my life seeing her tearing down the road in a company truck. What was she doing at the hotel?" Elle asked Reid.

"I don't know. I want to ask her the same question. Nurse, would you mind if I had a pair of scrubs to change into?" Reid asked. He didn't want to talk to Elle about Mallory right now. There were too many emotions roaring through him, and he didn't think he would be able to keep up the façade of cold indifference toward Mallory if Elle kept talking. He was already worried she'd been burned.

Seeing Mallory in pain ripped him to shreds. He'd thrown up after he saw her beaten by the man stalking his youngest sister a few months before. The sound of her scream when she held the hot windshield open for him to drag Troy out still echoed in his mind.

"Ladies, you can wait in the hall while your brother gets cleaned up," the nurse instructed as he retreated to the privacy afforded by a drawn curtain. He took a deep breath and undressed before washing Troy's blood off in the sink.

Mallory didn't pay attention to the doctor examining her. She was lying in bed in nothing but her bra and panties. She had a burn on her palm, one on her shoulder, and he was examining the ones caused by the windshield now. Her hand was covered in a cooling gel and wrapped in a sterile glove. They weren't bad burns, but they were definitely painful. However, that was not what she was thinking about.

The images of the plane wreckage kept flashing through her mind. The dynamics of the fire troubled her. The plane was arriving from Stromia, and the gas tank should have been low. Sure, it would explode on impact. However, if the plane went down because of an empty gas tank or a mechanical issue, the fire wouldn't have been as intense as it was. She'd been with the military enough to see what happened when a plane was blown out of the sky by a surface-to-air missile.

Mallory worried her lip as more medicine was put on her burns. It made sense. She had seen the plane coming in for a landing, and it had seemed fine. Surface-to-air missiles, or SAMs as she knew them, could be portable and hoisted onto the shoulder. She would never admit she knew firsthand it wasn't hard to fire one. It only weighed around thirty-eight pounds. You fire one of those as the plane comes in for a landing and what she saw today would be the result. There was only one way to be sure, though.

"Are you done yet?" she asked the doctor.

"Almost. I'll give you some pain medicine to help with

the burns," the doctor said as he wrapped some gauze around her stomach and back.

"I don't want any. I need to get going," Mallory said as she reached for her dress.

"Miss Westin, you need the antibiotics and the fluids. While these are only second-degree burns, they need to be treated."

"Fine, but I need some privacy to make a phone call. It's important." Mallory had dropped her purse in the suite when she had seen the explosion.

The doctor looked at the stubborn set to her mouth and gave a quick nod. "If you promise to come right back to bed and finish all your treatment, you can use the phone in my office."

"Done. Let's go."

Reid sat still as his hand was bandaged. It was the only injury he had sustained. There was a red mark on his hip, but it wasn't any worse than a minor kitchen burn. His sisters were all gathered around him, making him even more agitated than before. He couldn't listen to them. His mind was focused solely on Mallory.

"I'll be right back," Reid said suddenly. His sisters all stared at him.

"Back? Where do you think you're going?" Bree asked.

"It's not important. I'll be right back. If Mom gets here, tell her I'm fine. Give me five minutes. I just need some time." Reid pleaded with Elle with his eyes. She always was tuned in to him, and he hoped she would get the hint.

With a smile she let him go. "He's been through a lot, and I'm sure we're making it worse with all our chatter," he heard her tell their sisters.

He approached the first nurse he saw. "Mallory

Westin?"

"Over there, but she just left with the doctor."

"Left for where?"

"To his office. She had a phone call to make. There's her doctor now; you can ask him. Offices are at the end of the hall." The nurse walked off to check on the other patients, and Reid decided to bypass the doctor and head straight for Mallory.

He walked down the sterile halls to the row of wooden doors with glass windows. The offices were a wreck of paper, dirty clothes, and couches with pillows for the doctors to catch a quick nap. He found Mallory in the third office.

"I need you," Mallory said into the phone.

Reid felt a stab to his heart. So he had just been imagining her feelings. How stupid he was.

"I'm telling you, it's too much of a coincidence. I think it was a SAM. Probably shoulder-launched from a couple of miles away. It's a small plane, and the damage was so severe."

Reid stopped walking away and came closer to the cracked door.

Mallory let out a long breath. She was in a hospital gown, and he got a good look at her rear end in the sexiest panties he'd ever seen. But then his gaze dropped to the bandages around her thighs. She was hurt. He forced himself not to push into the room and comfort her. He had to find out what she was talking about because right now it sounded like she was talking about a missile, and that didn't make sense.

"They could have killed him. If he had been on that plane, Ahmed, I don't think I could handle it. You know how much I love him. Find out who did this, and I swear they won't take another breath."

Reid blinked in complete shock. Mallory's voice wasn't her own. She was hard, vengeful, and she was protecting him. She loved *him*? She was worried about *him*?

Mallory tried to control her emotions, but she was having a very difficult time. The more she analyzed the plane accident, the more she knew it wasn't an accident at all. Someone had tried to kill the man she loved.

"I'll do what I can. You need to keep your emotions in check. Keep your cover," Ahmed mentored.

"Screw my cover. I will find them and take them out, slowly. Trying to kill me is one thing, but no one touches Reid," Mallory said through clenched teeth.

"Do you think it could be your father or Ambrose?"

"I don't know. It has to do with our time in Stromia. It has to."

"Have you talked to Bowie?"

"No. Bowie's the only other person besides you who knows about Reid, and that makes him a suspect. I don't know why he would do this, but I won't discount it either. You're the only one I can trust. Just look into it and call me on the phone you gave me. I'm getting out of the hospital soon and will manage to talk myself onto the scene. I'll send you pictures. If there's shrapnel piercing the fuselage from the outside, then I have my answer. I just need a quick look to confirm it wasn't an accident."

"I'll put Nabi on it. He'll ferret any information out. If this has to do with the assassination, then you better be careful. Your cover may already be blown."

"I know. But I'm more concerned with Reid at the moment."

"Keep me updated. I'll drive down if you need me.

Right now, Nabi and I will work the back channels to see what we can find out. Stay safe."

"Thanks, Ahmed."

Mallory hung up the phone and let out a deep breath. Her mind was going a mile a minute, working on scenarios and running through suspects. She turned around to finish her treatment and stopped dead. "Reid," she whispered.

He was standing with his arms folded across his chest, and by the way he was staring at her, she knew he'd heard enough of the phone call that she wouldn't be able to lie her way out of it. Finally he shook his head as if coming out of a trance.

"I think it's time we talked. Now."

Chapter Nine

Reid studied Mallory intently. The way she talked and the things she said didn't match the fun-loving, carefree teenager he had fallen in love with. Standing in front of him was a rigid, cold woman with ice in her veins. Here he was worried about her, and she was making phone calls to deal with the threats.

"Yes, I guess we do. But it can't be now. It can't be here." Mallory lifted her chin in a stubborn tilt he did recognize and marched past him.

Reid didn't reach for her. He simply watched as she walked by. He turned and followed her down the hall. He tried not to smile at the view. The gown was flapping open, allowing him to gaze at her ass. He ran his eyes down to the bandages and then to that sweet ass of hers. After all these years, it was still perfect. Reid squinted and sped up to get closer. Peeking out from under the waistband of her panties was a scar that hadn't been there before.

Mallory pushed the curtain to her bed open and turned quickly on him. "Later, I promise. I can't talk about it here, and it would be good if you don't mention anything you heard. Promise me."

Mallory climbed back into bed and inserted the needle of her IV back into the port.

"How do you know how to do that?" Reid asked,

watching her hook the IV back up.

"I know lots of fun things. Inserting an IV is one of them. Now, as soon as this bag is empty, I can leave."

Reid took a seat in the chair next to her bed. "I'll just wait until you're ready to go."

"I don't think that's a good idea."

"Why not?" Reid asked as he rested his ankle on his opposite knee and leaned back.

"Because I'm here now." Bowie pushed open the drape and stepped into the small curtained room.

Reid clenched his jaw. It was the bastard from Stromia who was sleeping with Mallory. Great, just what he needed. Then Reid remembered Mallory's telephone call and her not fully trusting him.

"Sorry, Bowie. Not your problem anymore. I'll take care of her. You have a young aristocrat still warm in your bed in Stromia."

He noticed Mallory didn't seem surprised or even angry. "It's all right, Bowie. I've known Reid since we were kids."

"Oh, I know just how well you know him, and I also know he's an asshole."

Reid jumped up with his hand clenched into a fist. The sound of a sharp clap stopped him from advancing. Bowie moved and there stood Reid's mother. She was dressed in her pressed slacks with their ever-present perfect crease. Her red hair was in an up do, and the smile on her face was the one that meant someone was going to be in trouble. Reid just hoped it wasn't him. But it was her red-rimmed eyes that made him back down.

"Don't worry, gentlemen. I'm here to take care of our Mallory."

Mallory smiled and her whole body relaxed. "Thank

you, Margaret. I hope we didn't worry you."

"Of course I was worried for my two babies. Excuse me, young man, but since you're not family, the doctor has asked that you leave." Margaret stared pointedly at Bowie and smiled.

"I'm Mallory's fiancé. If anyone needs to leave, it's you."

Reid and Mallory sucked in a breath of air as Margaret's smile grew larger and her eyes smaller. "Young man, I don't give a fig who you think you are. Until you've sat at my dinner table, you're not family. Now, shoo," Margaret waved him away with her hands. Bowie stepped back, and Mallory's mask slipped for a second. Reid saw her hide the smile behind her hand.

"Is there a problem, Mrs. Simpson?"

"Oh, Aiden! It's so good to see you again. This young man was just leaving. Perhaps you can assist him with that endeavor." Margaret batted her eyes at the sexy-as-sin doctor who towered over Bowie with his sculpted body and killer smile. No wonder he was such an expensive escort on the side.

"Anything for you, Mrs. S." Aiden winked at her and Margaret blushed.

"Who do we have here? Oh, Dr. Starr, grr," Shirley growled. She pushed her way into the small room. A sign stating *I Make Cougars Look Like Amateurs* was taped to her walker. Aiden winked at her before she turned her attention to Bowie. She gave him a slow once-over that had Mallory hiding her laughter. "Hello, sonny. And just who might you be?"

Bowie blinked a couple times in shock. "I-I'm Mallory's fiancé," he stuttered.

Shirley leaned over and checked out his backside. "Aw,

isn't he cute when he's trying to lie?" Shirley reached up and pinched his cheek. "I'll happily pinch your other set of cheeks if you want to lie again."

Bowie's eyes widened even more and Reid thought he heard a snort come from his mother.

"Mallory, tell them," Bowie pleaded as Shirley winked at him.

"Bowie is an old friend from college. But we're not engaged. We decided we weren't suited as a couple when we were in Stromia. It's okay, Bowie. I'm fine. As you can tell, I'm well looked after. I'll call you later."

"Need a ride, sonny?" Shirley asked.

"No, thank you. I have a car."

Shirley's smirk widened. "That's not the kind of ride I'm talking about."

Yep, his mother definitely snorted. Bowie's mouth dropped open, and he started backing away, not daring to turn his back on Shirley. "I'll call you later, Mal. Glad you're okay."

The drape closed and the sounds of a man running echoed off the tiled walls. Shirley shrugged. "See, told you I could get him to leave faster than you."

Aiden just shook his head, his mom snorted again, and Mallory broke out in giggles. "Thanks, Shirley. I wasn't ready to deal with Bowie. And thank you, Margaret. But really, I am okay. And as head of security for the resort, I need to get back and check on things."

Reid's brow creased in confusion. "You're not the head of security."

"She is now," Elle said as she walked into the room with Bree and Allegra right behind her.

"Thanks for y'all leaving us like that," Allegra said with mock hurt.

"Sorry. I ran into Mallory and wanted to see how she was doing," Reid said apologetically to his sisters.

Shirley reached up and pinched his cheek. "Men really are so cute when they lie."

Elle looked between Reid and Mallory. He saw her mind actually working to figure out what was going on between them. He wasn't quite ready for that since he himself didn't know what was going on.

"Look, Mallory. Your IV is finished. Dr. Starr, is she ready to go now?" Reid asked.

Aiden picked up her chart and looked it over. He signed some papers and looked up at Mallory. "You're ready to go. Keep your bandages clean for the next week and apply the salve for two weeks. They should stop bothering you in just a couple days."

"Thank you, Aiden." Reid noticed that Mallory waited for Dr. Starr to unhook her from the IV.

"You're welcome, Miss Mallory. Now a nurse will be in to assist you in getting dressed. She has a pair of scrubs for you to wear since your dress was ruined. Remember, keep the bandages clean."

"Don't worry that nurse. I'll help her," Elle said as she stepped farther into the room. "You all can leave now. Reid needs to be discharged, and we can meet you in the lobby."

Reluctantly, Reid cast a quick glance at Mallory. He would just have to wait to talk to her. Urgency clawed at him as he forced himself to walk out of the room.

Mallory waited. She knew Elle's boardroom voice and knew she wanted privacy to talk. As soon as the nurse arrived with the scrubs, Aiden gave her some last minute instructions and her discharge papers. He left with a wink to the two of them. Elle waited a full ten seconds to get to the point.

"What happened between you and Reid?"

"What are you talking about?" Mallory asked as she turned her back and stepped into the scrubs.

"You know exactly what I am talking about. Right before college, something happened, and it hasn't been the same between you two since. In fact, it took me getting married before the two of you were even in the same room together. Now we come in here and he's ready to deck the sleazebag you thought you were going to marry. Add that to the fact he decked Finn's friend for talking about you . . ."

Mallory didn't turn around as she slowly worked the shirt over her burns. Reid had punched someone for her? But, Reid hated her . . . right? "I didn't know about any of that. I don't know why Reid would punch someone. It's my understanding he doesn't like me very much. To spare you having to walk a tightrope between us, we kind of came to an understanding that we would stay apart."

"What a bunch of malarkey. You've done a lot of things in your life you haven't told me about. But when did you start lying to me too?" Elle snapped.

Mallory spun around. "About sixteen years ago. There, are you happy?" Mallory stepped into her shoes. When she straightened up, Elle was glaring at her with hurt in her eyes. "What?" Mallory asked briskly.

"I have a right to know. Reid is my brother."

"Then ask him. Now, if you would excuse me, I have a crash site to get to. Unless you want to fire me too?" Mallory suddenly felt bad as Elle seemed to deflate.

"No, of course not. I'm just worried about you."

"I'm sorry," Mallory said softly as she walked passed Elle. "I'm fine, Elle, I promise. Just let me do my job."

Mallory plastered on her fake smile and headed to the

lobby. She made her excuses to the Simpson family and felt a sharp pain in her heart when she got into a cab. She wasn't their family. As Elle pointed out, Reid was her brother. For all they called each other sisters, they weren't. It was time for her to leave. It was time for her to give herself a chance to find her own happiness. As soon as this case was solved, she was out of here.

Reid fumed as he drove the truck back to the resort. A bush still hung from the grill, but as soon as he found out Mallory had already left, he didn't bother taking the time to pry it off. The conversation he overheard kept playing in his mind as he took the far entrance to the resort and drove toward the airfield.

Flashing lights and emergency vehicles filled the airstrip. The NTSB, FBI, and local authorities were all working the scene. Reid stopped the truck and stared dumbstruck at the remains of the plane. Troy was still in surgery. His mother was at the hospital waiting for news. How he'd even survived this long was a miracle.

He spotted Mallory instantly. She was on her hands and knees with a man who looked to be from the NTSB. She was crawling along the remains of the fuselage examining tiny bits of debris. Reid saw her point something out at the far end of the plane, and when the official looked away from her, she snapped some pictures on her cell phone.

"I'm sorry, sir, but this is a restricted area," a uniformed deputy told him.

"I'm Reid Simpson. I own this plane and resort. It's my pilot and friend in the hospital, so I would really like to know what's going on."

"Mr. Simpson." Agent Hectoria stepped from the crowd. She had helped his sister Allegra with her stalker. Actually, it was Mallory who had saved her life. And now it was Mallory who was trying to find out what had happened to his plane. It was always Mallory.

"I'm sorry to see you again under these circumstances. I let your head of security examine the wreckage as you requested. Mallory is very informative. She and the NTSB investigator are looking over some of the details now."

"Was it an accident?" Reid asked as he watched Mallory over Agent Hectoria's shoulder. She distracted the investigator again and took some more pictures.

"We won't know until the investigation is complete. The black box was recovered and has already been sent off for analysis," she told him noncommittally.

Mallory stood up and shook hands with the investigator and paused when she saw Reid. "Please keep me up to date. If you'll excuse me, I need to have a word with my head of security."

Agent Hectoria handed him her card and went back to the group of investigators as Mallory slowly made her way toward him.

"Reid."

"What did you find? You said on the phone, to whoever this Ahmed guy is, you would know instantly."

"Not here. Let's go back to the hotel. You drive."

Mallory walked past him and got into the passenger seat of the truck. He paused when she winced in pain. By the time he got in, she was on her phone sending all the pictures she had taken to someone. "Would you please . . .?"

"Hold on," Mallory reprimanded as she typed out a message. Moments later the phone rang.

Mallory's heart pounded. She had known it the second she saw the wreckage. The plane had been taken down by a SAM. The phone rang, and she answered it immediately.

"I got your pictures," Ahmed said. "We are of the same conclusion. My wife is looking at them now. Bridget has experiences with bombs as well."

"What did Nabi find?"

"An employee of Luxus was found murdered. Single gunshot to the front of the head. He was an assistant to their head of security. Dario was his name."

"There must be a link."

"Yes. And Bridget says it was a shoulder-launched surface-to-air missile for sure. One of the newer generations, too, since it hit the side of the plane as opposed to tracking the heat source and hitting from behind."

Mallory's mind raced as images from the previous seventy-two hours snapped into place. There were still some gaps, but it was a start. "Thank you. Let me know if you find out anything else."

Mallory ended the call and saw Reid watching her. "Take me to my car, please. I need to get some things from it, and then we can go to your suite and talk."

Reid looked at her suspiciously but turned the truck into the parking lot. It didn't take long for him to spot Mallory's car. He pulled into the space next to hers and got out. Mallory opened the purse she must have retrieved from upstairs and unlocked the car. She opened the hood and pulled out a small bag.

"Let's go. But not one word until I say so, okay?"

Reid pursed his lips but nodded. She tried to think of how to say all the things that needed to be said. Sixteen years of feelings, thoughts, and events that had been left unmentioned—ignored and pushed to the side.

Her heart was racing by the time she stepped into his suite. Mallory opened the bag; Reid went to the table and picked up his phone. She pulled out the scanner and turned it on. She swept the room for bugs while Reid listened to voicemails. She breathed a little easier when she determined the room was clean.

"I can't believe this," Reid said as he turned off his phone. "A member of my security team was found murdered."

"Dario. Yes, I know."

"How do you know? Who were you talking to? What is going on, Mallory?" Reid asked angrily.

"I think someone is trying to kill you."

Reid didn't know what to say. "Kill me? Why?"

"Your security assistant was murdered and your plane was shot down by a missile. You tell me why. What have you done that would warrant someone trying to kill you?"

Reid's phone rang again. He picked it up when he saw it was from Luke. "What is going on over there?"

"Thank goodness! I've been trying to get hold of you since they found Dario."

"I got your messages about his murder."

"I didn't want to leave this on a voicemail. Mr. Simpson, I pulled up everything Dario had been working on as soon as we found out about his murder. The last thing he did before leaving was to copy the high-stakes game, and then he wiped the system. All our digital files from the game are gone."

"I knew something was wrong. So I have the only file?"

"No. He made two copies. When the police found him, he didn't have it on him. I've, um, taken upon myself to search for it. It's not here, and it's not at his home. It's vanished."

"Thank you for calling me, Luke. Let me know if anything else happens."

"I will. If there is something here, I will find it."

Reid hung up the phone and looked at Mallory. She wasn't even hiding the fact she'd been eavesdropping. "Do you have hearing aids like Shirley?"

Mallory smiled and Reid gulped. Sixteen years and she could still turn him into a weak-kneed boy. "I have a lot of fun toys I'll show you sometime. What's on the file?"

"Security footage of the poker game you were at the other night. Your turn. Why is it worth killing for?"

Mallory took a deep breath and sat down in one of the armchairs. "Liam. This all has to do with Prince Liam."

Chapter Ten

"What do you know about Liam?" Mallory asked as she crossed her legs.

Reid thought for a moment and shrugged. "In all my business dealings with him, he comes across as a spoiled brat with a merciless streak. He throws a fit if he doesn't get what he wants, when he wants it. I know he hates his father, who is going to die any day now. But what does that have to do with me?"

"Nothing until you apparently showed an interest in the poker game."

"He was laundering money, wasn't he?"

"I think it was more of a payoff. The only thing we, meaning the CIA and Rahmi security, can't figure out is how they are connected."

"The payoff was to Black and Jonak. That was easy enough to see on the video." Reid blew out a long breath. He hated politics. And people thought casinos were a dirty business. "So he paid Jonak and Black to pull the trigger. When I asked for a copy of the tape, my guy sold me out. They killed him and then tried to kill me so there was no video evidence that could link them."

"Most likely. There's evidence of a plot to kill one of the presidential candidates. Liam somehow gave the identity of the target to one of them during the poker game."

"Let's watch the video. Maybe your eyes will see something I missed."

Reid pulled up the video on his computer and they leaned forward. He moved the video to the end of the game. "This is the part that caught me by surprise."

"Me, too. It was over so fast. Can you pull up all the angles?"

Reid nodded and the screen split into fours. They watched in silence as Liam went all in. He flipped his cards when he realized he lost. Then he slid his hand into his pocket so briefly it was hardly noticeable. He shook hands with Black and then Jonak. As soon as he let go of Jonak's hand, Jonak slid his hand into his pocket and smiled.

"There," Mallory called as she pointed. "He must have had the name on a piece of paper. I didn't see it because they were facing the dealer most of the time. It looked so natural."

"So, Jonak is the killer for hire?" Reid asked.

"It looks like it. I always thought it was both of them. I thought they were partners, but we can't find a connection between them."

"It's both of them. They're cousins." Reid saw the shock on Mallory's face.

"How do you know that?"

"Easy. Found it using our security software. The CIA doesn't hold a candle to the type of information casinos can get their hands on," Reid said with a little smugness of his own.

"Cousins . . ." Mallory stood up and sent a text. "If they are working together, then the outcome of the poker game didn't matter so long as one of them won. And if they are that connected, then their businesses must be as well. But all their records are clean. There is no money going from one to the other."

"Not into their new companies, no. But what about the company started by their grandmothers?" Reid asked.

"Amazing—years of research and all the CIA needed to do was go to a casino. You're running relationship awareness searches, aren't you?" Mallory asked excitedly.

"Sure am. I was suspicious and started pulling on threads this morning. Their grandmothers were sisters and started a small antiques store. Somehow this store grossed hundreds of thousands of dollars during the 1950s. They each had a son who started their own antiques store the next town over. However, when we pulled up the records, they were all owned under the same company name. That company is still run today by Black's and Jonak's fathers. It also appears Black and Jonak like expensive antiques. They've spent millions on old chairs from their fathers' stores," Reid told her.

"Their grandmothers ran the crime ring. After they passed, it was handed off to their sons. Black and Jonak have legit businesses as a cover. All illegal activity is laundered through antiques. The assassin must be in the fathers' employ," Mallory said as she snapped her fingers.

Reid shook his head in amazement. "Now it makes sense. When Luke and I watched the game, we thought they were possibly laundering dirty drug money. Instead they were laundering a payment for assassination."

"Exactly." Mallory started pacing the room as she snapped her fingers. "How is this for irony? The candidate, or candidates, who hired the assassin were there along with the ones meant to be killed. They lost too. And that money also went to Jonak. One of the candidates just paid for his own murder."

"What about the President of France?" Reid asked.

"I don't know. I'll pass that tidbit on to Bowie."

Reid narrowed his eyes. "What exactly is Bowie to you? And for that matter, who exactly are you?"

"Bowie is my CIA handler. I was recruited as an asset in college. I was just there to keep my ear to the ground and pass along anything interesting I picked up on the party circuit. Then I saved the lives of Princes Mohtadi and Dirar Ali Rahman. Prince Mohtadi's head of security, Ahmed, took me under his wing. He taught me how to be a spy and a lot more. I started getting orders directly from the President of the United States and the director of the CIA. I would say I was more of an off-the-books government asset. Somewhere, someone approved spending for a really expensive office chair, and that's who I was."

"What kind of orders did you get?" Reid didn't know what to think. Mallory had been kind as a teenager. She had so much love inside her he didn't know how she could be a ruthless contract agent.

Mallory shrugged. "I stole some government secrets. Got some stolen secrets back. Made sure some treaties were signed and some spies sent back to the US."

"How did you do that? Your face was on the cover of every gossip site."

"Give me some credit. I was never seen. An unmarked envelope would make its way to the desk of the king or president with some leverage in it, encouraging them to follow through with their promises. If I had to do something in person, I was in disguise. I know how to fool even your facial recognition software."

Reid shook his head as he tried to wrap his mind around this. "What kind of things did you have to do in person?"

Mallory took a deep breath. "You hate me anyway, so

it's not like I'm going to change your mind about me. When I had to kill someone, like this one warlord in Africa who was involved in the trafficking of little children, I was disguised as an international aid worker. There, I've told you and now you know. I'm not Mallory Westin, debutante, anymore."

"Did you save the children?" Reid asked quietly.

Mallory turned away but not before he saw her eyes tear up. "Most of them. One hundred seventy-three were saved. They killed forty-two before I could stop them and twenty-six have never been accounted for."

Reid stood up and walked over to her. Her head was down and her shoulders sagged. "I don't hate you, Mallory. And I certainly don't hate you for doing what you did to save people. You're a protector. Look how you protect my sisters."

He turned Mallory around in his arms and looked down into her cloudy blue eyes. Suddenly it hit him. Anger coursed through him at her betrayal. "Have you been protecting me without my knowing?"

Reid waited in silence. He felt her body close to his. He felt the feelings rush back to him. Sixteen years and they were as strong as ever. When she gave a simple nod he lost the tight control he'd been keeping on his heart.

"Damn it, Mallory. What have you done?" he asked as he held her tightly in his arms. Anger, love, hurt, and hope warred inside him.

"What I had to. I had to protect you and your family," Mallory said in a muffled voice. Reid loosened his grip on her so she wasn't talking into his chest.

"Protect us how? From whom?"

Mallory shook her head. "I can't. Not yet. You're not safe yet. I can't protect you until my birthday."

Her birthday? She'd be, what, thirty-five next month? Reid let his head fall back in frustration. All the talks they had had that summer came forward from the depths of his memory. It was the year she would receive her full inheritance. She'd be wealthier than her own father. She'd own all the farms, industries, and lots of old money.

"Your father said something to you that night. He bent over and whispered to you. He threatened us, didn't he? That's why you didn't go with me. You were protecting us the only way you knew how." Reid clenched his jaw. His hands tightened into fists. "I should kill him." He stepped away from Mallory and opened and closed his fists. He didn't know how to process all this new information. It clashed with everything he'd been telling himself for the past sixteen years.

"You may not have to. It seems our friendly assassin may help you out on that matter."

Some of the anger left Reid as he watched Mallory bite her bottom lip. She always did that when she was worrying about something. "I'm sorry. He's still your father. What do you want me to do?"

"Stay alive," Mallory tried to joke. "Okay, I think it may all go down here at the wounded soldiers charity event. It's what I would do. I need access to everything without being seen. I can't let the assassin know I'm on to him. It's the only way I can protect you both."

"What if it's your father who is behind this?" Reid asked quietly.

"I'll stop him just as I would anyone else."

Reid pushed aside his conflicted heart and pulled her into his arms. He allowed himself to savor the feel of her if only for a minute. "I can help with the access you need. But you have to do something for it."

Mallory looked into his eyes, and he felt the smile tugging at his lips. The same wild abandon that had raced away with his heart one summer so long ago swept over him once again. "You have to have dinner with me tonight."

"You want to spend time with me?" Mallory asked with both confusion and hope in her voice. Reid knew in that instant he was willing to let go of the pain he thought she had caused him. Tonight he would know if they would be able to get past it.

"We have sixteen years to make up for. Go home, get whatever you need, and then meet me here in two hours." Reid felt excited for the first time in a long time. Her father had kept them apart, and now he had a chance to prove to her he was worth coming back to; he was strong enough and powerful enough to take her father on. She was worth it and so much more. Mallory broke from his embrace and with a single nod accepted the invitation. Reid opened the door for her and watched her leave. Only this time he knew she would be back.

Black and Jonak leaned closer to the speakerphone. "What do you mean he's not dead?" Black demanded.

"He apparently flew home the day before. No one knew."

"You blew up an empty plane? Damn it!" Jonak slammed his meaty hand onto the table, causing the speaker to jump.

"I'll fix it."

"You better," Black snapped. "And you're not getting paid for this one. By next week, the candidate and Reid

Simpson better be dead. I don't care if you burn the whole fucking place to the ground so long as they are locked inside. We have too much riding on Prince Liam to mess this up."

"It will be done."

Jonak hung up the phone and turned to his cousin. "We should think about finding another base of operations."

"You may be right. Let's see how this plays out, though."

Chapter Eleven

Mallory picked up the ringing phone as she packed for her stay at Reid's resort. She stood looking into her gun safe, trying to decide between the Beretta and the Glock. She grabbed them both. Guns were like shoes: you could never pack too many.

"Lloyd, thanks for calling me back," Mallory said as she answered. Lloyd was the accountant to the stars—the criminal stars, that was.

"Mallory darling," he said in his prim British accent. After all, being an earl meant that manners were bred into him just like they were in the South. "What can I do for my favorite poppet?"

"I need some information. Someone wants to hurt my daddy, and I just can't let that happen," Mallory said as sweet as sugar. Lloyd loved it. If she was with him in person, she might even have thrown in a pout and a bat of her lashes.

"My poor poppet! Tell Lloyd what he can do to help."

"I need to know all about Prince Liam's finances."

"Prince Liam is involved? Then I daresay you do need some help. Spoiled whelp. I've seen my fair share of bad apples in royal families, but he's a blighter."

"I think he's the one arranging things with Black and Jonak. Have you heard of them?"

"By Jove, those two have quite the reputation as dirty up-and-comers. But, they still have a lot to prove. Their fathers are something of a legend, or a nightmare, in the underworld—ruthless to the core. Rumor has it Black and Jonak have gone all in with Prince Liam. If they fail their fathers . . . well, let's just say their fathers will cut their losses."

"I think Liam is using them to orchestrate this assassination, either through some off-the-books account I can't find or through their fathers' business."

Mallory heard Lloyd take in a deep breath. "I can look into Black and Jonak, but their fathers . . . that could be dangerous."

"Don't do anything that would put you in danger. Just keep your ear to the ground, will you?"

"For you, of course. It'll take some time because I'll need to be very careful. I'll call you when I have something. Don't fret, poppet. Lloyd will come through for you."

Mallory smiled at the phone as she pushed a pair of boot knives into the foam of the steel case. "Thank you, Lloyd. Kisses."

Mallory looked into the drawer and pulled out two combat knives along with two daggers. She placed them into the foam liner and closed the case. She set it by the door along with one bag of clothes, one bag of shoes, and one bag of guns. She looked back in her safe and saw the military combat tomahawk. Hmm, a girl never knew when she might need one of those.

Mallory grabbed it from the hook and slid it into her Prada tote. Feeling secure in her ability to protect Reid, she headed out the door. If only she was secure enough to tell him everything about her past. Maybe telling him about the number of people she had killed was like telling him the number of men she had slept with . . . best to divide it by three.

Reid headed downstairs and walked through his lobby. He was freshly showered and dressed in his typical suit and tie. He passed behind the front desk, saying hello to the people working, and headed back to some of the offices.

He knocked once on the partially open door of the event planner's office and walked in. Evelyn looked up from the computer and smiled at him. He smiled back and took a seat across from her desk. Evelyn was twenty-eight, stunningly beautiful, and would do anything to please. He didn't know from experience, but by the looks she sent him he knew he could if he ever wanted to.

"Evelyn."

"Yes, Mr. Simpson. What can I do for you today?"

"I have someone from my Las Vegas hotel coming today. Miss Winters is the head of events there, and I want her to come and take a look around."

Evelyn's eyes blinked rapidly. Her lower lip pouted just a bit. "Are you displeased with me?"

"Not at all. Miss Winters will be a silent observer only. And she's not here to comment on your job performance. She's solely here to see if there is anything the hotel chain itself can do or offer to improve our guest relations."

"Oh, like destination wedding and honeymoon packages?"

"Exactly. That's one of the things she's looking at—a package at the same resort or if we can offer a special for couples using one of our hotels for the wedding and another for the honeymoon. So, please feel free to write down any ideas you have and tell the staff to answer her questions, but don't draw too much attention to her. She's going to stay through the charity ball at the end of this week. Can you have the Star Suite made up for her?"

"Sure thing, Mr. Simpson. Is there anything else you'll be needing?" Evelyn asked as her tongue darted out to lick her bottom lip.

"No, thanks, Evelyn."

Reid headed through the lobby and entered the ballroom. In a couple of days, this place was going to be packed with people. Secret Service was scheduled to arrive tomorrow even though Agent Wallace had already done a preliminary report on the place and sent it to Washington.

"It doesn't look like there could be that many places to hide, but I can think of six ways right now to kill someone."

Reid turned and looked at Mallory, standing behind him. He blinked at the black wig she wore. With her porcelain skin, it made her look vampish in a sexy way. He cocked his head. There was something different about her nose too. It was pointier. She looked around the room with a critical eye that made Reid realize he didn't know anything about her anymore. He looked back where the stage was going to be and wondered how he felt about this side of her. He'd been shocked when he'd found Mallory bloody and beaten in an alley as she tried to protect his sister Allegra from a dangerous stalker. Once again when Mallory had killed the son of a bitch with a single shot to the back of his head.

He'd seen her at the hospital afterward. She hadn't shed a tear. She wasn't shaking. She didn't seem upset at all. He'd thanked her for saving his sister and never thought she should have been more upset after killing a man, even if he was a bad man. Did Mallory even have feelings anymore? From the limited interaction he'd had with her, he had thought she had turned emotionless . . . just like her father.

"Are you saying that for shock value? To make sure I know how much you've changed?" Reid asked as he looked her in the eyes.

"Yes and no. I'm not the same person I was, Reid. I don't know how to explain it. I've buried so much for so long, I don't know how to let it out—or if I should. You need to know that. And then, yes, I can also see those things happening. It's just like planning a seating chart for a society event. I can see it all laid out. Every angle, every possibility. See there," Mallory pointed to the air return vent. "I'd sit in there with a rifle. I've seen the plans, but tonight I'll need a way up there. I want to check it out for myself."

Reid looked up, way up, at the vent. "You want to go up there?"

Mallory nodded her head. "Where is the stage going to be set?"

"There." Reid pointed to the far end of the room.

"Miss Winters! I didn't know you were already here," Evelyn cried as she hurried across the ballroom.

"That's you. Event planner from Las Vegas. Trying to come up with ideas to implement across the hotels," Reid murmured before turning around to introduce them.

"A pleasure, Evelyn." Mallory smiled. Reid looked at her again as Evelyn talked. Mallory was telling the truth. She had no real emotion. She smiled and laughed, and none of it was true.

"Please let me know if there is anything I can help with. Anything at all," Evelyn said sweetly.

"I will. Thank you. Right now I'm going to head up to

my room. It's been a long flight."

"Of course, your key is at the front desk, and your bags have already been taken up."

"Thank you. I'll see you later, Mr. Simpson."

Reid stood and watched Mallory leave with Evelyn. His mind may have been wondering if Mallory was the same person he had fallen in love with, but his heart already told him she was. She just needed to be reminded what they shared.

Mallory wiggled into a pair of jeans and a tight-fitting black top. She slipped her feet into a pair of ballet flats and pulled her long hair into a ponytail. She wasn't going to get dressed up for dinner tonight. Not when she was going to be crawling around ductwork in a couple of hours.

Mallory looked in the mirror then looked away. It was all a lie. She was all a lie. She didn't even know who she was anymore. Her life had been one of vengeance. Anything it took to make her father angry. She didn't even know how she felt about her father's involvement in all this. When Ahmed had said her father was possibly in danger, she'd felt something. Guilt? She didn't know, and she didn't particularly want to think about it.

The knock at the door stopped her thoughts. It would be Reid. It was time for dinner. That was a whole other bag of worms she didn't want to open. He knew. He believed her. But, could she still protect him?

"Good evening, Reid."

Mallory swallowed. He was so handsome as he held out his arm for her to take. She giggled as she took it, and Reid smiled. Old emotions that had been buried deep struggled to awaken.

"There she is," Reid said with an achingly sweet smile.

"Who?"

"The Mallory I fell in love with." Reid pushed open his door and led her inside. Candles were everywhere. The table was set with linens and two covered plates. Wine was chilling. It was the most romantic sight she'd seen.

"I don't know if that woman exists anymore, Reid," Mallory confessed.

"She does. I see her every now and again. You've protected me long enough, Mallory. You should have told me. We could have figured out a way together," Reid said as he cupped her face with his hands.

Mallory felt her throat tighten with emotion. "No, we couldn't. It wasn't just you he threatened. It was your whole family. You know he's powerful enough to follow through with his threats of the IRS and SEC. But I'm proud of you. You and your family worked together, and look what you've accomplished. I'm so glad you found something you love doing."

"But what about you? Do you love working for the government? The same government your father works for?"

"I didn't do it for love. I did it for revenge. And I haven't done it in years. This just directly affected me, so I was brought back in. As for owning my security firm, it's something I'm good at."

"Are you happy, Mallory?"

Mallory looked into his eyes and shook her head. "For what I did to you, I don't deserve happiness. How could I ever be happy knowing how much I hurt you? The memory of the pain on your face when I told you to leave . . ." Suddenly her face was crushed against his chest. One hand cradled the back of her head while the other held her tight.

"Mallory, you sacrificed yourself for me. I was angry with you, hated you even, but my heart still wanted you. I've thought about nothing else for the past two hours. I was upset that you didn't tell me. But the more I thought about it, the more I understood your reasoning. If anyone deserves happiness, it's you—no, it's us," Reid corrected. "We deserve happiness. Or at least the chance of it."

"I can't, Reid. Not until this is settled. I can't lose focus now. Not when someone is out there trying to kill you."

"Let it go, Mallory. You've protected me long enough. Tomorrow I'm hiring a horde of private bodyguards."

"They won't be able to stop him. In fact, it will make it easier. Do you know how many times I slipped in to do a job as a bodyguard? Let me do this, Reid. Let me do my job. I'm good at it. It's my redemption. Please."

Mallory waited as Reid thought about it. "Fine. But I'm not wasting another moment. We have years to catch up on, and I'm not about to wait."

Mallory's protest was cut short by Reid's lips closing on hers. He was hesitant as if waiting for her to stop him, but when she didn't immediately push him away, he took control. Mallory moaned and clung to him as he reminded her with every caress of his tongue why they were destined to be together.

Reid felt as if the piece of him that had been missing was finally found. He was complete once again. His heart pounded with happiness. Every kiss, every sound, every taste was emblazoned on his heart and in his memory. Only now it wasn't in his dreams. It was real. Mallory had left him to protect him. She had loved him. It had to mean something that all these years later neither of them had been in a serious relationship. Neither of them had found love again.

He ran his hand down her side and felt the curve of her breast and the indentation at her waist as he carefully avoided her burns. His fingers flexed into her hip as he pulled her closer to him. There was no one else for him. It had always been her. It would always be her.

"Mallory, I love you," Reid said as his lips rubbed against hers. He felt her stiffen and cursed himself. He'd moved too fast.

"Reid . . ."

Reid pulled back and looked into her face. Gone was the mask; all that was left were vulnerable wide eyes. "I know it's too soon, but it's not soon at all. I've never stopped loving you. Don't give up on us. Believe in us, Mallory. Together we can stand up to your father. Together we can handle anything."

"I want to. But what if I can't protect you?"

"I can protect myself, Mallory. And you. Let me do this. Let me prove to you I can give you the life we've always dreamed of—one filled with love and happiness. I'll give all of this up, every single penny I've made, to protect us and to protect our dreams."

A tear rolled down her cheek. It was first time he'd really seen her cry. "I want to so badly. I want to believe in happily ever after."

"Let me prove it exists. We can take our time. I won't rush you."

Mallory's lip quirked. "I remember you saying something like that before. And you didn't rush me. I believe you, Reid; I'm just so scared to hope again."

"You scared?" Reid teased. "You're not scared of anything."

"I'm scared this is a dream. So many times I tried to talk

to you, and you shut me down."

"I thought you truly didn't care for me."

"I'm scared you won't love me for me, Reid. I don't doubt you love me for who I was, but what about who I am now?"

"I can't wait to hear all about who you are now." Reid took a step back and pulled out the chair. "Why don't you start by telling me about saving those princes?"

Chapter Twelve

Mallory covered her mouth with her napkin as she laughed. Reid had responded to her stories of danger and intrigue with stories of his own. Dumb criminal stories and casino escapades, causing her to laugh so hard her sides hurt. When she had confessed the darkest things she'd seen or done, he had listened while holding her hand across the table. She could tell he looked at her differently, but not in disgust, which was what she had feared the most. It was contemplative. It was as if he were seeing her for the woman she had become instead of the girl she had been.

Mallory's phone buzzed. "I'm sorry," she said as she tried to stop laughing. "I have to see what this is."

Nabi just heard from his contacts. The King of Stromia will be dead by Monday.

"What is it?" Reid asked with concern.

"Our time frame just got shortened."

Mallory typed back, *Assassin will be here on Friday. It's the only time that fits.*

"What time frame? Here?"

Mallory shook her head. "The King of Stromia is dying. Rahmi fears Liam will want his first act as king to be against his rival. It means there's now added pressure on the assassin to get the job done. It means he might not wait until the charity ball on Friday."

"But you said that was his best bet to kill the candidate."

"Yes, that's true. But not you. We have four days to catch him before the charity event, and I have a feeling those four days will be spent trying to keep you safe."

Reid grabbed her hand in his and held it until she looked him in the eyes. "Okay, we'll do this together. What do we need to do?"

"Let's start with moving my bags into your living room. I'm not leaving your side until this is over."

Reid shot her a grin. "I can't complain about that."

Mallory rolled her eyes, and Reid just chuckled.

"Before we go downstairs, I think I also need to tell my sisters," Reid said seriously.

"What? You can't do that. They can't know who I am," Mallory said desperately.

"Mallory, they'll love you just the same, maybe more."

"No, they won't. They'll be terrified of me. They'll be disgusted by the things I am capable of."

"I wasn't. Mallory, trust in us."

"I can't risk it. Tell them not to come to the charity ball. Tell them whatever to get them away from Atlanta. But please, Reid, I'm begging you, don't tell them what I am."

"Fine. Get your bags while I call them. Then we'll head into the ballroom. It's late enough that no one will be around."

Mallory stood up. "Thank you. I'll be right back."

Reid watched her hurry from the room before pulling out his cell phone. He dialed his oldest sister first and waited for Elle to pick up the phone.

"Hey, Reid. Any word on Troy?" Elle asked as soon as she answered.

"He's still critical. However, his chances improve every hour."

"Any idea what caused the crash?"

"Elle, I don't know how to say this, so I am going to just put it out there. The plane was shot down on purpose."

"What?" Elle yelled into the phone with surprise.

"I saw something I wasn't supposed to, and now they're trying to kill me. I need you to take the whole family to the Connecticut compound for a week. Call it whatever you want. Just don't tell them what's going on, okay?"

"Not okay. What are you going to be doing? And who is trying to kill you and what did you see?"

"I'm going to be staying here. I'm working with people to catch the person responsible, but I don't want you in danger. And you'll be in danger if I tell you anymore. Please, just take the family and leave."

"Mallory is helping you, isn't she? That's why she was with you in the truck. You would put Mallory in danger but not tell your own sister?"

Reid heard the hurt in her voice. "I didn't tell Mallory, she told me."

"How did she know?"

"Elle, I know you run the family company and feel compelled to run everything else, but this time you don't get to. Just do what I say."

"Reid, I . . ."

"Don't argue, Elle," Reid said sharply. "I'm begging you to trust me and do what I say."

His sister let out a long sigh. "Do I really manage everything?"

"Yes." She did. She wasn't pushy about it, but she'd tried to manage him her whole life.

"I'm sorry. I'll trust you, and I trust Mallory. Is it wrong I'm happy you're actually talking to each other again?"

"As long as it makes you happy enough to leave."

"I'll call everyone now. It'll be hard to get Mom to leave Troy, though. She hasn't left his side. We'll be gone by morning. Let me know when we can come back."

"I will. Thank you, Elle."

"I love you, Reid."

"I love you too, sis."

Reid hung up the phone and closed his eyes. He heard Mallory step into the room, but he didn't move yet. "They'll leave by morning."

"Good. Thank you for not telling them."

"Right. Eventually we need to stop being scared about what others will think and just live our lives."

"What do you mean?"

"I mean, if we hadn't been so scared of what our families would have thought of us dating all those years ago, the situation could have turned out completely different."

Reid turned around and found Mallory looking pensive. She shook her head, the end of her blond ponytail flipping back and forth. "No, it wouldn't have. It would have lessened our time together. We would never have been able to be together, to make love, or even kiss. As soon as my father found out about it, he would have stopped it. I'm just happy we had the time we did."

"I am too, but I'm not a helpless twenty-year-old anymore. I'm not going to hide from my family or yours. When this is over, it's all or nothing, sweetheart."

Mallory nodded. "If we survive this, then it's a deal.

Now, show me your ballroom."

Mallory tried not to laugh as Reid drove the scissor lift through the doorway. He cursed as it hit the wall and put it in reverse.

"Why did they build the ceilings so freaking high?"

"It's pretty. You did a great job with this hotel, Reid. Tall ceilings and all."

As soon as Reid cleared the doorway, she let go of the doors and locked them. She followed Reid into the room and to the one air return with a direct line of sight to the stage that had been erected that afternoon. She slung a canvas bag over her shoulder and stepped into the little lift.

"Can you go stand where the podium will be once I get up there?" Mallory asked as she used the controls to raise herself.

"Sure. Aren't you worried that will collapse, though?"

"Not if I'm lying down. It's up there pretty good." Mallory reached the top and took out a screwdriver. She slowly took out each screw and put them in her pocket.

Finally she popped off the vent and placed it onto the floor of the lift. She put her hands through the opening and pulled herself up. The metal was cool and thin. She immediately lay down on her stomach to prevent the ductwork from buckling. She put the canvas back in front of her and pulled out headgear with a flashlight on it. She turned it on and slipped it onto her head.

"Get up on the stage," she yelled through the opening. With the bag safely to her side, she turned around on her stomach and found a clear view of the stage. Reaching to the bag on her left, she pulled out her rifle. It was too big for the width of the ductwork. The angle wouldn't work.

Mallory put the rifle back in the bag and pulled out a

laser distance measurer. She aimed it at Reid and measured.

"Hey! That better not be a laser from a gun."

"Nope. I'm measuring the distance."

"Why?"

"A rifle won't work. It would be too cramped and hinder mobility. But, a Corner Shot would. It's a gun specifically made to shoot around corners. He could lie right here, headed in the escape direction, and do it all by looking on a screen. It's only accurate up to a certain distance, and we are well within that range. All he would have to do is make his way to the restrooms. I'm going to try it. Meet me in the lobby."

Mallory lined up the shot as if she had the type of gun where the trigger and barrel were at a ninety-degree angle. She heard the people clapping, saw the balloons and banners, and saw the people on the dance floor. She pretended to take the shot. Next she would put the gun in the bag to conceal it and make it easier to push around. She counted the time it would take her and started moving as fast as she could through the maze of ductwork. She had to look at the map she'd attached to her wrist to verify where she was going. First intersection from vent, turn left. Go past three intersecting ducts and then turn right.

She knew when she exited the ballroom and turned left into another section of the ductwork. It suddenly dipped, and she slid down the incline. Using her hands, she slowed herself to a stop over another return vent. She looked through it and saw the ladies' room. She unscrewed the vent from the inside and dropped onto a toilet before reaching up to replace the vent cover. She counted the time it would take to unzip a painter's bib to cover his clothes and then walk out of the restroom. She pressed her watch to stop the timer.

"One minute and ten seconds from the time of the shot to the time our man could walk out into the lobby in clean clothes," she told Reid as she approached him.

"But he has to get up there in the first place. Couldn't he be discovered before he even gets up there?"

"Could, but doubtful. A good sniper can sit for hours and hours and never move."

"So, what do we do?"

"I'm going to meet him in the ballroom—rather, over the ballroom," Mallory smiled.

"You're going to stake out the ballroom air ducts from the inside?"

"That's right. I'm going to spend the whole day up there. It should be fun. But I'll be in perfect position to grab him in case he gets by the people we'll have covering the main entryways into the air ducts."

"You're going to fight a trained killer in a closed space with no exit. Are you crazy?" Reid practically yelled.

"Shh. Don't forget I'm also a trained killer. A very good one. Plus, from that vantage point, I can keep watch on the setup of the party and the whole event itself. In case I'm wrong, I'll be able to see everything going on below me."

"But how would you get down?"

"Jump?"

Reid shook his head. "You're kidding, right? Please tell me you're kidding."

Mallory smiled. "Maybe I lied. Maybe this does make me happy." She gave Reid's shoulder a playful hit. "Don't worry. I got this."

"So what do we do between now and Friday? We have a couple days to just sit around?"

"Nope. I need you to have people you trust in here at all times. We need to renovate the restrooms and make sure no one can get in there until the afternoon of the event, then they will be guarded constantly. I don't want this guy getting any practice in or have a chance to slip up there before I do," Mallory told him as they headed back upstairs. "I'm going to have my crew in here helping with the setup to make sure no bombs get planted."

"Bombs? Suddenly I feel as if I am living in an alternate universe." Reid shook his head and let out a long breath. "Okay, so, what about me? They still need to try to kill me, right? Wouldn't it look strange if I were to die right before the party? There would be a chance they would cancel it."

"You're right. I've been thinking about it. Have you made it public that you will be at the party?"

"Yes. Very. I'm contributing a rather large check to the charitable organization."

"There are two possibilities. One, he kills you beforehand and disposes of your body so it just looks like you're missing. Or, two, he'll shoot you at the same time as the candidate and make it look like a bystander just got caught up in the fire."

"So it looks like we'll be spending a lot of time together. After all, you must protect my body," Reid said mischievously.

Chapter Thirteen

Reid couldn't sleep. He lay in bed and stared at the ceiling. He was willing himself not to get up and look at the woman sleeping on his couch. He tried to get Mallory to take the bed, but she insisted on being between him and the door. Then he tried to talk her into his bed. That didn't work either. And maybe that was the reason he couldn't sleep. There was a part of him still very much awake and eager to see Mallory as well.

Letting out a frustrated breath, Reid closed his eyes. A faint scratching noise caught his attention. What was that? Reid sat up and listened. He had to strain his ears, but he was pretty sure it was coming from the living room. Mallory was up! Maybe she was having trouble sleeping. A smile spread across his face, and the other part of him jumped up in anticipation.

Reid walked over to the chair to grab a pair of athletic shorts when the sound of glass breaking sent him running from the bedroom.

Mallory was counting sheep jumping a fence as she tried to get some sleep. But somehow those sheep kept turning into Reid, and he was winking at her. Then the next Reid to jump the fence was beckoning her with his finger. The next one didn't have shoes. The next one didn't have a shirt. The next one didn't have pants. And then those jumping Reids did nothing to help Mallory go to sleep.

She was flushed and wondered if Reid's offer to sleep with him was still open when she heard the unmistakable sound of a lock pick on the balcony door. Mallory slowly slid her hand under the couch cushion and pulled out her gun. She crept toward the door in her tank top and boy shorts. Taking a deep breath, she waited patiently behind the large sitting chair as the lock tumbled and the door opened.

A black-gloved hand reached through the drapes and pulled one back. A black-clad figure slowly slipped into the room. Mallory stood slowly and raised her gun.

"A little late for a visitor, isn't it?" Mallory asked.

The figure in black turned toward her.

"Hands above your head, now," Mallory ordered.

Mallory stepped around the chair as the person in a black ski mask complied. The zip ties were in a bag a few feet away. She glanced at the bag, and he leapt toward her. Mallory didn't have time to fire before the impact. She fell backward and grabbed onto the retreating arm of the attacker moments before crashing into the glass table.

Pain from landing on the thousands of tempered-glass granules shot through her a second before the attacker landed on her. The impact sent her gun falling from her hand as she grappled with the person sitting on her.

"Mallory!"

"Run, Reid!" she ordered as she blocked a punch. She wasn't so lucky and caught an elbow to her diaphragm, leaving her gasping for air.

The attacker sprang up and charged Reid. Mallory dragged in a ragged breath as she pushed herself up. She ignored the painful ovals of glass that dug into her palm.

Mallory saw the needle a second before Reid grabbed the black-clad arm, lowered his shoulder, and used momentum to send the attacker flying over his shoulder.

Mallory rushed past him as the attacker jumped up. They circled each other, both obviously trained in military combat and some other lesser-known martial arts. Mallory saw his hand unclench and move toward a boot knife. Mallory's was too far away to reach him in time to stop him from grabbing his secondary weapon. Instead she picked up a heavy coffee table book on the history of Atlanta and hurled it at the same time the attacker made his move.

The book hit him in the shoulder and caused him to stumble behind the couch. Reid took the opportunity and ran across the room. He hurtled the broken table and couch, landing right behind Mallory racing after the dark figure. As a group, they sprinted toward the open balcony door. The attacker didn't stop, but instead sprinted across the balcony and vaulted over the iron railing, disappearing from view.

"Where the hell did he go?" Reid asked as they raced toward the railing.

Mallory didn't answer. She was already jumping over the railing and sliding down the black nylon rope the attacker used.

"Wait!" Reid watched as Mallory slid as fast as lightning down the rope and ran after the shadow, tearing across the back lawn of the resort.

Mallory didn't hear Reid's shout. She was too focused on not losing sight of the figure in front of her.

She raced past the pool and onto the croquet field. With a burst of energy, she leaped after him. Her hand grabbed the back of the attacker's shirt and the unmistakable feel of a light tactical vest as they went down hard in the dew-covered grass. Mallory grunted as a boot connected with her ribs; a needle stabbed into her shoulder causing Mallory to cry out in pain.

Mallory couldn't let whatever was in that needle be injected into her. Her survival instincts kicked in full force as she struggled to prevent him from pushing the plunger. They fought frantically with each other. Each move was blocked and countered in a series of close-range combat moves. With the attacker straddling her and their hands on the plunger, Mallory used the only weapon left to her. She crunched up and smashed her head into his ski-mask-covered cheekbone.

It wasn't the right spot to knock him out, but it was enough to let her wrestle away control of the needle. Mallory yanked it from her shoulder. The sound of screaming and the bobbing of flashlights in the distance had the attacker jumping up. Mallory leaned forward to give chase, but a boot to the stomach had her coughing to catch her breath. There was nothing she could do but watch him disappear into the shadows.

Reid and hotel security raced into the garden. He heard Mallory wheezing as they trained their flashlights ahead. Her white tank top was covered with a sprinkling of blood as she lay on her back with her arms over her face. Her eyes were closed, focused on breathing.

"Mallory, are you all right?" Reid called as he raced barefoot and bare-chested toward her.

She coughed in response but gave a nod of her head. She pointed toward the woods before covering her face again.

"Search the woods," Reid ordered as security hurried

off.

Reid knelt down beside her and saw the dirt marks covering her body. Her forearms were scraped, and her knees were bleeding.

"Shh. That's it, deep breaths," Reid said reassuringly.

Mallory lowered her arms and glared before rolling her eyes. "Duh," she gasped.

Reid rubbed her arm gently and waited for her to catch her breath. He saw more injuries, but nothing looked too major. He also saw the needle on the ground next to her. "Did you get injected?"

Mallory struggled to take a deep breath. "No. It was in my shoulder, but I stopped him from injecting me. Learned two good things tonight. One, we'll find out what's in the needle and hope it leads to a clue on who it is."

"And the other good thing?"

"It's not Bowie. Bowie's taller and heavier. This person was more of a runner than a strength trainer. About five foot nine inches tall too. Bowie is just a little shorter than you, and you're what, six foot two?"

Reid nodded and slid his arm under her shoulders to help her sit up. "Let me take you to the doctor."

"No. I have someone I need to see. I'll also get him to identify what's in the needle. Just get me back to your room, and I'll call him."

Noise from the security team took their attention away from her wounds. The group was walking out of the woods empty-handed.

"Sorry. We couldn't find any trace of him."

Reid grimaced. "It's okay. Let's be on the lookout for any more thieves, though. Let's tighten security until after the ball. Anything suspicious, notify me at once. No matter how small it may seem. We don't want to let it get out we might have a thief on the grounds. We want our guests to feel safe."

Mallory let out a hiss of air as she stood up. When Reid shot her a worried look, she smiled. "Just a bruised rib, nothing too bad."

Reid refused to let go of her as he walked with her back to the hotel. He would never forget the feeling of watching her jump over the railing and run into the night after the attacker. There was a battle of conflicting emotions raging inside him. He loved her. He should be the one protecting her. But it was her job to protect him, and he wanted Mallory to know he trusted her to do that.

"Come on, let's call your doctor. I'll feel better knowing that you're not hurt too badly." Reid helped her inside and swore to himself he wouldn't turn domineering to her. It was hard, but he knew the right thing to do was work with her, not against her. Not only was he battling for her heart; he was now battling for her life.

Mallory smiled as Feng made his way into the room while bowing repeatedly to Reid. To say Reid was surprised to see the tiny Chinese man at the door early in the morning was an understatement. Feng was barely five feet two inches with a thin comb over and huge round wire glasses. He wasn't a day younger than eighty.

"Little missy, you've gotten yourself into trouble again." He shook his head. "No worries, Feng will take care of you," he said affectionately.

"You're a doctor?" Reid asked as Feng set down a bag half his size.

"I was a doctor in China, but when my family moved to the United States my training was not recognized even though I'd been a doctor for thirty years," Feng explained as he pushed up his glasses with his finger.

"What do you do now?"

"I own the Qigong studio on Peachtree."

"The yoga place?"

"Yes," Feng smiled as he pulled out his stethoscope.

Mallory smiled at Reid. "I met Feng at class there almost ten years ago now. When I found out he was a doctor and missed practicing, we made an arrangement. He would treat me for any, um, nefarious injuries I got. He gets paid and gets to practice medicine, while I don't have to go to the hospital and deal with all that paperwork."

"Take off your shirt, please," Feng said after listening to her heart, taking her pulse, and checking her blood pressure.

Finally Reid smiled, and Mallory just rolled her eyes and turned her back on him. She peeled off the tank top and Feng clucked again.

"You call Feng out early in the morning for this? This is nothing. You must be growing weak. You need to come back to class. I'll toughen you up."

"Nothing?" Reid asked surprised. Even though he was looking at her bare back, he could still see a bruise forming that ran across her side.

Feng shook his head. "Nothing for little missy. No bullet or stab wound. No broken bones," he said as he poked her in the ribs.

Mallory knew better than to make a noise while Feng examined her, or he'd just poke her some more. "But I do have this," she told him as she held up the needle.

Reid stepped closer as the little man was examining her and cleaning her cuts. He looked at her naked back and saw thin scars from knives and what looked like two bullet holes. A part of his mind had told himself what she did was nothing more than collecting gossip, despite the stories she had shared with him. It was something completely different to see the marks she bore on her body, proving the dangerous risks she had taken. It somehow made it more real.

The little doctor's eyes went wide though when Mallory held up the needle. They both smiled, and Reid wondered if he could ever fit into her world. This amused them while Reid was anything but amused.

"A mystery," Feng said happily as he took the needle.

"My attacker was trying to stab Reid with it and then, when we were fighting, stabbed me in the shoulder with it," Mallory explained.

"Was any injected?" Feng asked as he took a closer look at her shoulder.

"No. But, I need to know what it is. I'm hoping it will help me find out who was behind this attack."

"Sure thing. Feng will find out. Don't you worry."

The room froze when a knock suddenly interrupted them. Reid looked through the peephole before stepping back to open the door. The silver legs of a walker came through first. *Sexiness Never Gets Old* was hanging in between the bars as Shirley appeared. She looked around at Feng and a topless Mallory and then to Reid. "Looks like I'm missing the fun, but shouldn't you be where he is?" she asked Reid with a tilt of her head to where Feng sat in front of Mallory.

"I wish," Reid murmured. "He's her doctor," he said louder this time.

"I heard you the first time." Shirley winked before wheeling farther into the room. "And who are you, good-lookin'?"

Reid almost choked as Feng's cheeks turned red and he

ran a hand over the ten strands of hair covering his head. He decided right then Mallory was the best government asset they had when she turned with a straight face and introduced them.

"I heard Qigong is great for sexual exercising," Shirley said as she wiggled her eyebrows.

Feng nodded repeatedly. "Yes. Yes. Very good for it."

"Maybe I could get some private lessons?"

Reid stood staring. He didn't want to hear or see anymore of this octogenarian flirt fest, but it was like a train wreck. He couldn't look away. Mallory slipped on her shirt and smiled serenely at Feng and Shirley.

Feng placed the needle in his bag and pulled out a business card. "Here you go. You call me, and I'll teach you many techniques. You'll feel like a teenager again," he said with a wink.

God help them all, because Shirley already had the dirty mind of a teenage boy.

Feng turned to Mallory. "You're fine. Don't be a baby. I'll call you about the needle."

Reid did laugh as Mallory glared at Feng for calling her a baby. And it wasn't until Feng kissed Shirley's hand and left that Mallory finally cracked a smile.

"Shirley's going to get some," Mallory sang.

"I sure hope so. Do I need to get me one of those waxes? You know, the one down there," Shirley asked Mallory.

Dueling images entered Reid's mind. One he definitely didn't want to think about, the other he couldn't stop thinking about.

"I don't think so. I think Feng is a natural kind of guy," Mallory said straight faced. Yep, best spy ever to pull that off. "What brings you by this morning?"

"I want to know what's going on. Elle dragged everyone off to Connecticut at five in the morning—everyone except Reid and Margaret. Then I show up and you're flashing your bitties. Now, even more interesting is the fact that after how many years of just happening to have things to do when the other is around, you're flashing your bitties with Reid in the room . . . *his* room."

"I was hired to protect Reid, that's all," Mallory said simply with a shrug of her shoulder.

Reid didn't know if he liked that or not. She wasn't just protecting him last night when they had stayed up late talking and sharing stories of their lives. He wanted her for way more than protection. Not only was he trying to protect her, he was also trying to keep his desire for her in check.

"Humph." Shirley clearly didn't believe Mallory. "So, what's going on that requires you to protect Reid?"

"Oh, just an upset gambler wanting payback for the money he lost."

Shirley looked at the broken table. "Mallory dear, you are a horrible liar. Bless your heart."

At the sound of another knock on the door, Shirley raised a bushy eyebrow. Reid looked through the peephole and scowled. He opened the door and Bowie sauntered into the room. That is, until he saw Shirley. Then he froze and his eyes widened to near comedic proportions.

"Hey again, sonny. You ready for that ride?"

"You're like a porno granny," Bowie said as he continued to stare.

"Not yet, but maybe when I get done with that sex yoga stuff I will be. I could always stand to supplement my Social Security."

"Is she for real?" he asked Mallory.

"Want me to pinch you to prove it?" Shirley winked, and Bowie turned a little pale.

"Okay, Shirley," Mallory laughed. "He's a good guy, you can let up a little."

"Fine, take away my fun. This isn't the end of our discussion. I'll be back. And I'll see you in three days for the Veterans Ball. Margaret left me her ticket since she's taking care of Troy. Won't leave his side, she says."

Reid stepped back to open the door for her. "Don't worry about that. It's not going to be much fun. Maybe Feng will want a private lesson that night?"

"Well, if I'm not there, then I'm getting lucky. I'll talk to you soon."

The door closed, and Reid walked over to Mallory. He put a hand possessively on her shoulder and knew she wouldn't like it. But he was going to stake his claim. Bowie looked at his hand and raised his eyebrow.

"What happened last night?" he asked.

Mallory held up her hand to motion for them to wait. She stood up and made her way to the door. She quietly opened it and looked into the hallway.

"All clear. Shirley has eavesdropping skills the director would be envious of. Last night an attempt was made on Reid's life. I'm sorry, but I had to make sure it wasn't you. After a little hand-to-hand combat, I knew I could bring you back into the loop."

"You thought it was me?"

"You're close to Liam. I haven't worked with you in years. You could have easily turned, and you know that."

Reid enjoyed Mallory standing up to Bowie. She wasn't apologetic at all, and that was more reason for him to think he had a chance with her. If she were over him, then she would give him the brush-off just like she gave Bowie.

"After what we shared in Stromia?" Bowie said with blatant sexual innuendo.

"Knock it off, Bowie," Mallory stood up and faced her handler. Reid had to stop himself from punching him in the face—agent or not.

"Don't be a sore loser," Reid smirked. Mallory shot Reid a warning look, but he ignored her. He was upset he had to sit on the sidelines while Mallory handled things, and he was even more pissed Bowie got to do things in the elevator with her in the first place. Reid wasn't going to be pushed around anymore. Not by her father, not by Bowie, and not by some spoiled brat like Ambrose. He was going to fight for Mallory, and he didn't give a damn who knew.

"Enough, you two." Mallory stepped between them. "I called to give you an update. Reid, can you get Bowie a ticket to the Veterans Ball? Just put it under a different name."

Reid walked over to the phone and dialed an extension. "Good morning, Evelyn. Can you get a ticket to the veterans event for a Mr. Egbert Lipschitz?" Reid paused. "Thank you. He'll pick it up at the front desk later."

Mallory snorted, and Bowie fumed.

"You son of a . . ."

"Watch it or I'll put you at Shirley's table," Reid said as he took another step forward.

Mallory rolled her eyes. "Does testosterone suddenly make all men stupid? Come on. We have an assassin to catch, and you all are more interested in measuring dicks. I can leave if you want me to?"

"No," they both mumbled.

"Good. Now let me tell you what I have planned so far."

Chapter Fourteen

Mallory enjoyed the feel of hot water beating down on her. The wig she had worn was tight and made her head itch. It had been a long day of following Reid around the hotel as he worked, talking to Evelyn, and meeting with the rest of the hotel staff. The men from her security firm had been brought in to help with the setup of the ballroom. Bowie's CIA agents were brought in to be plumbers and work on the restrooms.

The hardest part was being so near Reid all day. He found any reason to touch her—a hand on her elbow or the small of her back as he directed her through the hotel, an arm across her breasts as he reached for a piece of paper. Mallory closed her eyes. She wanted things to happen so badly, but she didn't want to get distracted when his life was on the line.

There was a soft knock on the door, and Mallory looked over the stone half-wall of the shower toward it. Slowly, Reid walked in. "Mallory, I've been thinking."

Mallory smiled when she saw that Reid kept his eyes looking into hers and not roaming downward. "What about?"

"Us."

"Do you really want to have this conversation now?" Mallory asked as she looked down at her nakedness.

"Yes, I do. I know I told you I would be patient. However, there comes a time when patience is overrated. I have spent the last couple days with you. And while the feelings I had for you when we were younger have changed, they haven't wavered. It's not some teenage crush, Mallory. But then again, I think we both knew it was more than that even back then."

Mallory didn't say anything. Reid was right, though. Her feelings for him were as strong as ever. And they were different. She understood they would never go away. They just grew and changed as she did. Mallory was so afraid for her worlds to collide she didn't know if she could manage them together. Girlfriend and CIA operative? Girlfriend and bodyguard? There were too many fractions of her personality, each specifically crafted so she didn't feel emotion.

"As I said, my feelings have changed. They're deeper and more mature, just like we are." Finally Reid cast a quick glance down her body. She knew he only saw her bare shoulders but the way his eyes took her in made her think he could see all of her. "From the beginning, you've had the lead. You've always set the rules. I waited for you then, but I'm done waiting. I know you're a badass who gives orders, and I'm proud of you, Mallory. You are an amazing woman who has saved so many lives, protected so many innocent people, and who has loved my family with all her heart. I love you, I respect you, and that's never going to change. I know my feelings, and I know you do too. I'll be in the bedroom. Either come to me or walk out the door. But you have to decide now. I'm tired of putting my life on hold. I want to be with you, so it's now or never."

Mallory stood motionless as Reid turned and walked out the door. It closed with a soft click and Mallory finally remembered to breathe. She knew Reid had always been in charge of every aspect of his life, but it was different to see him take charge of hers. He never had before. Her mind rebelled against being told what to do, but her body was already turning off the shower and reaching for the towel.

Reid sat on the bed facing the bathroom door. He heard the water turn off and prayed she wouldn't walk past him and out the door. He knew he was taking a risk. His heart pounded as he listened for each little noise behind the closed door. He wondered what each one meant. If she was mad he'd taken control, or if she had to think about it.

The door opened, and he had his answer. Her wet hair had been brushed and twisted into a loose bun at the base of her neck. She stepped toward him wrapped in the plush white towel.

"I've made my decision."

"And what's that?" Reid asked, his voice rough with emotion.

Mallory dropped the towel, and Reid sat rooted to the bed. Mallory had changed since the last time he'd seen her naked. Her hips flared in a seductive curve that had him wanting to run his hands over her. Her breasts were rounder and fuller. When she moved forward, he opened his legs for her to step between. Slowly she bent down and kissed his upturned lips.

Reid had his answer. Sixteen years and she was finally his again. They fought madly to strip his clothes from his body. Mallory pushed him back on the bed and fell on top of him. He let her enjoy taking the lead as she rose above him to explore his chest. He cupped her breasts and relished their feel. He rose up and circled his tongue around one taunt nipple before sucking it into his warm mouth.

Reid's reward was Mallory's moan as she dug her hands into his hair. Reid wrapped his arms around her back and feasted on each breast. She tried to push him to the bed, but Reid flipped her onto her back instead.

"Next time you can take the lead, but it's my turn now," he said before kissing her passionately.

He used one hand to push himself up as he looked down at her. His erection was pushing against her, causing her to writhe against him. He slipped on a condom with his other hand before running his warm palm over the side of her breast and down her ribcage to squeeze her ass before guiding her to hook her leg around his waist.

Mallory followed the guidance and immediately wrapped her legs around him. She met his first thrust with one of her own as he entered her. The throaty moan she made had him struggling to control the pace. When she dug her nails into his back, he knew he didn't need to control himself or his feelings any longer.

"You'll never leave me again," he growled as their lovemaking grew frenzied.

"Never. You're mine now, Simpson," Mallory responded before tightening around him and crying out.

Mallory padded barefoot to the door the next morning and opened it for room service. She thanked the waiter and uncovered the plates. She was starving. If she thought her first time with Reid was good all those years ago, then there were no words to describe the previous night. It was sixteen years of built-up desires acting out.

The water turned on in the bathroom, and Mallory contemplated joining Reid. Instead, she grabbed her phone to check in with Feng. She took a sip of the orange juice as she typed her message. Grabbing a piece of bacon, she checked her other phone to see if Ahmed had any more news.

She took another drink and then set down her juice to reply to an email when a pain ripped through her stomach. It was so sharp she lost her breath and doubled over. She tried to call for Reid but could hardly breathe and felt a tightening in her chest. Clutching her phone, she called Feng.

"Hello?"

Mallory tried to talk but whimpered instead when the pain hit again.

"Little missy?"

"Feng," she whispered before the pain and lack of air dragged her into the depths of unconsciousness.

Reid turned off the shower and grabbed his towel. He was pretty sure the smile on his face was permanent. As soon as his family got back and this whole mess was over, he was never going to hide his feelings for Mallory again. To hell with her father. He wasn't afraid of him or the threats he'd made against him.

They were raised to believe family mattered more than their bank account. Even if Mallory's father came after them, he would soon learn the Simpsons would use every bit of the wealth and power they had accumulated to make sure none of their own were hurt. And Mallory was family . . . and soon she would be so legally. He was already planning a trip to the jeweler for the next week.

Reid opened the bathroom door and walked to the bed to put on his clothes. "Did breakfast get here yet?" he called out as he buttoned his black suit pants. "Mallory?" he called out again when she didn't respond.

Panic hit him hard as he ran into the living room. The sight of her curled up on the floor sent the world slamming to a stop. He raced forward and fell to his knees. She was ashen. He pressed his fingers to her throat and felt a weak, fluttering pulse. Leaning forward, he listened for her breathing. He sniffed and realized her breath smelled metallic. The door to the room splintered open and Reid's head shot up. He threw himself over Mallory to protect her from whatever threat was breaking in.

"Get away from her!" Feng yelled. He rushed in, opening his bag as he ran.

"I didn't do it. I just found her like this," Reid said as he grabbed her hand. He wasn't going to leave her.

Feng took in Reid's near state of panic and gave a nod. He brought out his stethoscope and pressed it to her chest. "Weak. She's having cardiac trouble. What happened?"

"I don't know. I was in the shower, and she was waiting for breakfast."

Feng looked at the table and then leaned forward to sniff Mallory's mouth. "Metal."

"I noticed that. What does that mean?"

"She was poisoned. Lucky I'm Chinese and not some city doctor. This poison is not from here." He reached into his bag and pulled out a container filled with black powder.

"What is that?"

"Activated charcoal. Get me water from the sink. Hurry."

Reid ran for the sink and filled a glass while Feng pulled out a needle and plunged it into a vial with Chinese writing on it.

"Here. What's that?"

"Put water in charcoal and shake." Feng measured out

the liquid in the vial and injected Mallory with it as Reid mixed the charcoal and water into a thick drink. "This is atropine extracted from nightshade. It will help her low heart rate. Now, hold her up. We need her to drink this."

Reid pulled Mallory into his lap and wrapped his arms around her to hold her up. Feng waited, and suddenly Mallory opened her eyes and took a gasp of air. Quickly, Feng pressed the charcoal to her mouth and pinched her nose closed.

"Drink, fast," he ordered.

Mallory didn't hesitate. She chugged the thick liquid and grabbed Reid's arms. He was reassured when her grip tightened. As soon as she finished, Feng leapt up and refilled the container with water as Mallory coughed and gagged.

"Drink," he ordered again.

Reid kept up a steady stream of encouragement as she drank down the remnants of the charcoal.

"Reid," she said softly when she finished.

"Yes, sweetheart?"

"Don't drink the orange juice. It's a killer." Mallory took another breath and Reid felt a tremor race through her body. "What was it, Feng?"

"Poison from Asia. It's from the Ranunculaceae family. Cousin to monkshood."

Mallory gave a weak nod. "Thank you for getting here so quickly."

"I was already on my way over. I discovered what was in the needle. I was only minutes away. Good thing too. If you had gone untreated for a couple of hours, you would be in a coma and dead by the weekend."

"What was in the needle?"

"The same thing you just drank, only a more

concentrated form. Very deadly plant, but my people have used it for centuries . . . well, mostly to kill people. It has symptoms like monkshood, just slower."

"What's monkshood?" Reid asked as he helped Mallory sit up a little more.

"It's a poisonous flower, and what Mallory ingested is in the same family. Monkshood will slow the pulse, give you shallow breathing, horrible stomach pains, and you will be dead in hours—even if you just brush it with your hand. Injected or consumed, it is immediate death. But this, this is a slower death. Same symptoms, but you linger until your body gives out."

"So, they decided not to wait to try again. We have to question the staff and pull the security video. This may be a hotel instead of a casino, but no one has any idea how many eyes in the sky I have here."

"Call Damien. I need to read him all the way in. I don't trust the Secret Service agents here with the candidates," Mallory ordered as she struggled to stand.

Reid held her down. "You need to get to the hospital. I'll take care of everything here."

"No way." Mallory shook her head.

"Yes, little missy. Feng doesn't have everything you need."

Mallory rolled her eyes. "Fine. Hand me my phone, will you?"

Feng reached the phone and handed it to her. Mallory pulled up a website and located the number she was looking for. "Hello. I need a male escort right away."

Reid had insisted on carrying her to the bed in her suite.

Feng fussed over her and Reid stood looking on as he used her phone to call Damien Wallace, a local Secret Service agent. She wondered how Reid felt about her calling her ex-boyfriend. She knew she wouldn't want to call one of his past girlfriends.

"Reid, it wasn't serious between Damien and me," she told him as he paced, waiting for him to arrive.

"Please don't tell me. I'm just going to pretend it never happened. I'm more concerned that you refuse to go to the hospital."

A knock sounded and Feng hurried to get it. He pulled a chair from the living room over to the door and stood up on it to look through the peephole. "Who are you?"

"Agent Wallace, Secret Service," Damien called through the door as he held up his badge for Feng to see.

Feng hopped from the chair, moved it aside, and opened the door. Mallory caught Damien's surprise as he looked down, way down, to the top of a head covered by a thin comb over. "I'm Feng. Little missy is in here."

Damien followed Feng with a look of amusement until he saw Mallory in bed. "What the hell happened to you?"

"She was poisoned," Feng told him.

"Poisoned? How? Why? Who are you?" Damien asked all at once.

Mallory gave a weak smile before she told him who Feng was and the full situation with Reid, her father, and the rest of the candidates. "I don't know who I can trust, except you."

Mallory saw Reid's jaw tighten as he looked away briefly.

"Just who are you, Mallory? Isabelle thinks you're some spook."

"Isabelle?" Reid asked Damien, not recognizing the

name.

"My fiancée. Y'all know her as Agent Hectoria. It's because of Mallory we went out. When she tried to find some information on Mallory, all she found were classified codes belonging only to the director of the CIA." Damien held up his hands to stop her from talking. "And don't give me that crap that I don't have the clearance to know."

Mallory smiled at him, and this time Reid omitted a low sound that resembled a snarl. Five minutes later Mallory had filled Damien in and watched as he shook his head in amazement.

"Okay, I think I get the picture. And you're sure the assassin will shoot from the air duct?"

Mallory shrugged. "As sure as I can be. I mean, it's what I would do."

"I'll station people inside the restrooms and let you cover the air duct from inside. The Secret Service from DC should be covering the mechanical rooms already."

"The CIA is already in the restrooms remodeling. Or at least pretending to."

"Damn, I don't like this. There are too many variables, yet it's the only way to catch the assassin. Once a contract is out there, it doesn't go away until either the assassin is killed or the target is."

A knock on the door had Feng hurrying from the room. "Who are you?"

"I'm from the escort company. Someone called for a sexy doctor?"

Damien's eyes flew to Mallory's and she smirked. Feng opened the door and Aiden sauntered in wearing a white button-up shirt, slacks, and a stethoscope hanging around his neck. "So, where is my client? Is this a stripper thing? Should I get naked?"

"You called a prostitute?" Damien asked incredulously.

"No, I called a doctor," Mallory said as she saw Reid was having a hard time not laughing.

Aiden, or Dr. Starr as he was known when he was at the hospital, paused when he saw Mallory and more specifically, Agent Wallace.

"I am going to have to arrest everyone here," Damien groaned. "I mean, you have an old man and an escort illegally practicing medicine, not counting the whole prostitute thing."

"Hey," Feng challenged as marched up to Damien and poked him in the chest. "I was a doctor for over thirty years in China. Good doctor."

"Yeah," Aiden said as he crossed his arms over his muscled chest. "And I am a doctor. I'm only an escort to pay off student loans. Do you have any idea how expensive medical school is? Now, what's going on?"

Aiden set his bag down on the bed and pulled out some supplies as Mallory and Feng told him about the poison. "I'm going to need some specific medicine. I'll call Barry to bring it over. Don't worry; we'll keep it off the books. By tonight, you'll feel right as rain."

"Who's Barry?" Damien asked as Aiden rattled off a list of supplies over the phone.

"He works with Aiden," Mallory informed him.

"As an escort or a doctor?"

"Both."

"I don't . . . Isabelle will never believe me." Damien shook his head and collapsed into a chair as they waited for the escort doctor to treat her.

Chapter Fifteen

Reid stood by as Dr. Barry and Dr. Aiden injected medicine into the IV bag they hooked up. Mallory's color was returning, and Damien was calling to order his most trusted agents to meet him at the hotel.

"Okay, Mallory. This last bit of medicine tastes very bad, but I need you to drink it all," Aiden told her as he handed her a plastic bottle. "It will help your system rebalance itself after the trauma it's gone through."

Aiden and Barry stood next to the bed as she took a drink. Reid watched Mallory's eyes widen, and then she spit the medicine back out. It sprayed Barry and Reid, the red dye from the medicine making it look like the doctors were covered in blood.

"I am so sorry! You weren't kidding that it tastes bad. I can't drink this," Mallory said as she eyed the bottled suspiciously.

Feng pushed the doctors out of the way and pinched her nose. "You drink now, little missy. Close your eyes and envision the most pleasant drink you've ever had. Good, now drink."

Mallory struggled, but she got it down. She coughed and gagged as she dealt with the aftertaste.

"If you guys want, I have some extra T-shirts in my room. I'll get them for you. I don't want you all walking through the hotel looking like you're covered in blood," Reid offered.

"Thanks, that would be good since we're both technically on an early lunch break. We have to head straight to the hospital after this."

Reid hurried to his room where his door was already in the process of being repaired. He grabbed two shirts and found Shirley staring at the worker hanging the new door. She whistled and the man blushed in embarrassment.

"Shirley, what are you doing here?"

"Came to check on you two. What happened here?"

"I'll explain inside. Mallory is in her room."

Shirley shook her head. "Trouble in paradise so soon. Don't you two muck this up. You've been waiting too long to have your chance."

Reid stopped at the door and stared at her. "Is there anything you don't know?"

Shirley moved her dentures around her mouth unconsciously as she thought about it. "Nope, I don't think so. Although, I've always wondered how those girls could pierce their hoo-hahs. I don't know about that, do you?"

Reid blinked. He couldn't form words so he just shook his head and opened the door for Shirley.

"Oh my lucky stars! And I just cashed my check. I know I have some ones in here someplace," Shirley cried as she reached for her wallet. "Who's going to dance first?" she asked as she held up the bills.

Reid stepped into the room and looked up to find Damien standing behind a shirtless set of escort doctors. Barry and Damien blanched, but Aiden just winked.

"What is it with you and dancing naked men?" Damien asked as he took in the spectacle.

"I like to watch their ding-dongs sway back and forth."

Damien shook his head. "I shouldn't have asked. I have to go meet my agents. Mallory, feel better, and we'll be in touch. Shirley, it's always . . . an experience to see you."

Shirley winked at him, and Reid decided Damien was a good guy for managing this situation. To say his life was abnormal was a massive understatement. But as he handed the shirts to the doctors, he made up his mind he wouldn't want it any other way.

Reid looked at the security tape as he waited for Damien to arrive. His people were now included in the plan for the charity event in two days. If only both he and Mallory could stay alive that long. She was doing better that afternoon. Between all the fluids and antidotes Feng and Aiden pushed on her, she said she had more energy than she did the previous night. She had said it with a wink and in a suggestive tone that had Reid waiting to rush back to her. He might have to toss out an old man, but he would do it if Feng didn't leave soon.

His head of security opened the door to the secure room, and Damien followed him in. "Is everything settled?" Reid asked as he motioned for his head of security to cue up the tape.

"Yes. How is Mallory?"

"Ready to get out of bed and into trouble. Feng is probably trying to control her with Qigong. Either that or he tied her to the bed." Reid stopped talking as his mind followed that train of thought.

"She's remarkable."

"What the hell does that mean?" Reid snapped, thinking Damien was picturing the same thing he was.

"It means she recovered quickly from her illness. Not that many people would." Damien snickered then. "Man, you have it bad, don't you?"

"Real bad . . . or good if you're in my place."

"I've known Mallory for over a year now, and I've never seen her like this. I'm happy for you both. Now, show me what you've got."

Reid shot him a grin and started the video. A person dressed in a waiter's uniform and wearing heavy padding walked into the frame. He managed to keep his back turned to the cameras at all times. He walked in one side of the room, past the tray waiting to go up, and simply poured something into the orange juice before walking out the kitchen door.

"Nothing. We can't even ID him," Damien said, annoyed.

"Ah, wait. Those were from the visible cameras. Now for the hidden cameras."

The video started again, and it was a clear shot of the face of the assassin.

"Damn it," Damien cursed.

"Exactly." Reid stared at someone who looked remarkably like one of the former presidents of the United States. "There is so much padding and prosthesis that I can only tell you the assailant is between five-foot-nine and five-foot-eleven inches in height. If he is wearing lifts, then I could be off on that. However, Mallory believes from her experience with him he's around five-nine, average weight, but with the padding we have no idea if that's even close."

"Smart and that's bad, really bad. Are you sure Mallory is up for this?"

"If there's one person I believe in, it's her."

Mallory was pissed off. She was amped up, and Feng was keeping her in bed. Every time she tried to get up, he pushed her down. Energy pumped through her system and she was ready to get to work. She was not accustomed to sitting in bed all day while there was a client to protect. Especially when that client was someone she happened to love.

"Lie still. Let Feng check you." He took her temperature and checked her vitals. The last IV bag of fluids emptied and he pulled the needle from her arm. "You are good now. Go take a shower. You smell."

"Thanks, Feng. For everything," she smirked as she jumped from bed. Her body took a moment to stabilize. She stood and weaved a bit, but then everything went back to normal.

"Anything for little missy. You'll feel better tomorrow. No strenuous activity tonight."

"Where's the fun in that?" Mallory asked with a smile.

Feng shook his finger. "No fun! None. Not until tomorrow. When you can stand and not be dizzy, then you will be good. Your body had a shock. Give it time to relax."

Mallory let out a long-suffering breath. "Fine," she teased.

"You call Feng if you need anything. I will wait until Reid comes back."

Mallory walked over to Feng, who was moving to the living room, and kissed his cheek. "Thank you."

She hurried back to the bathroom and closed the door. Her energy was back; she felt as if she were slightly drunk. Mallory turned on the hot water and stripped off her clothes. She brushed her teeth and stepped into the steaming shower.

"You know, I like finding you in my shower." Mallory looked up at Reid, leaning against the door.

"Funny, because I thought you would join me if you liked it so much."

Reid shook his head and pulled the T-shirt from his body. "Oh no, I got the full lecture from Feng. No fun. Good thing I find it completely unpleasant to help you bathe."

Mallory moved away from the entrance to the shower as Reid joined her under the water. When he wrapped his arms around her, she rested her head against his chest and listened to the sound of his heart.

"You scared me today," Reid whispered into her wet hair.

"I'll tell you a secret. I was a little scared too. The last thought I had was I would never see you again."

"Never again will we be separated. I hate this whole thing, but I'm going to do whatever you say until this is over. But then, we are going to take a very long vacation together. Just you and me. And we are going to get our lives back, free of any outside interference," Reid told her before squeezing some shampoo into his hands and working it into her hair.

Mallory turned and leaned her back against his chest as he massaged her head, neck, and shoulders. It was going to be very hard to avoid having any fun tonight. But as she felt the world rocking a bit, she knew she would have to enjoy just spending the evening together.

When Reid finished the massage, she rinsed off. He hurried to get her a towel and a fluffy thick robe. Wrapped in its warmth, she followed him out of the bathroom. She lifted her head and sniffed.

"What's that smell?"

"Pizza. I picked it up from your favorite place."

Mallory hurried into the living room as her stomach rumbled. She hadn't been allowed to eat anything all day. She looked at the box and laughed. It was from the small pizzeria near her parents' house. She hadn't eaten there since she lived at home.

"This is perfect."

Reid flipped off the lights, set the pizza on the coffee table in front of the couch, and took a seat. He patted the cushion next to him and turned on the television. "Date night in. Pizza and a movie. I know. You're overwhelmed by my romantic side."

Mallory just smiled and felt her heart flutter. She sat down on the couch, and he wrapped his arm around her. Even though she hadn't felt it for a long time, she knew exactly what it was—happiness.

"You failed again!" Black shot his cousin a worried look as Jonak yelled into the phone. "Take care of him! What the hell do you think we are paying you for?" Jonak clutched his hand in anger as their assassin told them Reid Simpson was still alive. "I don't give a shit. Kill him and that stupid politician by Sunday, or I'll send someone after you."

Black muted the phone. "Is that really a good idea to get an assassin pissed off at us?"

Jonak lifted a lip in a snarl before pressing the button on the phone. "By Sunday. Got it?"

"Yes, sir. It will be done. But don't you ever threaten me again. You forget I know more about you and your dealings with Prince Liam than your fathers know about. You push me enough, and you'll soon find out if your fathers are capable of filicide."

Black shot a warning glare to his cousin as the line went dead. "If our fathers discover we are branching out on our own, they'll kill us."

"Not if we complete this task and prove to Prince Liam we can handle any assignment he gives us. When the king dies, we will have Liam's protection. Our fathers won't be able to touch us."

Chapter Sixteen

Reid woke to the feel of a warm body pressed against his. Mallory's back was snuggled up against his chest while her ass hugged his erection. Her head lay on his bicep as his other hand cupped her breast. He wanted to wake up like this every morning for the rest of his life. He leaned forward and pressed a soft kiss to her temple. Her eyes shot open and her hand reached under the pillow.

"I moved your knife to the nightstand. I didn't want to be accidentally stabbed if we decided to have some fun this morning," Reid informed her as he brushed her hair away from her face. "How are you feeling?"

"Disappointed I had to wait until this morning to have fun."

Reid rolled her over onto her back and quickly covered her. "I would never want to keep you waiting. Although, I did enjoy sleeping with you in my arms last night." He leaned down and caressed her lips with a gentle kiss. He was so happy, so fulfilled. All he wanted to do that morning was worship her slowly. He didn't want to miss a single inch of her body.

Mallory stretched her arms above her and grabbed hold of each side of her pillow as Reid kissed his way down her throat, over her collarbone, and down each breast. His fingers whispered over her stomach and disappeared under the sheet. Soon after, his lips followed the same path, and he was rewarded with the sound of his name on her lips.

Mallory slid the black wig in place and fluffed the curls. She applied light makeup and a pink lip gloss to offset the "woman of the night" feel she got with this particular wig. Today was the day before the charity event. Secret Service from Atlanta and Washington were already in the building. They were checking entrances, exits, windows, sewers, and more. She just hoped Damien stood up to them enough to make sure he was in charge of the vents in the ballroom.

She looked in the mirror and saw Reid hang up the phone. "The prelim report on the plane will be complete next week. They were able to talk to Troy, and now they want to talk to me."

"I wouldn't be surprised if the FBI is also there. When do they want to talk?"

"Right now. They are in my office downstairs."

"Then let's not keep them waiting. Let me do the talking."

"And who are you today?"

"Who I am every day, the woman who protects you with her life."

Reid stepped forward and placed his hands on her shoulders. "And who protects you? When was the last time someone took care of you?" He didn't wait for her to answer. Instead he leaned forward and placed a kiss on the base of her neck. "It's no more *you* and *me*. It's now *we*. We will protect each other. We will care for each other. And we will love each other. Like it or not, you now have a very sexy new partner."

Mallory laughed when Reid winked at her in the mirror. She'd never been a serious "we" before. Bowie was the closest thing she had to a partner. While he was good-looking and good at his job, knowing Reid was standing next to her was a completely different feeling.

"I like the sound of that."

"Come on, let's go take on the world."

Mallory took his hand as they headed out the door. Since she was wearing flat, strappy sandals with a knee-length sundress, they took the stairs. Mallory dropped his hand as he opened the door for her. She smiled as she looked around quickly. She spotted the CIA and the Secret Service. The NTSB crew was the least of her worries as they headed toward Reid's office.

A woman with red hair in a stylish suit hesitantly stepped forward before they could leave the lobby. "I'm sorry, Mr. Simpson?"

"Yes?"

"I'm so sorry to bother you, but I've tried to get an answer out of the person at the front desk. They said they didn't know. I'm looking to hold a conference here next week and, well, with the restrooms closed, I'm worried I won't be able to."

"Don't worry, ma'am. The renovations should be over by tomorrow. We made sure to have them done before any of our events started. If there is anything else you need answered, please contact Evelyn."

The pretty woman smiled. "The events planner. Yes, I tried her first, but she wasn't there. Thank you, Mr. Simpson."

The woman batted her lashes and Mallory felt the need to slip her hand into the crook of Reid's arm. This woman was sending him blatant come-hither looks. Reid smiled back and patted Mallory's hand. He laughed as soon as they were out of earshot. Something about the redhead's laugh had just sent Mallory's nerves firing warning signals.

"What?"

"You are so jealous, and it's adorable," Reid teased.

Mallory dropped her hand from his arm. "I am not jealous."

Reid chuckled again, clearly not believing her. Before she could respond, they walked into his office. She recognized the investigators from when she had met them as Mallory Westin. Most were NTSB, but there were two from the FBI.

"Hello again. This is Miss Winters—"

"His counsel from Las Vegas," Mallory lied easily.

The investigator gave a surprised look before starting the questions. "Why do you feel you need an attorney, Mr. Simpson?"

"I was here already on business and thought I would tag along," Mallory said nicely as she drew the investigator's attention away from Reid.

"Hmm, we have a tentative cause for the plane crash. Would you like to know what it is?"

Reid nodded even though he and Mallory already knew. She knew the second she had seen the plane and was sure the investigators did too.

"Your plane was shot down with a shoulder-launched missile."

Both she and Reid acted surprised as they were supposed to with the situation. Mallory asked questions and discovered the real reason they were here.

"Your pilot said you were supposed to be on the plane, yet you weren't. Why not, Mr. Simpson?"

Reid put his hand on Mallory to stop her from answering. "I needed to get home right away. As you can see, I have a million things going on in anticipation of this charity event with both presidential candidates here. I called Troy. He was flying to Seattle for Elle, so I caught a commercial flight. I have the boarding pass on my phone if you would like to see it."

"Who knew you were leaving early?"

"Only my head of security in Stromia."

"Where were you when the plane was shot down?"

"He was in his suite," Mallory answered for him.

"Can anyone verify that?"

"Yes," Mallory said before Reid could answer. "Not only is it recorded with the use of his key card, there's also the fact that he was with Mallory Westin. It's my understanding you met her already."

She felt Reid's shoulders vibrate as he restrained his laughter. The investigators closed ranks and whispering ensued. Reid cast a glance at Mallory, but she shook her head. There was no evidence supporting that Reid had anything to do with shooting down the plane.

"This luxury hotel was a major project, wasn't it?"

"Yes. It took longer than I thought it would. But I'm very happy to report we are solidly booked from the grand opening on with a few of these private events before then."

"This probably cost you hundreds of millions . . . and your jet, wow, that was worth sixty million dollars. Good thing you have it insured."

Mallory shook her head when Reid went to talk. "If you are trying to hint that Mr. Simpson is having financial difficulties, then think again. Or better yet, don't think it until you've provided us a shred of evidence supporting that theory."

Another investigator stepped forward in what she was sure was a two-pronged attack. "For the safety of the presidential candidates, we are waiting to release the results until after the charity event. The Secret Service and FBI have been apprized that we believe someone targeted your plane on purpose. If not for the insurance money, why would anyone want to do that?"

"I don't know," Reid said as if pondering the question.

The investigator stepped forward and handed Mallory and Reid his card. "If you think of anything, please let us know. We will be in touch soon."

The investigators filed out of the office on that ominous threat. Reid waited until they were in the lobby before closing the door and sitting down with a sigh. "Great. Not only do I have people worried their events can't be held because of the restrooms, now I have the FBI thinking I somehow had a hand in the plane crash."

"Don't let it bother you. We already know who was at fault, and we will take care of it."

Reid grinned and pulled her down into his lap. "Look who is saying *we* now."

"Yeah, yeah, yeah," Mallory grumbled before kissing him.

"Phone," Reid managed to say.

"Huh?"

"Your phone is ringing."

Mallory reached into her purse and pulled out her phone. "Lloyd. What did you find?"

"Hello, poppet. Nothing good, that's for sure."

"How so?"

"Well, I looked into Black and Jonak for you. I wasn't the only one asking. My source told me another person had asked just a couple of days ago."

"Why are people looking into them?"

"It wasn't just people. It was two very specific people. After promising my source a very expensive bottle of brandy, he told me it was their fathers. And what they found didn't make them happy."

"What did they find?"

"That Black and Jonak have been taking jobs from Prince Liam and the French president on the side. They haven't been paid in cash but in property in Stromia and French weapons."

"A different country and different suppliers from their businesses and their fathers," Mallory said more to herself than to Lloyd.

"They have gotten themselves into a very sticky wicket."

"Very sticky. Thank you, Lloyd. I don't want you to look into it anymore. I don't want their fathers to get wind of it."

"You don't have to say that twice, poppet. Whatever you are tied up in, be careful."

"Aren't I always?"

"Ha!" The phone call ended with Lloyd's deep chuckles still ringing in her ears.

Reid looked concerned as he waited for her to tell him the news. Mallory let out a long breath. "It looks like we all have daddy issues."

"What?"

"Liam and his father, Black and Jonak and their fathers, me and my father . . . this whole thing is about gaining freedom, power, and control from them."

Mallory conveyed her conversation with Lloyd to Reid as she paced. "I don't understand what Liam has to do with this. It seems like he had no dog in this fight. Why would he hire out his goons for a United States problem?"

"Would your contact know?" Reid asked.

"I don't know. I'll call Ahmed and find out."

Reid came over and slid his hands up her arms to her shoulders before placing a kiss on her forehead. "I have a meeting next door. You can use my office to call. I'll be in there most of the morning. Let's meet for lunch?"

"Fast food. Remember, don't eat or drink anything from the hotel," Mallory warned.

"I don't think you need to worry about me forgetting that."

Mallory watched him grab a leather portfolio before heading through the connecting door. She dialed Ahmed and waited for him to pick up. Once he did, she filled him in and waited as he processed it all.

"I have an idea. I'll get back to you."

"You'll get back to me? Wait!" But it was too late. Ahmed had already hung up the phone. Sometimes dealing with other government agents sucked. No one trusted anyone and they never told the full truth.

Mallory strode from the room and went to find Damien. She might as well get all the bureaucratic bullshit out of the way.

"Miss Winters!"

Mallory groaned as Evelyn hurried over. Mallory hadn't had enough coffee yet to deal with someone so perky.

"Oh, I'm so glad I caught you."

Mallory smiled. "What can I do for you, Evelyn?"

"Well," she said conspiratorially, "I was hoping you would join me for coffee and some old-fashioned girl talk. When I saw you, I just knew we'd be friends."

Stab her in the eye with a fork—she was done. Mallory plastered on her fake deb smile. "Sounds like fun."

Mallory couldn't fit a word in as they walked to the hotel restaurant. "I got Reid, I mean, Mr. Simpson, to put in a full coffeehouse. We even hired the best barista in Atlanta. You'll just die when you taste her cinnamon spice latte."

She had been right. Mallory knew this would kill her. "Yum," she smiled at Evelyn who hurried off to place the orders. Mallory took a seat at the window table and had never been so relieved to see Damien.

"Mallory," he said as he approached the table.

"Shh. It's Miss Winters."

"Whatever. How are you feeling?"

"Great. Thank you. Any news before our perky event planner gets back?"

"No. It's been quiet except for a few people needing to use the restroom. Are you sure this is going down tomorrow? I'm getting major pushback from DC. They don't understand my involvement and definitely don't like that I'm issuing orders."

"I am so tired of people and their power struggles. I'll take care of it."

"Thanks. I don't have the kind of power you do to get the higher-ups to back off."

He smiled and walked away as soon as Evelyn came over with two hot lattes. "Oh my gosh. Who was that hunk? I didn't know you had a boyfriend, but I am so happy you do. I thought you had a thing for Reid. I mean, Mr. Simpson. I was so afraid we wouldn't be able to be friends then."

Mallory took the offered coffee and looked in horror at the smiley face the barista had made in it. "Oh? You and Reid, I mean, Mr. Simpson," Mallory smiled back, "are an item?"

"Not officially, but it's going to happen. I know he has this strict no-dating-employees rule, but when we are together . . . phew, I get hot just thinking about it."

"I bet you do," Mallory said as she put down her latte without taking a sip.

"I just know he's going to ask me to dance at the charity event tomorrow. It's going to be so romantic. I have this killer dress and killer heels. Yum, this latte is killer good."

Mallory smiled blandly. How many times could she say *killer*? It wasn't making her any more inclined to take a sip of the drink Evelyn had brought her. She read the message loud and clear. Stay away from Reid.

"I thought Mr. Simpson was dating that security woman."

"Mallory Westin?" Evelyn asked as if the name were a curse. "Don't tell anyone, but I know all about her. She's an ice princess. Reid would never go for her. She thinks she's too good for him. Which is ridiculous because he is so much better than she is."

Mallory's smile grew tight. All this talk about killing was giving her an idea. She looked at the spoon and thought of three ways she could kill Evelyn right this instant.

"And when he looks at me with those eyes," Evelyn sighed. "But, your guy is totally dreamy too."

"Damien? Yes, he is," Mallory said tersely. Was it possible this woman was behind the poisoning?

"Aren't you going to take a sip of your drink?"

Mallory smiled and lifted the cup to her lips. "Mmm," she said as she pretended to take a drink.

"So, have you had many complaints about the restrooms being closed? I know we ran into someone who was worried if they would be open for their event."

"It's always something. But Reid told me they would be done by tomorrow. If he says it, then it must be true. Oh, here he is now." Evelyn waved. "Hello, Mr. Simpson."

Mallory clutched the spoon in her hand as Evelyn dropped her voice to a seductive purr.

"Good morning, ladies. Miss Winters, I need to go over those reports you have for me."

Mallory stood and smiled at Evelyn. "Thanks for the drink. It was wonderful."

Reid hid his smile as he waited for Mallory to stand up. He took a step back and followed her from the room. He felt Evelyn watching them so he didn't dare touch Mallory. When he had come into the room, he had seen the way Mallory was smiling and then her hand go to her spoon. He recognized that look from high school. She was about to murder Evelyn, and Evelyn had no clue she'd come so close to death.

"What was that all about?" Reid asked once he had Mallory safely in the lobby.

"Your girlfriend was warning me to stay away from you. She said the word *kill* over three times in one sentence."

"Evelyn? Please. Not my type."

"Apparently ice princesses are." Reid raised an eyebrow as he opened the door to the ballroom so they could check the progress. "She thinks nothing is going on between Mallory and you. Mostly because Mallory is an ice princess."

Reid laughed. "Well, if that's true then I must be the sun because she melts for me every time."

"Look who's getting cocky."

"My cock does have something to do with it."

Mallory smacked him on the shoulder before switching into business mode and looking around the ballroom.

"Excuse me," a tall man called out from the door. "I'm looking for the owner."

Reid took in the man's strong build and height. "You found him."

"I have a complaint, and no one at the front desk can tell me anything. I'm having my mother's eightieth birthday here next week. I just came to drop off the deposit, and I saw the restrooms are closed. I can't have a bunch of senior citizens here for a party without a restroom. Can you imagine?"

"I'm sorry for the worry, but the restrooms will be complete by then. Nothing to worry about. You have my word."

"When exactly will they be done? I can't leave this up to chance."

"They will be done before the charity event this weekend. I guarantee it."

The man didn't look all the way convinced but finally gave a nod of acceptance and left the ballroom.

Mallory looked amused. "Having problems?"

"Yes. That's the fourth person to stop me and ask about the restrooms. Apparently Evelyn forgot to tell the front desk that the work will be done soon."

"Well, that's not the only problem we have. Damien said he's getting resistance from the DC crew. I'll need to make a call when we get back to your office. The stage looks good, but tonight, when no one is here, I want to look over it again—especially the podium. You could easily set a bomb in there."

"I've hired private security to come in with a bomb-sniffing dog and clear the place before the party starts tomorrow."

Mallory nodded. "Good idea. It looks like it's coming along. There haven't been any reports of anyone suspicious."

"What does that mean?"

"It means I'm probably right about the assassination attempt."

"Come on. I have a few emails to send, and you have your phone call. Then let's go get lunch. I feel as if we are in a holding pattern just waiting for someone to kill me. It's getting very boring."

"I'm sorry it's boring to be stuck in your room most of the day. I know you would rather be walking around the property. You're more of a hands-on man," Mallory apologized.

"You misunderstand me, sweetheart. It's the fact we have to leave the room that's getting boring. I very much enjoy my hands-on activities when we are there."

Reid enjoyed the slight blush to her cheeks. He'd always had such fun teasing her.

Chapter Seventeen

Reid opened the door to his Aston Martin Vanquish for Mallory. They were starving after a little hands-on activity in his office. He walked around the car and then slid into the low seat. Looking at Mallory, he shook his head and smiled.

"What?"

"With that wig on, I felt as if you were going to bite me at any second while we were making love."

"I didn't know you were into that," Mallory teased back.

"Woman, you are killing me," Reid whispered as he leaned over and kissed her hard and fast. "Now, what should we do for lunch?"

"Sushi!"

"Done." Reid started the car and turned out of the hotel's property onto the winding country road. The nearest sushi restaurant was twenty minutes away in Atlanta.

Reid reached over and took Mallory's hand in his. He looked at her briefly and smiled. He was happy. He was fulfilled. The thought of driving in an SUV with blond children in the back and Mallory at his side flashed into his mind. Instead of panic, it filled him with eager anticipation.

"Mallory, how do you feel—?" Reid was about to ask about children when he pressed on the brake pedal going around a turn. "I don't have any brakes!"

Reid grabbed the steering wheel with two hands as he navigated the tight turn. He reached for the emergency brake, but nothing happened either.

"Reid, truck ahead," Mallory said calmly.

Reid swerved into the opposite lane and passed the truck, but traffic was starting to pick up the closer they got to the city. He looked frantically around for someplace to run the car off the road.

Mallory cursed. "We have another problem."

"What?" Reid asked as he passed another car.

"We are being followed by a large black SUV. And it's closing in on us. You need to speed up."

Reid looked where the country road ended and turned onto a larger highway. Taking the turn to get onto the highway at this speed was going to be tricky enough.

"They're closing in." Mallory unbuckled her seatbelt and reached into her purse to pull out her gun.

"Keep your seatbelt on. Are you crazy?"

"Just a little, but in a good way, which means I'll try something kinky in the bedroom at least once," she winked before rolling down her window and pulling herself out. Reid heard the sound of the gunfire as he grew closer to the intersection.

"Hurry up and get inside," Reid yelled.

"Don't rush a woman with a gun, Reid," Mallory called back before firing off another round.

Reid saw the windshield to the approaching SUV crack, and then it swerved, slamming on the brakes to control the large vehicle. Mallory slid back into the seat and buckled her seatbelt.

Reid kept both hands on the wheel as he made a sweeping turn through two lanes of traffic. Horns blared, tires squealed, and Reid struggled to keep the car under control.

"They are still back there. Lose them in Finn's old neighborhood," Mallory ordered.

"Seriously? I can't drive that fast through there."

Mallory was already pulling out her phone. "I'll take care of it, just do it. Terrell, Mallory Westin. I need a favor."

Reid kept control of the highly responsive sports car through traffic. He sped down the highway toward the neighborhood he'd normally never drive through in a $250,000 car, hoping they were making the right decision. Mallory had been on the phone issuing orders as he swerved from lane to lane, confusing the SUV that was still following them.

"Take a right," Mallory ordered.

Reid turned the wheel as the tires searched for grip on the pavement. As soon as he straightened the wheel, he saw they had turned into a neighborhood he'd never been in before. It looked strangely like the neighborhood he grew up in.

"There," Mallory pointed straight ahead. "Come on," she chanted as she looked in the mirror for the SUV. "Yes!"

"It's behind us?"

"Sure is. Go to the end of this street and take a left. It'll pop out at that rundown industrial park. You can just slide it into neutral, and we'll coast to a stop."

"That sounds like a good plan except for the person following us, who is trying to kill us." Reid kept his eyes on the road and prayed no one would step out into the street. Somehow the neighborhood was strangely deserted.

"You won't need to worry about that much longer," Mallory said as she flashed him a grin. "Ready?"

"For what?"

"For me to give Terrell the cue."

"I'm the expert at driving. You be the expert at whatever you're doing."

"I like the sound of that. Except I think I may be the better driver."

"Faster, sure. Better, not so sure."

"Are we having our first fight as a couple?"

"As long as we can have our first round of make-up sex." Reid grinned as he kept his eye on the road.

Mallory rolled down the window again as soon as they passed a stop sign. She fired at the windshield of the SUV. She slid back in and rolled up the window as an explosion of gunfire erupted behind them. Reid caught a quick glance in the rearview mirror as the SUV took on heavy fire from both sides of the street.

"Terrell," Reid said with appreciation.

"Terrell," Mallory grinned. "Now take a left. We're only a couple miles away now."

Mallory wouldn't admit it, but she was kind of mad she wasn't driving. Sure, her Porsche was nice, but Reid's car was orgasmic. And he looked so sexy as he handled the car.

"Stop sulking. I'll let you drive my Zenvo ST1 when this is over. It goes from zero to sixty in under three seconds."

"You get to have all the fun," Mallory pouted.

"Come on, isn't this romantic?" Reid grinned. "And don't think for one second I forgot you said you would try something kinky in the bedroom. I have this great idea for when I have you blindfolded . . ."

Mallory felt herself flush pink as Reid told her what he wanted to do to her. Okay, the car didn't sound nearly as orgasmic as that.

"It's been fun, Simpson. But next time I'll drive." Mallory winked.

"Then who will hang out the window and shoot?" Reid asked as the car slowed down. Cars flew by him into the large industrial parking lot and stopped. The Aston Martin cruised to a smooth stop right where Terrell had parked.

Mallory laughed as she opened the door and stood to meet Terrell and some of his guys. "Thanks for the help back there."

"No problem. Anything for my angel." Terrell tossed a smirk to Reid. There seemed to be some kind of tension between them. She didn't know if they had met before. Sure, they were both at Allegra and Finn's wedding, but she never saw them talking. "Do you two know each other?"

"Nah, we just had a little chat at the hospital once. It's all good." Terrell tipped up his chin in acknowledgment to Reid.

Reid stiffened but held out his hand. "Thank you for the help. It looks as if you have a habit of saving the members of my family."

Mallory watched as Terrell looked at Reid's outstretched hand. He looked over to her, and she gave a quick smile as she took a step closer to Reid. Terrell grinned and shook Reid's hand.

"That's a nice car, man." Terrell ran his hand over the hood of the Aston Martin and whistled.

"I'll make you a deal. After I get it fixed, you can meet me at the speedway and drive it."

"Damn. Seriously?"

"Now you're letting him drive it before me?" Mallory teased in mock outrage.

"Don't worry, sweetheart. I'll give you a ride you'll

appreciate."

Mallory automatically dropped her eyes down his chest, past his narrow waist, and to his—

"Whoa, so that's how it is." Terrell interrupted her thoughts. "I'll take you back to the hotel before you two get into any more trouble."

"I need to wait for my mechanic to get here," Reid protested.

Terrell gave a quick nod of his chin to his guys. "Don't worry about your car. We gotcha covered. What's your mechanic's name?"

Mallory waited as Reid gave his mechanic's card to one of the guys staying behind to watch his car before heading over to Terrell's car. The ride back to the hotel was only prolonged long enough for them to run through a drive-thru.

"Are one of you going to tell me what's up? My angel is looking a little devilish today. Not that it's not hot, but combined with the car incident . . . do y'all need Terrell's help?" Terrell asked as he pulled his car up to the front door of the hotel.

"Basically, someone is trying to kill Reid because of something he's seen, and somehow my father is involved in an assassination plot."

"Damn, y'all got problems. Call me if you need me."

Mallory leaned across the console and gave him a quick peck on the cheek. "Thanks again."

"Anytime, angel. Reid, good luck, man."

Reid shook his hand, and Mallory missed a quick exchange they had. But then Reid thumped him on the shoulder before joining her to walk into the lobby.

"What was that about?" Mallory asked as she looked around to see if anyone was surprised to see them still alive.

"Guy stuff." Reid shot her a wink before putting on his business face. "Let's check out the ballroom again. It should be almost done for the day."

Damien saw them as soon as they walked in and headed toward them. "Thanks for the phone call. It worked. DC is pissed about it, but they've backed off challenging every one of my orders."

Mallory looked around at the work being done. Tables were being wheeled in. The stage was complete. Someone was working on the wiring of the microphone at the podium. "No problem. It's always nice to talk to the director."

"Talk?" Reid joked after Damien headed to do a final check on his people.

"Okay, threaten. Same thing."

"How did you know about him and that prostitute in Costa Rica?"

Mallory shook her head. "I swear, they hire me to dig dirt up on people, but never once assumed I will get any on them. Politicians, they think the higher they are on the ladder, the more indestructible they are. Reality, in fact, is just the opposite."

Reid chuckled. "You should run for office. Take your father's seat."

"Have you lost your mind?" Mallory asked, horrified.

Reid sent her a wink. "I'd be willing to trade sexual favors for votes."

"Mr. Simpson! I'm so glad you're *finally* back. I was so worried about you." Mallory rolled her eyes before turning around to see Evelyn hurrying forward.

"I ran into a bit of car trouble. Nothing to worry about," Reid said smoothly, if not a little irritated. The way Evelyn put her hand to her heart and let out a relieved sigh convinced Mallory she hadn't heard the irritation.

"Oh, thank heavens."

It seemed Evelyn was auditioning for a role in *Gone With the Wind*. If she swooned in a fit of vapors, Mallory was going to shoot her.

"What was so important?" Reid asked.

"Golly," she blinked quickly before giving him a dazzling smile. "I need to finalize all the details for tomorrow—timing of arrivals, if we feed all these lawmen, stuff like that. I have ordered dinner in the private dining room. It's all set up."

Reid grimaced. "I just ate, I'm sorry. However, you can email me your schedule, and I'll send it back with any notes."

Evelyn's eyes narrowed briefly at Mallory. She smiled innocently back and batted her own lashes. "I see. May I have a word in private, Mr. Simpson?"

"Of course," Reid answered as he sent Mallory a pained glance before stepping away.

Mallory took the time to examine the podium. The wiring was good, and she saw the CIA had exchanged the normal wooden podium with a metal one wrapped in a faux wood laminate. If a bomb were placed inside, it would act to contain the explosion.

Reid watched Mallory bend over and examine the podium. He was still riding high on adrenaline, and the last thing he wanted to do was stand here listening to Evelyn whimper over him. She knew there was a no-dating policy between higher-ups and their employees, but that didn't seem to stop her from trying. She was doing everything she could to convince him to have coffee or a drink with her to look over the schedule. The same schedule he'd approved yesterday.

"Evelyn, is there anything new you actually need?" She blinked her eyes and placed her hand on his arm. "Evelyn, you're a nice woman, but I'm in a relationship. And even if I wasn't, it's against the rules to date an employee. I'm sorry."

Evelyn gave a nervous laugh. "I know. Did you think . . . Oh, my. I didn't mean for you to think that. I just want tomorrow to go perfectly. It's my first major event."

"Everything will be fine," Reid said with his fingers crossed. Fine so long as an assassin could be caught before it started.

"Thank you, Mr. Simpson. Your support calms my nerves. So, you're dating someone? Anyone I know or another famous model?" She tried to make it a joke, but Reid heard the tightness in her voice.

"Mallory Westin. Now, if you excuse me, I have a lot of work to do before the party tomorrow."

Evelyn took the hint and hurried back to the front desk. Reid let out a long breath. He didn't want to hurt her feelings, but his days of playing the field were over. The only woman he wanted knew how to blackmail, shoot, and drive fast, all with a smile on her face and pearls around her neck.

"Miss Winters?" Reid asked with a smile across his face. Mallory was on her hands and knees looking under the stage. She wiggled her ass as she scooted back, and his laughter turned to a groan.

"Coming," she called and stood up, dusting off her knees. "How is everything with Evelyn?"

"I'm afraid you're right. She's angling for a relationship. But I told her I was already in one." Reid leaned forward, and Mallory swatted him.

"You're in one with Mallory Westin, not Miss Winters."

"As if a wig and some makeup is going to stop me from wanting to make love to you."

"It will if people think you're having an affair. That would be bad for business and draw too much attention to me. As far as everyone else knows, Mallory is off playing detective with the plane crash. They don't need to think she's here. They talk much more freely around Miss Winters."

Reid held open the door for her as they left the ballroom. "I just need to get some things from my office."

"Reid."

Reid heard his name called and both he and Mallory froze. For a split second, her eyes widened before her cover fell back into place.

"This idiot is telling me there are no suites available for me since I don't have a reservation. Fix it."

"Prince Liam. What an honor it is to have you visit my newest property. What brings you here?" Reid asked as he strode toward the front desk where Evelyn was rushing from the back to help the attendant. Mallory stood far enough away to blend into the background of the lobby, but still close enough to listen. Reid smiled and moved so Liam was looking in the opposite direction.

"I'm here for the charity event tomorrow. Someone mentioned it in Stromia, and I thought it would be a good show of support. I want to show America that King Liam will be a friend to them."

"King?" Evelyn sighed with round eyes.

"Isn't your father very ill?" Reid asked.

Liam lifted his lip in disgust. "He's always ill. I'll go back after the charity event. Father would approve of me solidifying political alliances, and that is what tomorrow is all about."

"Your Majesty, I'm so sorry not to have a room ready for you," Evelyn cut in. "Mr. Simpson, I can get the penthouse ready, but it will take thirty minutes." When Reid gave a quick nod of his head, Evelyn turned her eyes back to Liam. Reid felt a gentle breeze from all her batting.

"Your majesty, I feel awful about the wait. I have a private table set up in the dining room. I would love to have you join me for a meal, and you can let me know if there is anything at all I can do to make your stay more pleasant."

Liam cast a glance at Evelyn who had moved her hand from her heart to push up her breasts. "I would like that very much."

Evelyn gasped, and Reid knew he had just been replaced. He waved to the doorman who hurried over and took the bags to the penthouse while Evelyn ordered the room to be prepared.

"I hope you enjoy your stay, Prince. I'll see you tomorrow at the party." Reid turned away after shaking his hand. "Oh, and I don't know if you are aware, but I am donating a rather large check to the foundation. Maybe you should consider doing the same. Then you can stand on the stage with me during the candidates' speeches and even give your own when you present the check. It would look very good in the media."

Liam nodded his head. "That is a good idea, my friend." Liam turned to a man standing behind him and ordered it to be done.

Reid smiled and headed for his office. Mallory was already walking that way. What was the saying? Keep your friends close and your enemies closer? If Liam was behind the assassination, then Reid wanted to stick to him all night.

Chapter Eighteen

Mallory walked past the office and into the stairwell. She watched through the small window as Reid went into his office and came back out a few minutes later with an armful of folders. She tapped softly on the glass, and his head whipped around to the doors. Seeing her, he headed toward the stairwell.

"What the hell is Liam doing here?"

"I don't know, but are there any other ex-boyfriends I need to know about? Damien, Bowie, Liam . . ."

"First, I dated Damien, but not for long. Second, I never dated Bowie or Liam . . . or at least I never *really* dated them. It was my job."

Reid let out an aggravated breath. "It's not that. I'm just being jealous when I have no right to be. The past is the past, but our past just can't seem to leave us alone."

"We have our whole future together. Let's just think about that. What did Liam want? Why is he here?"

"That's the thing; he says he's here to make alliances with America. After what Lloyd told you, I think he's here to make sure the job gets done. If this is really about alliances, he and the candidate could be making backdoor deals for when their time comes. As we both know, most deals come about behind closed doors."

"Shit," Mallory cursed. "Liam mentioned they would

no longer be weak—that they would have weapons. This could be about the French arming Stromia."

"But what would the candidate get out of it?" Reid asked before shaking his head. "I know. What's the one thing Stromia, as small as it is, is known for?"

"Your casino?"

"Money. You probably don't know this since you haven't been over there much, but they are quietly changing their banking laws to make them more secretive. They want to become the new Switzerland. Or, in this case, a dirty version of the Swiss banking system."

Reid unlocked his fully refurbished suite and tossed his key on the side table. Mallory nibbled on her lip as she pulled off her wig and started pacing. She couldn't help but think about her father. Did her father hire an assassin to take out his competition and ensure his presidency? Did Liam do it to get weapons?

"I'm so stupid," Mallory cursed. "It's so easy. I was overthinking it. What are the two things people like Liam and my father are always after?" Mallory didn't give Reid a chance to answer. "Money and power." It was clicking into place now. "Every candidate is incredibly wealthy and powerful. But they are never satisfied with that money and power. They are always trying to earn more, gain more."

Reid immediately caught on. "And in the United States, when you gain the ultimate power of the presidency, you lose all of your business interests. The president doesn't make much money compared to what these guys make now. And Liam has a way to hide that money. Foreign laws will make it nearly impossible for the US government to find out whose money—and how much—is in Stromia banks."

Mallory grinned at Reid. "But Liam needs weapons to

wage a war against their rival, Rahmi. Because he is such a sore loser, he will attack King Dirar in a power play for embarrassing him."

"So, we figured out the *why*. Now the last question we need answered is the *who*." Reid paused and took her hand in his. "Are you afraid your father is behind this?"

Mallory felt as if someone was reaching into her chest and squeezing her heart. "I don't know. How horrible is it for a daughter to not know?"

"It's not horrible, Mallory. We both know he's not above carrying out threats and using the power he has worked so hard to gain against someone."

Mallory stepped into Reid's embrace and laid her head on his chest. "I hope he's not behind it. I used to idolize him. It all changed when he was elected senator and became so ingrained in national politics, he stopped caring about the people around him. I don't remember the last time my mother laughed. Of course, I also don't remember the last time I was with them. After what happened to us, I couldn't stand to hear my mom lecture me on my family duty. She blindly followed my father's lead. I think she got a high from the power and notoriety as well. But then if it's not him behind it, that makes him the target and the thought of him dead—"

"Shh. It'll be all right. We will work together to stop it before anything bad happens. I'll stick with Liam tomorrow. Bowie will be in disguise with the candidates, and you'll be the badass I love sitting in a hot air duct getting all sweaty and stuff."

Mallory felt her chest tighten, her shoulders shake, and then she laughed out loud.

"Now, we have done, redone, and accounted for just about everything possible. Tomorrow is going to be a long day, and you promised me something kinky," Reid joked as Mallory felt her shoulders relax. Maybe having a partner wasn't so bad.

"Kinky, huh?" Mallory slowly unknotted his tie and pulled him into the bedroom.

In the early morning hours, Liam slapped the girl's ass as she left his room. He had to hand it to Reid; he knew how to hire some fine women. Evie, Ellie, or something like that. He didn't need to know her name when he was done with her. He got what he wanted, and she got to say she screwed a king.

Liam waited until the door closed before talking. "Did you enjoy the show?"

"I always do," the voice said from the shadows.

"When did you get here?"

"About an hour ago."

Liam sat down heavily on the couch with his robe falling open. "Is everything on schedule for tomorrow?"

"Yes. But Black and Jonak are wavering. They're upset I couldn't get to Simpson yet."

"Well, Black and Jonak think they are running things. But you and I both know that's not the case. I just need someone to run my illegal activities through. They are easily replaceable. Reid wants me on stage with him tomorrow to give some money to these . . . *people*. So, don't miss," Liam warned. "Now, tell me about Reid."

"He has a woman with him. I fought with her the first night. She stopped the poison attempt. I don't know what happened the other times. I mixed the poison in their drinks for breakfast, but nothing happened. I rigged his car this morning, and he lost control, but then another woman fired at me so I couldn't get too close. Right when I thought I had them, we drove through this neighborhood, and I got ambushed. I had to retreat. A couple of hours later, he and the woman sauntered into the lobby as if nothing happened."

"Who are these women?" Liam asked. It figured Reid would have some deadly black widow with him instead of beefy security guards. Reid never did what was expected.

"The woman with black hair from today is Miss Winters. He claims she is with his company out of Las Vegas. The woman from the first night had blond hair. It was so dark I didn't get a good look at her. I know it sounds crazy, but she kind of reminded me of Mallory Westin."

Liam sat up. "Mallory Westin?" Now he was interested.

Mallory slid the black, long-sleeved spandex shirt over the Kevlar vest she had already put on. Reid watched her as he tightened his tie. She bent over the open metal case, pulled out the two knives, and slid them into her combat boots. Next, she slid the daggers into the X-shaped sheaths at the small of her back before strapping her gun to her thigh. Reid lifted his eyebrow, though, when she attached a tomahawk to a shoulder harness.

"Seriously?"

"Deadly."

"That's for sure."

Mallory was in the zone. She ignored her emotions, shut off her mind, and focused solely on the job at hand. She slid on her boxy suit coat and pulled up the wide-legged pants. She looked in the mirror and then gave her black wig one more brushing. She wouldn't draw any attention walking through the lobby as Miss Winters. "I'm ready."

"I'll come down right behind you. I want to see you safely in the air duct before I return to my job."

"Do you want one of my men to accompany you?"

"Not necessary. I'll be around everyone until I have to change. And then I'm meeting with Damien when I come up here. We are going over any last-minute details. Hopefully, everything will be over with by then anyway."

Mallory stuck her earpiece in and tested it. When Bowie responded, she snapped the communications device into place. "Fingers crossed."

Mallory turned and gave into her feelings long enough to kiss Reid. It was quick, powerful, and then she was gone. She couldn't look back. She couldn't think this was the end—that this was the last time she might see Reid. She had trained with the best, and she refused to fail. She had a lot more riding on this than the approval of the CIA. Her entire future rode on it.

Reid waited until the door closed before he clicked open the metal case Mallory left on the vanity. He pulled out the one remaining combat knife and felt its weight. Then he opened the second, larger metal case. She had already taken one of the guns from it but had left two. One was a rifle, and the other was a handgun. He picked the handgun up and checked to see if it was loaded. Finding it empty, he looked for the ammo and found it in another bag. He loaded the gun and slid it into the waistband of his suit before covering it with his jacket.

Mallory may have changed a lot over the years, but she forgot one very important thing about him—he'd grown up on the wrong side of the tracks, as her dad liked to remind him. Whether his mother liked it or not, he'd been shooting a gun since he was a kid. Well, his mother did say to let the other kids have a choice in what to play. His poor mother. She was trying to promote a sense of community by making nice with the neighbors. If she knew he learned to shoot, Allegra learned how to hotwire a car, Bree was a good tattoo artist, and Elle cut her teeth on settling drug disputes, then she would faint.

True, it had been a while since he had shot a handgun, but he'd been shooting clays for the last eight years. Hopefully, he wouldn't need it. But it if looked like Mallory was in danger, then he would do anything to protect her.

Chapter Nineteen

Mallory walked through the lobby without garnering any attention. It was common for Miss Winters to be going to and fro, so no one paid her a bit of attention. She headed down a side hallway and pulled out the key Reid had given her for the mechanical room. She knocked twice, then opened the door. The Secret Service agent stood inside with his hand on his gun.

"Agent, I'm Winters. Code word, *quack quack*." Mallory rolled her eyes as the agent grinned. "Agent Wallace assigned me to the air duct inside the ballroom."

The agent smiled as he watched her undress. "Yeah, Wallace told us. You expecting trouble?" He laughed as she stripped the suit coat and pants she'd used to conceal her weapons and tossed them in an empty box.

"I always expect trouble. It's why I'm good at my job." Mallory eyed the large return vent and the ladder already set up for her. She looked at her watch. Ten fifty-one in the morning. What was eight hours in an air duct?

"Has there been any change to the standard operating procedure?" Mallory asked as she started to climb up the ladder.

"Just a little. The prince believes he should have some of our men guarding him, which we agreed to do. That leaves some of the low-priority rooms unprotected. But, that's all."

"The restrooms?"

"That's right. We pulled our two agents from the lobby restrooms. We still have all the agents stationed in the lobby, though."

Mallory dropped the vent cover to the agent. How could they not listen to her? "I told them the restrooms were high priority."

"No offense, but Washington was tired of hearing what you, a local non-agent, think. This is a foreign dignitary. When they ask for protection, we give it to them. Enjoy your day, Agent Winters."

Mallory pulled herself up and began the long crawl to the ballroom. She didn't need a map this time. She'd studied the whole system enough to know every turn by heart. She heard the vent behind her being sealed before the ladder was removed. As she navigated the ductwork, she pressed her coms. "Bowie, you there?"

"Copy," her handler responded.

"Where are you?"

"I'm checking all the trucks as they come in to unload the food and decorations."

"We have a problem. The Secret Service pulled their agents from the restrooms to guard Liam."

"I know. I tried to get some of my guys on it, but there's some major dick-swinging going on in DC. The only director who knows what's going on is ours. The FBI and Secret Service are throwing fits. They don't want foreign intelligence operating on their turf."

"I'm starting to hate this super-secret spy shit."

"True, and we both know the best of operations get blown with this interagency cooperation crap. I swear, no one can keep their mouths shut anymore."

Mallory agreed. While it would seem better to have all these shared resources, the more people you involved, the more chance of a screw-up. She crawled past the women's restroom and took a peek through the vent. The remodel was wrapping up. They were scooping up the fake debris and sheets of cardboard into trash cans to make a big show of exiting. The restroom did look nice with its fresh coat of paint and new light fixtures.

"I hope we can end this before lunch," Mallory whispered as she crossed the ballroom.

"Me, too, but it's not looking like it. I don't see anything. It's a strange feeling, this one."

"I know what you mean." Mallory felt the familiar tingle down her spine when she became anxious. "I know I've been out of the game for a while, but this is different."

"Copy that. I have to check another truck. Stay alert and be ready for anything."

Mallory took the last turn, crawled past the vent, and then slowly turned around in the nearby intersecting ductwork. She was careful not to put too much weight in one place or to knock the walls. She didn't want anyone to get suspicious and look up. When she finally got in position, she slid forward on her stomach to look out the vent.

Reid stood in the middle of the ballroom with Evelyn. She was directing, and he was nodding. As if feeling her eyes on him, he turned around and looked right at her. It lasted only a split second, but she could tell he knew she was there. He gave another nod and then headed out of the ballroom. He didn't look up at her as he left.

Reid couldn't see Mallory, but something told him she was there. He looked at his watch. Eight hours until the candidates arrived. He crossed the lobby and saw the fake construction men clearing out of the restrooms.

"Oh, thank goodness," Evelyn said as she hurried up behind Reid. "I've had so many questions about whether the restrooms would be opening soon or not. That makes tonight much easier."

"Reid," a familiar voice called out.

Reid plastered on a smile and tried not to get upset by the way Evelyn started simpering when Liam called out to him and sauntered over.

"Prince Liam. Is there something I can do for you?"

"Why, yes, there is. I am going riding. Join me."

Reid smiled. Even he wasn't careless enough to head outdoors right now. Not after multiple attempts to kill him. "I'm so sorry, Prince. I am too busy with preparations for tonight. But, may I recommend you try out Atlas? He's the best horse in the stables."

"Are you sure? A ride could do you good. Help you relax before the big night," Liam said as he tried to convince Reid.

Reid smiled tightly. "I'm sure. Thank you, though."

"I'm sorry for the loss of your company. I shall see you tonight then. And thank you for the suggestion. I will give Atlas a try."

Liam walked past him and out the door with his entourage trailing behind. A luxury golf cart picked him up to whisk him to the stables.

"Maybe I should help him?" Evelyn asked hopefully.

"I'd be careful of him, Evelyn. He's not the marrying kind, and I have a feeling you are. Anyway, the linens should be arriving soon. Why don't you handle that instead?" Reid suggested kindly. Sure, it annoyed him when she flirted. But she didn't deserve what Liam would dish out. Evelyn sniffed and then nodded before walking quickly to the new restroom to compose herself.

Reid headed to his office but was intercepted by Damien, carrying a bag from Reid's favorite sandwich shop.

"I know it's only eleven-thirty, but this is the last chance I'll be able to eat. I grabbed you a sandwich, too."

"Thanks, Damien." Reid unlocked his office and decided Mallory had excellent taste in men, especially since she was now with him.

"No problem." Damien pulled out a sandwich wrapped in wax paper and set it on the desk. "How are your sisters doing?"

"They're good. Mallory convinced them to go to the Connecticut compound. I'm sure Elle is madder than a hornet. She doesn't like to be away from the office much. And Allegra and Finn are still on their honeymoon. Bree and Logan seem to be enjoying their time away from the city, but it's my mother who has me the most worried. While she's not at the hotel, she is still in town. She's checking in on Troy every day and sending me updates."

"How is he doing?"

"Really well, given the circumstances. He's improving every day, and they're even talking about releasing him to a rehabilitation center soon."

"So you are the last man standing. I bet your mother is on a mission," Damien chuckled.

Reid laughed before taking a bite of his sandwich. If she were coming, she would introduce him to every single woman or mother of a single woman at the charity event tonight.

"I guess you don't have to worry about that much longer the way things are going between you and Mallory.

How do you think your family will feel about you and Mallory as a couple?" Damien asked interrupting Reid's nightmare of never-ending ladies being foisted on him.

"I don't know. I'm thinking of not telling them," Reid joked. "I just know as soon as I do, they will all warn me not to mess it up. And if I do, I fear they may kick me out of the family and keep Mallory."

"Good luck with that. Mallory is a wonderful woman." Damien stood up and tossed the empty wrapper into the trash. "Given what's going on, keep your office door locked at all times, and no venturing out onto the property."

"I have a lot of work piling up here. It'll be another couple of hours before I'm done."

Damien looked at his watch. "I'll meet you in the ballroom at five. The string quartet for the lobby should be setting up and the band in the ballroom will have arrived. We can go over everything then."

"Guests will start arriving in the lobby at six for drinks. The ballroom doors open at seven. Let's hope this whole thing is over by then. I hate just sitting here, waiting." Reid crumpled his trash into a tight ball and threw it away. His nerves were shot.

"I do, too. I don't like feeling helpless while Mallory is up there. It's why I'm going to head back in, now that I know you're safely locked up."

"If you think of anything I can do, please let me know."

"I will. I'll see you this evening."

Reid walked Damien to the door. At each end of the hallway was an armed guard. Between his security guards, the Secret Service, and undercover CIA, he had a sinking feeling nothing was going to happen tonight. And that meant he was going to have to stay in hiding. The air kicked on and blew lightly down from the vent. He wondered how

Mallory was doing. He agreed with Damien. There wasn't anything worse than knowing the woman you love was putting her life in danger for you and all you could do was trust and support her. It didn't change the fact that he hated it.

Mallory looked at her watch: 4:45. She rolled over onto her back and did some leg pulses to keep the blood flowing in her body. Her body was stiff, and she was getting very hungry. She'd kept an eye on the ballroom all afternoon. Quite frankly, she was shocked nothing had happened yet. The ballroom was filled with florists, caterers, decorators, and now a band had just arrived to start setting up.

"Checking in." Bowie's voice sounded in her ear. "How are you doing?"

"Stretching now. Anything?"

"Negative. And this wig is killing me," Bowie complained.

"Really? You've been wearing it all of a few hours. I've been stuck in mine all week. Crybaby," Mallory teased.

"Damn Liam for showing up," Bowie muttered.

"You know him really well. What do you think he's up to?"

"I don't know, but I'll be sticking to him like a tick on a deer."

Mallory rolled back over onto her stomach and looked out at the ballroom. "Someone is testing the microphone at the podium. Make sure you recheck it when they are done."

"Copy that."

Five minutes later, Mallory saw Bowie disguised as an older

gentleman in overalls approach the stage.

"All clear," he whispered into the coms. "It's almost five. Reid will be here soon and the bomb-sniffing dogs will be walking through in a couple minutes. You don't have any explosives on you, do you?"

"Damn, I knew I forgot something," Mallory deadpanned.

The ballroom doors opened and slammed shut. A couple of seconds, Mallory saw Reid, Damien, and a dog with its handler walk in. The dog and handler went to work while Reid and Damien walked around the room.

Mallory felt like banging her head on the thin metal. How could this not be over yet? She was so sure the assassin would hide here. This whole thing would be resolved by now. Reid would be safe and she would know whether or not her father was capable of murder.

Mallory fought down her emotions and doubt. She had to trust her training. She had to trust her instincts. If it meant she spent the whole night here making sure Reid was protected, that was what she was going to do.

Chapter Twenty

Reid opened the door to his suite and let Damien walk in first. Damien reappeared a minute later and told him it was safe to enter. He cast a quick glance at the clock. It was five-forty. He had twenty minutes to get dressed and meet the arriving guests.

"Have you talked to Mallory?" he asked Damien, who was unzipping his own garment bag.

"No. Everything is radio silent. I don't even know where Bowie is. They didn't want anyone to pick up on their plan. They're worried any of their communications might get picked up on the coms network by my team, so they are on their own secure channel."

"I have a bad feeling, Damien. I don't know why, but I feel as if this whole thing is falling apart."

"I couldn't agree more," Damien said as he reached into this garment bag. "That's why I got you this."

Reid caught the bulletproof vest Damien tossed at him. "This will look nice under my tux."

"Yeah, just don't dance with anyone. They'll be able to feel it and wonder why you're wearing it. Now, for tonight's schedule. We've heard from both campaigns. Graham and Orson will arrive at seven o'clock. Westin and Childs will arrive at seven ten. At seven-thirty, you will begin your welcome speech and introduce Graham.

Graham will talk for five minutes and introduce the head of the charity. Sandburg will speak and introduce Westin. Westin will talk for five minutes. Sandburg will then make a closing remark and accept your and Liam's checks. Clapping and then dancing starts."

"And somewhere during that time, someone gets shot," Reid said dryly.

"Could be. Let's hope only Mallory does the shooting."

Reid closed the door to the living room and undressed. He thought over and over that he was glad he took Mallory's gun. He double-checked it and slid the gun back in place.

Mallory felt her head sweating under her wig. She was sure the makeup she had on to change her features was running. Both were a hindrance to the job, but she needed to be in disguise when she joined the party, which was in full swing. Graham and Orson had made their entrance and were currently circling of the room. She looked at her watch: seven-ten. Her father would be pulling up to the front door right now.

The ballroom was packed. There were veterans in service uniforms with spouses in formalwear. There were businessmen, philanthropists, and society types all mingling together to raise money for veterans' needs. Newspaper, television, and magazine reporters took pictures and interviewed the who's who of local and national fame.

The room erupted into polite applause, and Mallory knew her father and Ambrose had arrived.

Reid didn't bother shaking hands with Mallory's father or Ambrose Childs as they strode into the room like a pair of peacocks. The fake "Oh, hello! Good to see you again" look followed by a wave was getting on his nerves.

He also didn't smile when he saw Shirley wheel into the event with Feng next to her. She spotted Reid and sent him a wink. He watched as they moved to the table nearest the side exit. He'd given orders to his security to take care of them in case anything happened tonight.

Reid smiled to each guest who walked past him and was surprised when he saw Senator Westin heading right toward him, fake smile and all.

"Reid, I need to have a word," Senator Westin whispered.

"I don't think so," Reid smiled back as people pressed in to shake the senator's hand.

"Where's Mallory? I need to talk to her. It's important."

"Why should I know? Don't you manage her—telling her who she should marry, that kind of thing?" Reid felt his voice cut into the senator but didn't care. He forced himself to smile at another patron who passed by.

"You know," the senator said, surprised.

"Look at the time," Reid said with a show of looking at his watch. "I need to give a speech."

Reid headed toward the stage and in his peripheral vision saw Evelyn rounding up the candidates and the head of the charity, Mr. Sandburg. Reid's heart raced from his talk with Senator Westin. As he approached the stage, he felt his footsteps slow. It was going to happen, and he didn't know if he'd be able to live through it.

He fought the urge to look up to where Mallory was. Instead he took the black stairs one at a time, each one a step closer to the end of his life. He cast a quick glace behind him to see the other candidates walking a little way behind him. One of them was supposed to die with him.

Mallory pulled her gun from her thigh. She didn't hear movement, but she sensed it. She focused on controlling her breathing and tuning out the applause. Reid's voice spoke to the audience, welcoming them to the first event to be held at his new resort.

She closed her eyes and focused on the metal. She felt it. A vibration. She put her finger on the trigger of her gun and slid backward a couple of feet into the *T* intersection in the ductwork. She didn't want to be a sitting duck for the assassin coming around the corner from the restrooms. It was just like she had thought. So far, so good.

Mallory pressed her com. "We're a go," she whispered.

"Copy that. Moving into position," Bowie whispered back.

Reid smiled and clapped along with the hundreds of people sitting at their tables. The candidates, the prince, and the head of the charity were lined up behind him across the stage. Secret Service flanked the front of the stage.

"Military veterans and their families sacrifice so much . . ." Reid continued with his speech. Out of the corner of his eye, he saw an older man move forward. Reid faltered. Was that him? Was this it? The man gave his head a very tiny shake of his head and a quick glare before casually scanning the audience.

Reid cleared his throat. "As many of you know, Governor Graham proudly served his country for nearly ten years before he decided to run for political office. Please join me in welcoming Governor Graham."

Reid took a step back and watched Graham step toward him to shake his hand. Reid smiled and shook hands before coming to stand next to Liam. Liam shifted nervously, and Reid had a sinking feeling it was all going to go down tonight after all.

Mallory counted off the seconds it would take for the assassin to make it from the turn in the air duct to be fully visible. Mallory made her move. She pushed herself partially out from the intersection she was hiding behind and aimed her gun.

"Stop where you are," she said to the figure who surprised her by being just inches from her.

"Or you'll shoot?" replied the feminine voice. "Oh, please. That's so dramatic. Besides you're not the only one with a gun."

Mallory's mind raced as she came face to face with the barrel of a gun. The voice of the owner sounded familiar. "Who's your target?" Mallory asked as they kept their guns aimed at each other in the narrow confines of the air duct.

The woman with red hair just laughed. "Honey, as if I'd tell you. We're in a bit of a standoff, aren't we? I must say, I'm surprised, Miss Winters. I thought someone else would be trying to stop me. I'm kinda glad. I liked the other woman, and now I won't have to kill her."

Reid stood with his arms behind his back while Governor Graham started his speech. He took a moment to look at the rest of the men on stage. None of them seemed to be worried. None except the man standing next to him. Liam continued to fidget and repeatedly tried to take a step away from Reid. Every time he did so, Reid found a reason to lean over and whisper something to him, moving even closer to Liam's side.

The old man Reid had spotted earlier in the audience kept moving closer to the steps of the stage. The Secret Service continued looking straight ahead. Damien must have picked up on Reid's worries, because he saw him moving closer to the vent Mallory was in. Reid looked at his watch. Graham had two more minutes left in his speech—if he lived that long.

Mallory took in the red hair, the full lips, and the tight black dress with two large slits up the sides that allowed access to a knife she saw strapped to the woman's thigh. She could try to slide back into the intersecting air duct where she just was, but they were too close. The woman would easily be able to fire.

"No so fast, Winters," she said as she moved to press her gun against the side of the metal. "You move and I shoot. I'm bound to take out some innocent lives. It's awfully crowded down there. I could maybe even get a whole table by the time your bullet enters my brain. Is your mission really worth that?"

Mallory kept her hand on her gun as she thought about her next move. "You know my name, but I don't know yours."

"I like it that way."

"You seem like a sweet, young girl. Why don't you just tell me who you were hired to kill. Then we can call it a night."

"Has that ever worked for—" Mallory didn't let her finish talking. She made her move. She dropped her gun and lunged forward, grasping the woman's gun hand. She wrenched back her trigger finger, and the young woman grunted in pain.

The next thing Mallory knew, it felt as if a hammer had been slammed into her chest. She hadn't seen the woman grab the gun Mallory had tossed aside before the redhead fired it into Mallory's vest. Mallory's breath was torn from her body, and she fought the panic of not being able to breathe. She lay helpless on her side, struggling for air, as the assassin opened a leather bag from over her shoulder and pulled out a Corner Shot.

Reid watched the old man in the crowd step closer to the stage until he was right in front of the Secret Service. He saw Damien's brows furrow as he looked up at the air ducts and talked into his communication device at his wrist. Governor Graham finished his speech and started to step away from the podium. Suddenly there was a loud *crack* and Ambrose crumpled to the ground.

Senator Westin stood staring in shock at his fallen counterpart. Reid knew by Westin's expression it had to have been Graham or Orson who orchestrated the assassination. Westin was innocent and in danger. Secret Service was scrambling to the stage. The old man pushed his way onto the stage as people screamed in horror and a second shot rang out.

Reid jumped. He saw Senator Westin's eyes go round as he vaulted toward him. In a split second, Reid felt the impact of the bullet meant for Senator Westin hitting the back of his vest. The force of the shot, combined with his momentum, sent Reid crashing into Westin. The two men slammed onto the floor of the stage at the same time an agent jumped to cover them. The sharp pain hit him with every breath.

Fear for Reid's safety caused the final adrenaline surge needed to overcome the pain of being shot. Mallory propelled herself forward and grabbed the Corner Shot before the assassin could pull the trigger a third time. Mallory ripped the gun from the woman's hand in a move she was sure broke the woman's trigger finger.

Mallory tossed the gun behind her and rose up onto her hands and knees to deliver a hard punch to the assassin's temple. Her face knocked onto the metal floor of the air duct, causing it to shake.

"Who hired you?" Mallory screamed as she grabbed the woman by the shoulders.

"Screw you," she spat before moving quickly onto all fours in order to grab Mallory by the throat.

Mallory snarled as she wrapped her hand around the assassin's. She dug her thumb painfully in at the pressure point between the woman's thumb and index finger. With a flick of Mallory's wrist, she twisted the woman's hand from her throat. The woman shouted out in pain as Mallory wrenched her arm.

"Who hired you?" Mallory yelled over the screaming coming from below. She didn't get a chance to ask again as her world shook and suddenly disappeared from beneath her.

Reid sucked in a painful breath. His rib had to be broken. The Secret Service agent was pulling Senator Westin out from underneath Reid as the old man he saw in the audience was fighting with Liam.

The sounds of metal scraping caught his attention. Was Mallory still alive? He pushed himself up as he saw his answer fall from the sky. The bottom of the air duct fell to the ground, followed by two women.

"Mallory!" Reid called in a panic as he watched her and the redhead who had asked him to dance fall in a tangle of limbs and crash onto a table.

China shattered, food went flying, the table collapsed in broken pieces, and guests who were running for the door screamed in surprise as they saw the weapons strapped to both women.

"Mallory? Where?" Senator Westin asked as he pushed off his security detail. Reid didn't bother answering but knew when the senator saw who Reid was looking at.

"Help me," a weak voice said from nearby.

Senator Westin and Reid shot a look at where Ambrose was being dragged past them by two Secret Service agents.

"Senator, we need to go right now." An agent grabbed the senator and pulled him along the stage.

"No!" Ambrose and Westin yelled.

"Is that really Mallory? We can't leave her," Ambrose whispered as blood seeped from the gunshot wound through his right shoulder. He clung to the agents and slowly sat up. "Help me up," he ordered.

Reid didn't care about Ambrose. He cared about Damien's team surrounding Graham and Orson. And he was worried about the redhead climbing on top of Mallory.

Mallory remembered to exhale as she hit the table. The woman fell slightly on top of her, giving her the upper hand. People were screaming, and the screams grew more panicked as the assassin pulled out the knife strapped to her thigh.

Military veterans pushed forward to stop the fight, but as they closed in, the redhead threw the knife. It landed in the leg of one of the soldiers and the others fell back to help him and to protect the civilians.

"Get back," Mallory called out before the woman straddled her and landed a hard punch to her face. Mallory blinked back the stars and heard the distant shout of her name. It was Reid! Reid was still alive.

Mallory responded by rolling her hips and sending the two of them tumbling off the shattered table and onto the floor. The two women stood up and circled each other. Mallory reached for one of the daggers strapped to her back. With a flip of her wrist, she sent the knife sailing at the woman. The woman lunged to the side and it flew past her, lodging inches away from the wife of a veteran. The veteran pulled his wife to safety and started yelling to everyone to evacuate.

"So, you like knives. Let's see what you've got," she said as she pulled another knife from her other thigh.

Mallory pulled her last dagger from her back as they circled each other. In a blink, they both lunged.

"Shoot her," Reid ordered the Secret Service agent.

"They're moving too much. I can't get a clear shot. There are civilians all around. I can't."

"Reid," Senator Westin yelled to get his attention. "Are you telling me that girl with the black hair is my daughter?"

"Yes, now get somewhere safe," Reid ordered as he pulled his gun from the small of his back.

"Like hell." Westin shoved off his security and rushed across the stage.

"Who hired the assassination?" the old man yelled at Liam. Bowie was the old man.

"Diplomatic immunity. You can't touch me," Liam said with a haughtiness that implied he thought he could walk out of there with no consequences.

Reid staggered forward, ignoring the sharp pain in his

back. He stopped in front of Liam and raised the gun. Bowie's surprise was evident even through the heavy makeup. "Who hired her?"

"I have diplomatic immunity."

"Ah, but I'm not a government agent. I am a private citizen and don't give a shit about your immunity." Reid lowered the gun and pressed it against Liam's thigh. "Tell me now or I shoot you. The next time you don't answer, I will shoot higher."

Bowie struggled to keep back the prince's security back as Reid put his finger on the trigger. The sound of blades crashing against each other in a deadly battle drew Reid's attention, and it cost him.

Chapter Twenty-One

Mallory sliced through the air, and the redhead blocked. Their blades slid along each other before being pulled away. It was a deadly, beautiful dance they shared—lunging, slicing, and spinning as they fought. The world fell away until it was just the two of them.

The assassin stabbed and then spun the other way. Her hair whipped into Mallory's face, causing a second of blindness. It was all the woman needed. Mallory felt the knife pierce the skin of her hand and dropped her dagger. A four-inch gash ran across her hand, but luckily she could still move her fingers.

"Sorry about that, honey." The assassin smiled with pure joy.

Mallory felt her training slip, and her emotions burst to the surface. She closed the short distance between them and slammed her head into the woman's nose. The impact of the hit sent both women stumbling back. Mallory felt her fake nose and wig slip from position. She reached up and tore off the wig and props. She stared in surprise as the assassin's red hair lay on the ground. Instead of being a redhead, the woman was a bottle blond. They looked up at each other and blinked.

"Mallory, it is you."

"Tilley, darling. Fab seeing you again," Mallory said with ice in her veins as she looked at the young party girl. Mallory reached for her shoulder harness and unhooked the tomahawk. "Totes sorry we won't have time to chat."

Reid felt Liam's fist slam into his face. His head snapped back, and Liam made a move to bolt. Bowie fired his gun, taking down two of Liam's guards, leaving two confused Secret Service agents standing there. Reid spun and leveled the gun. He only had a moment before the agents would tackle him. He pulled the trigger and saw Liam stumble as the bullet ripped into the back of his leg.

Mistaking the situation, the agents attacked Reid. The punch to Reid's stomach made him fall to his knees, and another agent tackled him to the ground.

"CIA," Bowie shouted.

"I command you to stop. They are with me," Senator Westin yelled, climbing off the stage with a bloody Ambrose leaning on him.

"But, sir . . ."

"No buts. Let them go."

"Liam—you must stop Liam," Reid shouted. The prince was limping through the crowd.

"Go," Westin ordered. The two agents bound from the stage and gave chase.

Bowie grabbed Reid's arm and hauled him up from the ground. Reid saw his security team organizing the evacuation of the ballroom with the help of the veterans, who provided a wall of bodies protecting the civilians as they filed from the room. He could see Secret Service and CIA moving people into the restaurant. No one would be allowed to leave until this was all settled.

"Dear God," Senator Westin gasped the moment

Mallory head-butted the assassin.

"Holy shit," Bowie said in shock. "That's Tilley Vanderfield."

"And that's my daughter with a tomahawk. Where did she learn this, and who are you?" Senator Westin demanded.

"This is Bowie, her CIA handler. Your daughter has been a government asset since college," Reid said, pushing through the ring of veterans and other agents who had formed a large containment circle around the two women.

"With them standing there, we can't shoot," Damien cursed as he rushed over to Reid and Bowie. "We grabbed Liam as he was pushing his way through the crowd. My men moved him to a secure armored prisoner transport."

"Asset? But, but . . ." the senator mumbled.

Reid almost felt bad for Senator Westin as he stared at his daughter. He cringed as Mallory swung the tomahawk at Tilley. Tilley leapt agilely back, and the dance was back on.

Bowie pressed his finger to his ear. "They have Graham and Orson in custody."

Reid couldn't move as he watched Mallory. She was beautiful, elegant, and deadly. Was this the same woman he had fallen in love with? Yes, and he'd be damned if he didn't love her even more as he saw her completely focused on her task.

Tilley blocked a chop and jumped back. Mallory's weapon was far superior in a close combat situation. Mallory fell to her knees and swung out with her tomahawk when Tilley swiped. She felt it connect with Tilley's leg before she could jump back. The slice cut off part of her dress and left a deep wound.

Tilley cursed and hobbled backward. Mallory didn't let up. With singular focus, she advanced and sliced again. Tilley blocked, but barely. She was fading, and Mallory wasn't feeling sorry for her. She was going to finish this.

"Are you working for Liam or Black?" Mallory asked as she advanced again.

Tilley grunted as she blocked Mallory. Her arms shook as Mallory pressed the tomahawk against her blade. Tilley's weakness spurred Mallory on.

"Who hired you to assassinate Ambrose and my father?"

"Who said I was to kill them? They're still alive, aren't they?"

"It just means I'm better at your job than you are." Mallory pulled back and swung again. Their blades clanged together and Mallory stepped forward until they were only inches apart. She pushed down on her tomahawk, causing Tilley's arms to shake where she was holding the knife above her head.

"I want immunity," Tilley said through clenched teeth.

"How about I just let you live?" Mallory smiled.

Bang!

Mallory gasped and jumped back in surprise as warm blood splashed across her face and chest. Tilley's arm went lax, and she dropped her knife a second before crumpling to the floor. An agent grabbed his chest a short distance away as he stumbled backward and cursed. The bullet that had gone through Tilley's head had also hit an agent protecting the remaining partygoers as they left the room.

Reid and Senator Westin stood side by side as they watched Mallory press her advantage. Mallory swung down with the tomahawk and Tilley blocked. Her arms started to shake, and everyone leaned close to hear what Tilley was going to say. Reid didn't pay attention to Ambrose pushing forward to hear.

The gunshot caught Reid by surprise as well as the agent whose gun had been taken.

"Mallory! Thank God!" Ambrose dropped the gun he'd taken from the agent he had been leaning against, rushed forward, and wrapped her up in a hug. "It's okay, you're safe now."

Reid and Mallory's eyes connected, and she looked as bewildered as he did. They were safe. That was what mattered. Mallory pushed Ambrose from her and stared daggers at him.

"You idiot! She was about to tell me who hired her."

"Well, we know that, right? It was Graham and Orson."

"You killed the only evidence of it. Now they are going to say they didn't do it, and we have no one to prove otherwise."

"I'm so sorry," Ambrose stuttered. "I was just trying to protect you."

"We have Liam," Reid said as he stepped around Ambrose and wrapped her in a hug. "You scared me to death."

"I thought she had killed you," Mallory said with a break in her voice. It was hard to keep her feelings bottled up anymore. She leaned forward, buried her face in his chest, and came face to face with his vest. "This is how you are still alive. Smart man."

Cameras flashed and video cameras were pushed forward. Reid cursed but didn't let go of his hold. Ambrose was already talking to a reporter about how he saved Mallory Westin's life. Her father came forward and touched her gently on the shoulder.

"He saved my life, dear. That bullet was meant for me, but your man saved me."

"You saved my father?" Mallory asked as she was pulled away from Reid and into her father's tight embrace.

"I figured you'd want him around after he apologized to us. You are planning on doing that, aren't you?" Reid leveled a glare at him. Their eyes met over Mallory's head, and he gave a soft smile.

"An apology and a whole lot more," the senator said quietly.

"We need to talk to Liam," Mallory told them, stepping away from her father. "We'll talk later."

Reid saw her mask go back in place as she set her jaw, determination filling her eyes.

"He's already calling for diplomatic immunity and demanding to be returned to his plane. The trouble is, we're going to have to let him go. We just got word his father died. Liam is now King of Stromia. There's no one left to grant us an exception to the immunity. Besides, we don't have any proof of a crime he's committed. I've been telling him we are holding him for his safety, but soon I will have to let him go," Damien told them as rejoined the group.

Mallory nodded. "Let him go. Bowie and I have this. Reid, stay here with my father, please. I want to make sure you two are safe. I won't be gone long."

"No. I can't let you go again. You're finally safe," Reid said as he grabbed her arm.

"I have to, Reid. This is my last job, and I'm going to see it through."

"Your last job?" Bowie asked as he came toward them, carrying Tilley's bag.

"My last job. I have something more important to do

with my future," Mallory winked at Reid. "Come on, Bowie. We've got a job to finish."

Reid pulled out a handkerchief and dunked it in a crystal water glass at a nearby table before wiping it slowly over Mallory's face. He didn't say a word as he cleaned the blood from her face and neck.

When he was finished, he leaned down and kissed her. "Come back to me. We have our whole lives to start living. Together."

"I can't wait."

Mallory strode from the room with Bowie on one side and Damien on the other. She saw Reid escorting her father and Ambrose from the ballroom with television cameras surrounding them. Ambrose was eating it up, while her father looked contemplative. It relieved Mallory to no end to know he wasn't the one behind this.

"Bowie, get the king's car. Damien, give me three minutes, and then release him." Mallory watched as Damien walked over to the windowless box truck Liam was in.

"How do you want to handle this?" Bowie asked.

"Let's see what I can get from him in the car. Then we'll have to see. But I'm thinking Plan 32."

"Ah, good ol' Plan 32," Bowie said before taking off for the garage.

Three minutes later, Liam burst from the back of the truck, pushing off the EMT wrapping his bleeding leg. He cursed, he threatened, and he preened as Damien apologized and swore they were just trying to keep him safe.

"Liam," Mallory called out as she walked over to him. "I've ordered your car to be brought around. I think it's safer for you to go back home. Sadly, we have become too politically unbalanced to guarantee your safety any longer."

"Mallory? What is this? Who are you?"

"I'm doing a favor for the government. Right now I need to see you to safety. We have the assassin in custody, but we need to get you to your plane."

"Of course. But, I can't believe you . . ." Liam looked down at her with surprise.

"It was my job to look after you, Liam. I was to protect you so you may become a strong king with favorable US ties."

Bowie drove up and stopped the limo. His cap was set low to disguise his face as he opened the door for Liam. Liam didn't even look at him as he climbed in. Mallory slid onto the seat next to him and grabbed his hand.

"I'm sorry to tell you, Liam. It's your father. We just got word he passed away thirty minutes ago."

Liam's eyes lit. "He did?"

"Yes, you're the new King of Stromia. No one can touch you now." Mallory had to force herself not to flinch as his eyes took on an evil, powerful glint.

"Yes. Yes, I am. I am king." He smiled as he patted his pockets. He found his phone and held it in his hands. He stopped short of dialing. "You have the person in custody? The lady you were fighting with?"

"Yes, but she was able to finish her job. We didn't stop her in time," Mallory said sadly.

Liam patted her hand. "I'm sorry we both lost our fathers tonight. But, I know you are like me . . . held under the thumb of a powerful father. It must be a relief to you."

Mallory swallowed. It was supposed to be her father. The thought sent a chill down her back. "So, Tilley was right. You did know about it."

Liam looked at her as if she were a child. "Are you really mad at me? I thought you would appreciate being free from him?"

Mallory let out a shaky breath. "I am. I'm just surprised you went through all this trouble for me, especially since I know you were depending on US support when you took the throne."

"As much as I would like to take credit for it, my dear, I'm afraid I can't. I did this for just that reason."

"But, Tilley is saying only you were behind it . . ." Mallory said with confusion. She batted her eyelashes and pushed back her long hair. Liam never thought women were smart enough to compete with him. It's what surprised her most about his hiring Tilley instead of a man.

"Me? Tilley said it was me?" Liam asked with surprise.

"Yes, she told us it was all your idea."

"She didn't even mention Ambrose?" Liam slammed his hand in his fist. "Stupid whore. She spread her legs for him, and now she's being loyal to him instead of me. She had these grand ideas he would marry her and eventually make her First Lady. Stupid woman. Besides, she's not my employee. She's with Black and Jonak."

Mallory nodded to hide her surprise. It wasn't Graham or Orson behind it. It was Ambrose. "Well, Ambrose is very attractive. And she is so very young. I'm not surprised she fell for his charms. It's hard not to."

"Well, it doesn't matter. I am king and so powerful no one can touch me. Ambrose will keep his end of the bargain and supply more weapons to Stromia in exchange for the banking we can provide him. And I'll be king and have you by my side."

Liam reached for her and pulled her against him. "I read your letter. I'm glad you told me you loved me but were scared of the pressure of being queen. Don't worry, I'll teach you everything. I'll be by your side telling you what to do. You know, I think Ambrose thought this would endear you to him. I think he wanted to make you First Lady. Too bad for him. You were destined to be my queen. Before I finally make you mine, I just have to make a quick phone call."

Liam reached for her thigh and started stroking upward as he pressed a contact on his phone. "Is it true? Is my father dead?" Liam asked into the phone. "Good. Contact Black and Jonak. I want them to kill King Dirar by the time my plane lands in Stromia."

Liam leered at her while he hung up his phone. "Now I think it's time for us to pick up where we left off on our last limo ride."

Mallory had had enough. "I don't think so." With a swift uppercut, she connected with the tip of his chin. His eyes rolled back into his head and he fell back against the seat. Mallory rolled down the window. "Did you get all that?"

Bowie grinned in the rearview mirror. "Sure did," he said as he held up his phone. "I think Plan 32 was a great choice." Bowie pulled the car to a stop in front of Liam's plane at the airport.

"Do you need me to go with you?" Mallory shouted as Bowie moved the stairs to the plane door. Liam's pilot and flight attendant were still cozy in their hotel room nearby without a clue the plane was about to be confiscated.

"No, I'm good. Head back and take care of Ambrose." Bowie locked the stairs into place and walked over to her. "It's been fun, Westin. I look forward to next time."

"There won't be a next time," Mallory said as she

hugged him.

"There's always a next time. Be good, kid."

Bowie kissed her cheek and pulled Liam from the backseat. Mallory watched him carry Liam up the stairs of the plane and disappear. It was bittersweet saying goodbye to Bowie again. But now she had Ambrose to deal with.

Mallory pulled her phone from the strap at her waist and drove away from the airport.

"Ahmed, you need to be prepared. Liam issued the kill order on King Dirar."

"We knew the king died but didn't know the order had already been placed. I'll let the king know, and we'll be waiting for him."

"It's Black and Jonak. I captured their first assassin but don't know who else is on their payroll."

"We've got it covered. Thank you. I think I'll give their fathers a call. What about your father?"

"Ambrose hired the assassin to wound him and kill my father. His plan was foiled when Reid saved my dad. I'm on my way to take care of it now."

"And Liam?"

"He's being taken care of as well."

"Good. King Dirar and Prince Mohtadi thank you for your help."

"It was good talking to you again, Ahmed."

"I have a feeling it won't be the last time either."

Mallory grinned and hung up the phone. She had one more thing to complete, and then she could do what she wished she'd done all along . . . run away with Reid.

Chapter Twenty-Two

Reid paced his office floor while a paramedic left after dressing Ambrose's wound. Senator Westin was on the phone with the president. The door opened and Mrs. Westin came running into the room.

"Where's Mallory? She won't answer her phone! What did you do to her?" she spat at Reid.

"She's safe. I shot the person responsible before she could kill our Mallory," Ambrose said quietly as Mrs. Westin rushed to his side.

"What are you talking about?" Reid asked. "Mallory had everything well in hand. She didn't need you to save her. All you did was kill her lead."

Mrs. Westin, in her gown and pearls, rounded on him. "It was more than you did. I always knew you were worthless."

Reid straightened to his full height and stood staring down at Mallory's mother. She'd always been the quiet one. Her vitriol surprised him. "Quite frankly, I don't give a crap what you think."

"Dear," Senator Westin said as he hung up the phone, "we have been gravely mistaken in our beliefs. This young man saved my life. He jumped in front of a bullet meant to kill me."

"To kill you? But I thought Ambrose was the one who

was shot." Her perfect makeup wrinkled slightly as she looked at the men in the room. She'd been dragged from the room so fast she didn't see what happened.

"I would have been dead if not for Reid. And I fear I was wrong about him all those years ago as well."

"But," Ambrose whined, "Mallory is mine. I saved her."

"I don't think so, son. I don't think she was ever meant to be yours," Senator Westin said sadly.

"She's mine!" Ambrose slammed his hand on the desk. He stood up and slammed his hand against Reid's shoulder. The jarring motion caused a sharp pain from his broken rib, and Reid let out a hiss of pain. "Now that she's done with this silly government stuff, she will take her place by my side and be the First Lady. She will serve me, and we'll be the next John and Jackie."

"See, that's why she never wanted you. You can't stand the idea of her being her own woman," Reid shot back as he gave Ambrose a shove.

"She's had enough time to gallivant around. She'll settle down and do what she's told. She is her mother's daughter, after all. And no one, not even Mallory, can resist the power of the presidency. I can give her that. What can you give her? Money? Well, between my trust and hers, we'll have plenty. But you would never be able to garner the kind of power we could have."

"That may be, but I can give her love. I'm man enough to be proud of her instead of intimated by her success. See, that's the difference between you and me. I want her to be happy, and I want to stand *beside* her for the rest of her life, not in front of her."

"Thank you, darling. It's one of the many reasons I love you."

Reid turned to his side and saw Mallory leaning against

the door with a smile on her face. "I love you, too," Reid said as he rushed to kiss her.

"Mallory Westin! What are you wearing?" her mother interrupted.

"Stop it, dear," the senator warned. "Mallory has been a government asset these past years. I've just finished talking to the president who filled me in. Our daughter is a hero for her service. She's saved countless Americans and innocent civilians around the globe."

Reid smiled at her father before wrapping Mallory in his arms and kissing her.

"We'll see how long this lasts. Reid won't be able to handle Mallory having more connections and more power than he has," Ambrose spat.

Mallory stepped away from Reid's embrace and placed her hand on the gun Bowie had given her. "Too bad you won't be around to find out. You know, I had this interesting talk with Liam before he flew home. Remember, he left before you shot Tilley."

Ambrose froze. "You talked to Liam?"

"Yes. Why don't you tell my father how you banked on him dying and you being elected president? And while you are at it, why don't you tell him how all your money has been transferred to banks in Stromia and how you promised Liam weapons as soon as you were voted into office."

Her father stood quietly as he watched Ambrose. Reid blinked and her mother sputtered, "But Ambrose was shot."

"I know. Clever, wasn't it? He'd look like a hero for living and carrying on the campaign. He'd be a candidate Graham and Orson would be accused of trying to murder. Ambrose arranged for Tilley to shoot him in the shoulder.

She was too good a shot to miss."

"How do you know that?" Ambrose tried to laugh it off.

"Because I wouldn't have missed," Mallory said with a smile on her face. A hint of seriousness in her voice led everyone in the room to know she wasn't joking.

"As if you have any evidence of such a crazy idea," Ambrose sneered.

Mallory pulled out her phone and pressed a button. Liam's voice filled the room and Ambrose went white. Her father turned red, and her mother fainted.

Reid stepped forward as Mallory turned off the voice recording. "You know, there is something I am better at than Mallory." Reid punched Ambrose so hard his eyes rolled back, and he crumpled to the floor. "My right hook."

"True. You always did have a nice hook." Mallory winked at him. "Damien, he's all yours." Damien and three agents filed in from the hallway.

Reid saw the weight lift from Mallory. The mission was over. He and her father were safe, and now they could move on with their life—together.

"Marry me?" Reid asked with a grin on his face. He took both her hands and looked into her eyes. Relief, excitement, hope, and love shone through. "We've waited long enough. We've accomplished enough. And we know we love each other enough. Marry me and let me spend every day showing you how much I love and cherish you." He saw a tear run down her cheek and he brushed it away. "Say yes. Marry me, Mallory. Together we have everything we need. I don't care about your father or the money we've made. All I care about is us."

"For crying out loud, Mallory, say yes," her father

laughed as he wiped a tear from his eye.

"If this is finally real and not just my dreams, then yes, yes, yes!" Mallory cried. Reid smiled and kissed her hard. He pulled her tight against him, not caring about the pain in his ribs as he deepened the kiss.

"Mallory, dear, ladies don't kiss like that in public," her mother murmured as her father filled her in after her swoon.

"How very right you are, Mrs. Westin," Reid grinned in between kissing her. He bent down and scooped her into his arms. "We'll just cut through the conference room on the way to my suite. No one will see us or hear very unladylike kissing."

"Do hurry, Reid," Mallory ordered.

"Yes, ma'am." Reid unlocked the conference room door and hurried inside.

"Oh my God!" Reid and Mallory froze and gasped at the vision on the conference table.

"Hello, little missy. Good to see you lived. If you need Feng, it will be a little while."

Mallory buried her head in Reid's neck and started laughing. "I think we're good, Feng," Reid smiled. He looked between Feng and Shirley. "Um, please excuse my fiancée and me. Carry on."

"Fiancée?" Shirley's head popped up over Feng's bare shoulder as Reid hurried from the room.

Mallory couldn't stop laughing. She was happy. She felt as if she were a teenager again. The pain of the past fell away, and all the hope of the future shone bright as Reid unlocked the door to his room and carried her inside. He placed her gently in the middle of his bed as he stood and slowly loosened his tie. He kept his eyes on her and unbuttoned his tuxedo jacket, tossing it aside, followed by his shirt.

Reaching up, he undid the Velcro straps of his vest and let it drop to the floor. He kicked off his shoes, and Mallory couldn't tear her eyes from his chest and the ridges of his stomach. He'd matured over the years. His body was thicker, stronger, and he seemed even more confident in his own skin. When his hand reached the button of his trousers, Mallory stopped comparing him to their first time. Instead, her eyes followed as he unzipped his pants and crawled naked onto the bed.

She smiled when he lay next to her and slowly started undoing the thigh strap and shoulder harness. They didn't say anything as he helped her sit up so he could pull the shirt from over her head and unstrap her vest. He kissed his way around the bruise that had formed over her right breast as he reached behind to unhook her bra.

Mallory closed her eyes and felt the feather-light touches of his fingers slipping the bra from her arms before cupping her breasts in his hands. His teasing touches caused her to arch her back. Instead of giving her what she wanted, Reid pushed her back against the pillows with his kisses and slid his hand farther down. His fingers slid the tight fabric from her hips, and she kicked off her pants while his lips followed the path of his fingers. Mallory closed her eyes and arched her hips against his tongue as he pleasured her. Her fingers tightened on the sheets as she felt the orgasm building. She cried out his name and twisted the sheets as she tossed back her head and enjoyed the waves of pleasure rolling over her.

Reid lifted his head and crawled slowly on top of her. His paused, his erection at her entrance. With achingly slow movements, he ran his hand up her side to cup her face. Mallory instinctually nuzzled against him and placed a kiss on his palm before he claimed her lips in a searing kiss. Reid pulled his mouth from hers and looked down at her face. "I love you now and forever," he said before sliding into her. Mallory's mind clouded with pleasure. As she felt her body spiral out of control, she knew Reid would always be there to catch her.

Chapter Twenty-Three

Reid woke slowly. The shift between him and Mallory was palpable in the air. She was plastered against his side with her head on his chest and an arm thrown over his stomach. Gone were the outside influences preventing them from enjoying each other. Gone were the threats. Gone were the lies of the past.

Reid stroked Mallory's long hair as he held her in his arms. He rested his cheek against the top of her head and cherished every moment he had with her. They weren't going to leave the suite that day unless he could talk her into eloping. At least then he would have a stay of execution in having to confess all to his family. Yes, that was perfect: an elopement with a nice long honeymoon. He wouldn't tell anyone where or why he was gone. They would just enjoy each other for as long as possible.

"I don't care, Drake. Give me the freaking key!"

Reid's eyes went wide. Elle? What was she doing here? He didn't have time to wonder as a second later the door to his suite was thrown open.

Reid grabbed the bed sheet and pulled it over Mallory's bare breasts. Mallory's eyes popped open, and her whole body tensed, but Reid held her tight against him as he sat up to lean against the headboard.

"How could you?" Elle demanded as she stormed into

his bedroom. She shot daggers at him and as if that weren't bad enough, his whole family plus Shirley trailed in behind her.

"Me? You're embarrassing Mallory. Get out!" Reid yelled. His grip on his temper was sliding. He was finally happy and now he had to deal with three, no, *five,* demanding women.

"She's my best friend, not some simpering society type who just wants her picture in the gossip rags." Elle's hands were on her hips, and Drake was desperately trying to convince her this was none of her business.

"Listen to your husband and get out, Elle." Reid grew impatient.

"You're my brother!"

"And you're my *younger* sister. That doesn't give you the right to storm in here and dictate my love life," Reid said threateningly. He loved his sister, but this was exactly what Mallory and he had feared since they were teenagers.

"Elle, this isn't what it looks like," Mallory stated calmly as she turned to face the closest thing to a family she'd ever had. She leaned against his chest with Reid's arm around her.

"Isn't what it looks like? Really, Mal, you're going with that line?" Elle snapped.

"That's enough!" Margaret clapped as she pushed forward. "Elle, I know you're concerned for Mallory. We all are. But Reid would never hurt her. He's loved her since high school. Isn't that right, dear?"

Reid was shocked. He'd been so careful not to show his feelings. He could only nod at his mother who smiled happily.

"What?" Elle, Bree, and Allegra gasped.

"It was as clear as day they loved each other. What I

don't know is what happened at the end of summer that one year to change all the sneaking around you were doing," Margaret said pointedly.

Reid looked to Mallory and let out a long breath. "Do you want to tell them?"

Mallory nodded. "It's about time I did. Reid and I have been attracted to each other since I was sixteen. After graduation, we spent one wonderful summer together. Reid asked me to go to Europe with him, but my father stopped us. He threatened not only Reid's scholarship, but also to rip apart Mr. Simpson's company and send you all to jail for tax fraud if I ever saw Reid again."

"Why, that son of a biscuit eater!" Shirley slammed her hand into her fist.

Reid saw his whole family stiffen in outrage. His sisters' husbands all took a step backward, knowing the women were about to let loose. But Mallory held up her hand to stop them. "I know. I broke it off with Reid very harshly so he would never think he had a chance with me. Then I ran off to England to be a government asset."

Allegra looked at her sisters and then stepped next to Elle. "What's a government asset?"

"Um, welcome back from your honeymoon," Mallory smiled meekly.

"Don't change the subject. What have you not been telling me? I'm your best friend. Or at least I thought I was. Obviously," Elle motioned to her and Reid in bed, "you didn't feel the same way."

Reid felt horrible for Mallory. He felt her shoulders slump, and he couldn't stand it anymore. "Knock it off, Elle. Mallory is still your best friend. You're not being a very good friend to her right now. Stop thinking about yourself and think about how hard this has been for Mallory. She lost her family. She lost the man she loved. She spied for the United States, ran covert operations in dangerous places, and had no one to talk to."

"Is that true?" Elle asked quietly.

Mallory nodded. "I couldn't tell anyone. If I were caught, well, it would make things very messy. I love Reid very much. Since he saved my father's life last night, and Ambrose, the man my father wanted me to marry, turned out to be the bad guy . . . well, I think we're in the clear to be together. And, Elle, I'm sorry if you can't handle it. You're my best friend. You all are my best friends," Mallory said to the group standing at the end of the bed. "But I have lived in fear long enough. It's time for me to be happy. Reid makes me happy. If you can't handle that, then I will understand. But it's not going to stop me from being with him."

Elle let out a long breath. "I've been a bitch, haven't I?"

Drake patted her shoulder. "It happens to the best of us, babe."

"I'm sorry, Mallory. Reid, when Shirley called last night telling us she saw you carrying Mallory upstairs, I thought the worst. I thought of all the things that could go wrong instead of right."

Shirley coughed and sucked in her dentures. "Did I forget to tell you that when he was carrying her up the stairs, he mentioned she was his fiancée?"

"Fiancée?" they all said together.

Both Reid and Mallory laughed at everyone's shocked faces. "Yes, fiancée," Reid said before picking up her hand and kissing it.

"Shirley! How could you leave that out?" Margaret asked as happy tears started to fill her eyes.

"Oh, I know. She was a little busy in the conference

room. It probably slipped her mind," Reid teased.

Everyone turned to look at Shirley and then each other when they noticed the blush on her cheeks.

"Shirley?" Margaret asked slowly. "What were you doing in the conference room?"

"I think the better question is *who* she was doing." Mallory snickered. "Sorry, Shirley, payback's a bitch!"

"Who?" The women gasped as Logan, Drake, and Finn took a sudden interest in the floor, but not before Mallory noticed their shoulders shaking with laughter.

Margaret clapped her hands. "Well, obviously we have a lot to catch up on. Family dinner tonight—including all our *whos*. Everyone be there at six. Now, shoo." She pushed her kids out of the bedroom. "We have another wedding to plan, after all."

"Quickly," Reid called out. "I won't wait more than a week to marry Mallory."

"A week?" his mother cried in dismay.

"Come on, Mom. I know all of Mallory's favorite styles. We'll get everything ready for them tonight." Elle smiled before running back into the bedroom and throwing her arms around Mallory.

"Now we really will be sisters. I love you. Both of you." Elle kissed her brother and squeezed Mallory's hand before running out the door yelling at Drake to call the musicians for the band.

Mallory and Reid sat staring at the door for a long time. Finally she turned to him and slumped against his chest. It was over.

"That was very traumatic," Reid mumbled as he pulled her against him.

"At least it's over. Our relationship has not only been accepted, I think they actually are happy about it," Mallory said as she ran her hand over his light smattering of chest hair.

"Happy, shoot they're thrilled. Mom's married us all off. Elle, Bree, and Allegra get the sister they've always wanted, and I get you," Reid said, grabbing her and pulling her onto his lap.

Mallory sat on top of him as he leaned against the headboard. "I'm pretty thrilled about it, too. I have a house in St. Barts. No one knows about it."

"Why, Mallory Westin, you've been keeping secrets," Reid teased before pulling a nipple into his mouth.

"And if you keep it a secret, we can honeymoon someplace completely private where no one will be able to find us," Mallory moaned.

"I think you need to convince me to keep it a secret."

Mallory grinned. "Only if you do everything I say."

"Give up power to you?" Reid smirked. "Any time. Have your way with me."

Mallory lifted her hips and took him inside her in one motion. The smirk fell from Reid's face as his hands tightened on her hips. He moaned in pleasure, and it was her turn to smile. Who said sharing power couldn't be fun?

Chapter Twenty-Four

Reid reached over and took Mallory's hand. They walked up his mother's sidewalk hand in hand and smiled at each other. They had locked the door, put a chair under the handle, and hadn't left the bed all day. Well, until the shower.

The front door opened and Margaret clapped her hands excitedly before grabbing Mallory and pulling her in for a hug. "Finally I can officially introduce you as my daughter. Oh, Reid, you made a wonderful choice for a bride."

Reid grinned as Mallory blushed. "I think I did, too."

"Now, dear, the women are all in the kitchen with wedding ideas. Narrow them down before we ask Reid's opinion. We learned that after Logan's little meltdown." Margaret stepped out of the doorway and let Mallory go inside. Reid tried to follow, but Margaret pushed him back outside.

"What is it, Mom?" Reid asked after she quietly shut the front door.

"You love her so much, don't you?" She smiled up and ran her hand over the stubble on his face.

"More than anything in this world."

"You two remind me so much of your father and me." Tears started to pool, and Reid felt his heart clench. His mother had been so alone these past years without their father. "Well, except for that international secret agent stuff. Your father and I also took a little while to get together. When we did, my heart was full. And then to be blessed with all these wonderful additions to my family—I have been truly blessed."

Reid reached over and wrapped his arms around his mother. She rested her head against his chest, and he rubbed her back gently. "We are the blessed ones, Mom."

Margaret pulled back and looked at the tiny chip of a diamond on her ring finger. "When your father and I fell in love, we knew it was forever. No matter how hard it was at times, we were happy because we had each other. Even through the long absences while he was away at work, just like you and Mallory have had, our love only grew. I want you and Mallory to know that love. Now, I know it's not much," she said as she wiggled the ring from her finger, "and I know it's nothing compared to those honkers your sisters are wearing, but if you want it, it's yours to give to Mallory. To bring you the happiness your father and I had."

Reid felt his throat constrict as he reached out to take the small gold ring in between his fingers. "It's perfect, but won't you miss it?"

His mother patted her heart. "I have your father right here. And in all of you. It will feel strange not to have it on my finger, but it will give me, and him, such joy seeing Mallory wear it. Besides, maybe it's time for me to take it off."

"What do you mean?" Reid asked. Was his mother ready to start dating again? The thought had him slightly nauseous. He'd just made sure his sisters married men who deserved them; what would he do with his mother? He was going to break out in hives at the thought of it, but the sound of a honking horn prevented her from answering him.

"What in Sam Hill?" His mother's eyes went wide, and he turned to see what had surprised her.

Feng parked his car half on the sidewalk and half in the street. Shirley and he were necking. They were accidently hitting the horn over and over again. "They must not have their hearing aids turned on."

"Oh, that's just not right!" Margaret covered her eyes and hurried down the sidewalk.

Reid opened the door and called to his family. "Y'all have to see this. Mom's about to bust Shirley!"

Everyone rushed outside, including Finn who pushed Troy in a wheelchair. Reid saw their pilot and patted his shoulder. His face was still bruised and his leg was in a cast, but he was alive, and that was all that mattered.

"It's good to see you, Troy. You had us worried."

"It's good to be here, thanks to you and Mallory. And, of course, your mother, who has been taking care of me this week. She stayed with me at the hospital, nursing me back to health. Now that's a good woman and more than this old flyboy deserves," Troy said as he shook his head. "Did Shirley just . . .?"

"Sweet magnolia," Allegra whispered as they all took in the sight of the windows fogging up.

"Is your mother . . .?" Logan started. "Yep, she's really going to interrupt them."

"I need my camera." Bree laughed as she reached into her pocket.

"Eww. Do you really want this on your camera?" Elle asked.

"She has enough to blackmail us; it's only fair," Finn said as he shuddered.

"It's okay, babe. I saw the picture she took, and you

couldn't see a thing," Allegra cooed.

Mallory shot her a look, and from behind Finn's back, Allegra shook her head and used her hands to demonstrate that the picture showed a whole lot more than nothing.

"Oh no, here we go." Drake snickered as Margaret rapped her knuckles on the passenger window.

"Shirley Louise, you stop that this instant!" Margaret shrilled out in her best mom voice. The window rolled down slowly, and Shirley's tussled hair came into view.

"Margaret, the well has not runneth dry, and I plan on haulin' water as long as the pipe is working."

"I don't need to know that," Margret groaned.

"I think you do. You need to prime your pump and have some plumbing done."

Reid and his family all looked at each other and made gagging noises—all except Troy who just smiled.

"What kind of example are you setting? Why buy the cow when you can get the milk for free?"

Shirley laughed and held up her hand. "I'm not free. We got married this afternoon. After seeing Mallory and Reid, and how happy they were, we decided to stop wasting time."

"Married?" the group on the stoop all asked at once.

"Yes, married. Now, stop interrupting the honeymoon!" Shirley rolled up the window and Margaret turned, stunned as the horn began to honk again.

"I have a bottle of bourbon behind my *Southern Lifestyle* cookbook. Reid, be a dear and grab it. I think we all need a shot after that."

Mallory couldn't stop laughing as she and the girls took shots of bourbon and picked wedding dresses out of magazines. She and Reid decided they would marry next

Saturday at the hotel. Reid had called Evelyn, who was gracious enough to be happy for them both and was now busy calling all their contacts for flowers and food.

The men were clustered around the television, watching sports and initiating Feng into the family. Mallory picked up a picture of a beautiful dress and smiled. It was simple, understated, and elegant. It would be perfect with her wild, five-inch red heels. "This one. It's perfect."

"We will go to the boutique tomorrow. I already called them and the designer and everyone will be there to find you *the* dress," Allegra told her as she handed her another magazine.

"What's going on in there? It suddenly got quiet," Bree said as she leaned forward to look into the living room.

"Mallory, I think you'll want to see this," Reid called out.

The women stood and hurried into the living room. On the television she looked at President Nelson standing next to King Dirar.

President Nelson stepped forward and spoke into the camera. "We are all saddened by the tragic loss of King Liam Vidmar Markovic. King Dirar of Rahmi was in the United States visiting family when the news broke that King Markovic's plane crashed into the Atlantic Ocean upon its return from a charity event last night. This is a sad day for Stromia and her people, having lost two kings in just two days. We, the American people, grieve with you. And we promise to stand by you and assist the new king in any way necessary."

President Nelson stepped back and King Dirar stepped to the podium. "Such loss of life is tragic. It is widely known that King Liam and I did not get along, but that does not change the fact that I wish only the best for Stromia, a small country so much like Rahmi. I have already talked with the new king and have pledged Rahmi's full support."

The television panned back to the reporter who looked sadly into the screen. "This tragedy follows on the heels of vice presidential candidate Ambrose Childs's arrest in a bizarre assassination attempt on his running mate. It has been leaked by an unnamed source from within the FBI that this assassination may have been orchestrated by King Liam, who they say was actually fleeing the country before he could be arrested. In an unprecedented move, Senator Westin made the following comment earlier today about the assassination attempt made against him."

Mallory bit her lip as she saw her father and mother come on the screen. Reid stood up and hurried to her side. He wrapped his arm around her as they watched her father speak to the camera.

"I still have not processed Ambrose's betrayal. This has given me the wake-up call I needed, though. In any case, where there is such darkness, you must search for the light. The light I'm clinging to is my family. My daughter, Mallory Westin, is newly engaged to Reid Simpson of Simpson Global—the same man who saved my life. I plan to take the next few weeks off from campaigning and help my daughter with her wedding. I am so proud of all she and her fiancé have accomplished in their short lives. Their enduring love and never-give-up attitude are truly inspiring. After discussing it with my family, I will decide how and if I should continue with my campaign. Thank you, the American people, for your outpouring of support as I strive to never let you down."

Mallory felt tears running down her cheeks. Reid pressed a gentle kiss to her temple. Margaret sniffled, and Troy reached up to hold her hand. The sound of the doorbell startled the quiet room.

"I'll get it," Shirley said as she moved to the door with her walker. Her *Just Married* banner made Mallory smile. Shirley opened the door and hissed, "What are you doing here? You think some fancy words on television will make up for all the years you neglected your daughter and threatened my family?" Shirley shoved her walker forward and smacked Senator Westin in the shins. He cursed and hopped away as Mrs. Westin stared in astonishment. "Don't get me started on you, missy. You stand by while your husband threatens to bankrupt us and send us to jail all because Mallory was in love with Reid. They were young. You were supposed to support them, not shove aside your daughter's happiness."

Mallory and the rest of the room stared open-mouthed as Shirley railed against her parents. Fresh tears poured down Mallory's face. As she wiped them away, she came up behind Shirley and hugged her.

"Thank you, Shirley, for all you've ever done for me. I think my grandmother sent you to be my angel."

"Devil is more like it. Your grandmother was a spitfire just like Shirley here . . . and you," her father said as he kept a wary eye on Shirley.

"Look, Dad, I don't know what you are doing here. But if you think one pretty speech changes what you did, then you're wrong," Mallory said, putting her hands on her hips and staring her father down. She wasn't a meek teenager anymore.

Reid stepped up beside her to offer silent support while Margaret stormed forward to give her two cents' worth. "Senator Westin, you and your wife are despicable. How could you not see how happy our kids were together? Instead, you banished them to years of pain. We could have been happily sitting together bouncing babies on our knees by now. But, you only cared about yourself and your status. You never had faith in your daughter or my son. And I want you to know one thing," Margaret stepped forward and wagged her finger in their faces. "If you ever threaten my family again, I will destroy you. No one threatens my family, bless their hearts, and lives to tell about it. I don't care who you *think* you are. I will make your life a living hell if you so much as say a cross word to my son. And why should you listen to me? Because I cherish family above all else, and I will walk through fire to protect them—something you know nothing about. As for living on the wrong side of the tracks, you're damn right I did. And I learned just where to hide the bodies. Don't you *ever* mess with my family again."

Reid and Mallory looked at each other with astonishment. They had never heard Margaret say anything mean, much less go into a full rage. Her red hair flared, her eyes were sparking, and Mallory's parents could only turn paler.

"Mrs. Simpson, you are right," Mallory's father said slowly. "I was wrong then, but we've come here to ask for a second chance. I don't want to miss those moments you were talking about. I want to see her and your son madly in love. I want to be there to spoil our grandchildren rotten. I want to walk my daughter down the aisle and eat Sunday dinners together. I'm here to see if that's still possible. But first, I must apologize to all of you. I wronged each and every one of you with my attempt to control everything. And look at what it got me," her father shook his head. "A person I thought of as a son tried to kill me. To say I'm looking at the world differently is an understatement."

Margaret crossed her arms and stared him down. "I've

said my piece. The rest is up to Mallory. If she can forgive you, then so can we. If she can't, then I'll help her bury you beneath a mountain of future happy memories."

Mallory looked behind her at her adopted family. Elle and Drake glared at her parents. Bree and Logan had their arms similarly crossed. Allegra and Finn had their jaws tight and fingers fisted. They would all defend her if she just asked. One week ago, she would have taken them up on the offer. But not anymore.

"Dad, Mom, I'm happy now. I'm tired of looking back. I'm looking forward to my new life with my husband. We're getting married next week at the hotel."

"Next week! I can't plan a wedding by then," her mother cried.

"I'm not asking you to plan it. In fact, we've already started. I'm offering you a chance to show me you've changed. I've seen enough politics to know saying and doing are two different things. I'm going to be happy in my life, with or without you. The choice is yours. I hope you choose to join us on this journey."

Her mother looked at her father and they smiled. "We'd like that. When do we start, and what do you need us to do?"

"Well, we are going dress shopping tomorrow," Allegra said softly from behind Mallory. "I can give you directions to the boutique."

"I'd like that," Mrs. Westin said, suddenly a little shy.

Mallory smiled and leaned forward to kiss her mother on her cheek. "I'd like that, too."

Margaret's scowl switched to a smile as she opened the door wide. "Then come in, we have lots to plan. Now, y'all must call me Margaret . . ."

Mallory watched her parents hesitantly follow

Margaret into the kitchen. Elle, Bree, and Allegra started showing them the plans they had made while Shirley wheeled her way over to her.

"I think we set them straight."

Mallory laughed. "I think so, too. Thank you, Shirley. How about planning my bachelorette party for me?"

"What?" cried the women from the kitchen along with the men in the living room.

"Sweetheart," Reid started, "do you think that's the best idea?"

"Nope, but it will make me happy." Mallory smiled at him as Shirley pulled out her phone. "Besides, can you imagine my mother's reaction?" Mallory whispered.

"Well, we lived through it once. We can live through it again," Margaret said with false optimism. She turned to Mallory's mother. "If you have heart medication, make sure to take it beforehand. You'll have never seen anything like this before."

Jonak and Black threw the bags of cash into the back of the car along with their suitcases. Jonak got behind the wheel and started the engine.

"Hurry up," he called to his cousin.

Black slid into the passenger seat and slammed the door. "We have just enough time to stow away on your boat headed to the Philippines. Our fathers will never find us there."

Jonak pressed the gas as they shot away from their offices in Stromia. "I can't believe this went all to shit."

"At least we are getting out before our dads find out. We'll rebuild." Black looked down at his phone when it buzzed. "Shit."

"What?"

"It's a text from my dad. They know."

Jonak turned and looked at his cousin a second before the explosion sent the car flying into a million fiery pieces.

Chapter Twenty-Five

One week later . . .

Reid stood nervously in his office and waited for the guests to arrive. They were being shuttled from the hotel to the gazebo on the lake. Chairs lined a walkway and flowers adorned the gazebo. The senator pulled in every favor he was owed and got Reid and Mallory's favorite band to play at the reception in the silk tent by the lake. Her parents were putting forth the effort, and Mallory was basking in it.

Allegra told him Mallory's dress was beautiful, and Mallory seemed happier than he'd ever known her to be. She was at peace, and it showed. She laughed—a lot—and he loved it. They made love both tenderly and with wild abandon. Best of all, they were together. Nothing seemed impossible with her by his side.

Reid started pacing. Twenty more minutes. His brothers-in-law were all serving as groomsmen opposite their wives who were the bridal attendants. They were making sure the women didn't need anything—at least that's what Drake told him. He was pretty sure they were just looking for a couple minutes alone with their spouses before the party.

A knock at the door had Reid spinning around, away

from the window. "Come in," he called.

The door flung open, and Troy wheeled himself into the office. Reid smiled and hurried over to help him clear the door. Troy was still getting used to his temporary mode of transportation. As soon as his bones healed, Troy's internal injuries would also be healed enough to start physical therapy.

"Reid, I hoped I could talk to you for a minute."

"Of course."

Troy fidgeted with the sleeves of his tuxedo before putting his hands in his lap and looking up at Reid. "I've been with you all for almost eight years now. It was shortly after your father died that I was hired on. I've seen you grow up into a fine young man. Of course, you took some detours to get there, but don't we all? You would have made your father very proud. You have taken care of your sisters and made your mother happy. As the male of the Simpson family, I have come to ask you something."

Reid shook his head slightly. "Anything; you've been like a father to me since I lost mine. You were the one who pulled me out of the dives I buried myself in after his death and put me on the straight and narrow."

Troy gave a weak smile. "We won't mention I was in those dives with you. But, thank you. I'm glad you could think of me as a father. It's why I'm here. I want your permission to marry your mother."

Reid blinked. "Excuse me?"

Troy took a deep breath and soldiered on. "I have loved your mother for seven years. It's why I was in those bars with you, drowning our sorrows. Your mother was so in love with your father, I thought I would never have a chance. And I didn't until my accident. I had given up hope. Then, like an angel, she was there when I needed her most."

"And does my mother love you, too?"

Troy smiled then. "She does. She told me she fell in love with me two years ago at the Simpson Christmas party when she saw me with you kids. She saw how I love each of you as my own family. She didn't say anything because she wanted to see you all settled first."

"She would put us first," Reid sighed. "Of course you have my blessing. And I'm sure my whole family's." Reid stepped forward and shook the relieved man's hand. "Welcome to the family, Troy. Officially."

The door opened and Reid's brothers-in-law all came in, wearing goofy grins. They stopped and looked at Reid and Troy.

"Are we interrupting anything?" Logan asked.

"Troy here just asked permission to marry Mom." Reid sent them a smirk in reply to their shocked faces.

Finn was the first to pick up on the look. "Well, I don't know about that. I think we need to have a talk first."

Drake nodded and stepped forward. "We need to know how you plan to support her."

"And make sure you have good intentions toward her," Logan said as he crossed his arms.

"Because if you don't . . ." Reid smiled.

"You'll deal with us," Finn, Logan, and Drake said together.

They stared him down. When Troy didn't back down or look away, they all clapped him on the back and laughed.

"And I thought hazing in the military was bad," Troy grumbled.

"It's an initiation we all had to go through, but the Simpson women are worth it." Drake smiled.

"But, now we have to get Reid to the altar or face

Mallory. Quite frankly, she scares me," Logan joked.

"Yeah, we should have said, 'You hurt Margaret and you'll deal with her.'" Finn laughed.

"We'll save that one for our daughters." Reid grinned. "Now, let's get me married."

Mallory slid her hand into the crook of her father's elbow and smiled up at him. Her sisters had helped her dress in the beautiful trumpet gown. Margaret and her mother had shed tears as they fastened the veil. Her father had even shed a tear when he had come in to escort her down the aisle. All was not forgotten, but she was beginning to forgive. And who could dwell on it when Reid was standing at the end of the aisle in his tuxedo, waiting for her?

As she walked down the aisle, Mallory saw her friends wink at their husbands. Soon, she and Reid would have their own winks and their own family. That thought, along with the look of pure desire on Reid's face, filled her with joy. Mallory let go of her father's arm, and Reid took her hand in his. She looked up into his eyes and smiled as he squeezed her hand.

The minister started the ceremony. Before she knew it, she was saying, "I do."

Reid smiled and pulled her close. "I love you, Mallory Simpson," Reid whispered in her ear before commanding all her attention with his lips. Mallory wrapped her arms around his neck and matched him kiss for kiss. This was going to be one wild ride, and she was determined to enjoy every up and down it held in store for them.

"I am proud to present Reid and Mallory Simpson," the minister said to the cheering crowd.

Reid grabbed her hand and, with a laugh, they ran

down the aisle. Who knows, maybe married life would soften her. Even if it did, she was just happy to have the man she loved sharing it with her. But then again . . .

Reid closed his eyes and enjoyed the warm sun and the sound of the waves crashing against the shore. Mallory squeezed his hand and he looked over to where she lay next to him on the beach.

"I'm going to go inside and make another margarita. Do you want one?"

Reid smiled at his naked wife. It was good to own a private beach. "I'd love one."

Mallory leaned over and kissed him before heading into the house. She had bought it before they married. The private, gated home afforded them the seclusion they wanted to enjoy on their honeymoon. And what a honeymoon it was. They hadn't left the house in a week.

Reid pushed up the lounge chair and looked out over the ocean. Movement to the left caught his attention as he squinted against the sun to see better. A person in black was climbing the rocks that marked the end of their private beach. On the other side of the rocks was jungle. It's one of the reasons Mallory had bought the place—it had great hiking. What was a man doing coming onto their property, though?

Reid stood up and watched in amazement as the man in a suit and loafers carried a briefcase as he jumped off the boulders and onto the soft sand. He straightened his tie, dusted off his pants, and smiled at Reid. The man walked through the sand and Reid wrapped a towel around his waist before moving to meet him.

"You're trespassing," Reid said with a cold edge to his voice.

"Are you Reid Simpson?"

"You know damn well I am. Now you are on private property. I suggest you leave. Now." Reid blocked the man's view of their house. He didn't want Mallory sauntering out nude for this man to see.

"Oh, I know. It's why I had to hike through a jungle to get this to you." He held out an envelope and Reid stared at it.

"What do you want?" Reid demanded. He was growing angrier by the second.

"Just to do my job. I'm Mallory's attorney and I was charged with delivering this to you on her thirty-fifth birthday." The man shoved the envelope into Reid's hand. "Please sign here saying you've received it. I have held onto it since she was eighteen."

Reid signed the receipt and stared at the envelope. Mallory had told him she had written him a letter. He just hadn't thought about it since.

"Thank you. You can go out the front entrance if you'd like," Reid gestured to the path that led to the gate, all the while not taking his eyes off the letter he held.

"Thank you kindly. And congratulations on the wedding. Give Mallory my best and let me know if I can be of service to you."

"If you're a lawyer willing to trample through the jungle for a client, then I'll hire you right now." Reid shook the man's hand and grinned. The lawyer wasn't even sweating. That was the kind of lawyer you wanted. "I'll call you when we get home."

"Look forward to it. Enjoy the rest of your honeymoon." The man shook Reid's hand and then he was gone.

Reid turned the envelope over and slid a finger into the seam to tear it open. He pulled out the paper and slowly unfolded it. It was dated a couple of days after she had kicked him out of her house at her father's insistence.

Reid-

I know I can never begin to ask for your forgiveness for what happened the other night. All I can do is explain and hope that you will understand. I did it all for love . . . for your love and for the love I have for your family.

My father threatened not only you, but also your family if I did not stop seeing you. I did what I thought I had to do to protect the man I love and the only real family I know. It was the hardest thing I have ever done and I have spent the past days second-guessing myself. Should I have stood up to him? Should I have risked the chance of him sending your father to jail or bankrupting your family just for us to be together? I wish I did, but I couldn't be that selfish.

In my dreams I run away with you every night. For in my dreams is the only time I can live out my fantasy of being with you. I have thought about you constantly since I pushed you away. About how you loved me and how we had all the hope of a future together. When I am thirty-five, I will be able to stand up to my father. I will say all the things I longed to the other night. I will have money and power to protect you and your family then.

I know I don't deserve it. I can only imagine how you will think of me over the years, but I beg you to forgive me or at least talk to me so I can tell you how much I love you. I beg you to understand that I hurt down to the bottom of my soul with the pain I have caused you. I will always love you and I will always be here waiting for the moment I can share that love with you again.

If you can bring yourself to give me a chance, then find me. You don't have to say anything. I'll know the second I see you if you forgive me or not. For myself, my love for you will always be true and steadfast.

Love,
Mallory

Reid stared at Mallory's handwriting on the page and took a deep breath. She had told him what happened that night so many years ago. But to see the anguish it caused made his heart clutch.

"Honey, I have your drink."

Mallory stepped out of the house with two margaritas. Reid turned and he saw her freeze. Her eyes were locked on the piece of paper in his hand.

"Is that my letter?"

Reid nodded and walked up the beach to stand in front of her. He took the drinks and set them down on the table.

"Say something," Mallory pleaded.

"You said I didn't have to," Reid said, quoting her letter before running his hand down her arms and then up her sides. He brushed the sides of her breasts with his thumbs as he pulled her closer. "Let me see if I can find you and then you can decide how I feel."

He smacked her butt and her eyes shot open. Her mouth tilted into a smirk as she took off down the beach and toward the ocean. Reid chased after her and their laughter echoed off the rocks.

Some time later, Reid's towel was tossed on the beach next to the margaritas as he held Mallory in his arms. They floated in the water and he leaned forward to kiss her. "I think I found you."

"I think you found me twice," Mallory murmured with her eyes closed. Her arms were wrapped around his neck as they bobbed peacefully in the water.

"I love you, Mallory. And I think we are going to have a very exciting marriage."

Epilogue

Stromia, three months later . . .

"I don't give a shit if you want a lawyer. Do I look like a police officer?" Mallory asked as she slammed her fist onto the metal table in the dark room of the basement. The table reverberated, and the man in the chair jumped.

The room was purposely hot. The one light was dim and cast shadows menacingly about. It smelled of fear, and Mallory loved it.

The twenty-something man sitting in the chair on the other side of the table audibly gulped. He looked down at her evening gown and shook his head.

"You will tell me everything I need to know, and you will tell me right now," Mallory said coldly as she tossed a pad and pen on the table.

"Yes, ma'am." The man trembled under her glare.

The door opened and Mallory strode out of the room. Reid pushed away from the cement wall and grinned at his beautiful wife. "You are so sexy when you interrogate people trying to steal from my casinos."

Reid pulled his wife into his arms and kissed her hard. Like always, she matched him stroke for stroke and kiss for kiss. She was perfect for him.

"Why, thank you, husband," Mallory murmured against his lips before kissing him again. "Here's his signed confession. He named the mastermind and even told us about another group of card counters he ran across in college. Shoot, once he started talking, I couldn't shut him up. Do you want me to go after the rest of them?"

"Would that make my new head of security happy?"

Mallory looked down at him in his tuxedo. They had been about to leave for the coronation party for the new King of Stromia. She let out a sigh. "I guess I have to let Luke have some fun. He sure was sweet, letting me do the interrogation."

"I think it's because he gets a kick out of watching you work. All the guys rush over to the monitor to watch the helpless bastards tremble in their seats."

Reid held out his arm for her and escorted Mallory from the basement to their limousine. He opened the door and watched as Mallory's leg flashed when she sat down.

"That slit is giving me very naughty ideas," he whispered as he pressed the button to close the privacy divider.

"I sure hope so. It's the whole reason I wore it," Mallory challenged.

Reid was never one to back down from a challenge. He ran his hand up her leg and pushed aside the material to expose her bare center. He looked at her and raised an eyebrow.

"No panties?"

"I like to keep things interesting," Mallory said seductively.

Reid pulled her onto his lap and walked his fingers up her thigh. "We have a lifetime of interesting ahead of us."

Mallory leaned forward and kissed his lips. Her hand wrapped around the nape of his neck as they lost themselves in the kiss. Without saying a word, he could read her. The love, the passion, the future . . . she said it all with her kiss.

"I love you," Reid whispered into her neck.

"I love you, too," Mallory whispered, sliding off him and straightening her dress a second before the door opened.

Mallory smiled widely for the cameras as Reid escorted her up the red carpet in front of the palace. The four-hundred-year-old palace gleamed with gold details, rich reds, and shining crystal chandeliers. She was blind to all of it, save for her husband.

They made their way up the stairs and through the entranceway before Reid bent down to whisper in her ear, "See that alcove over there? We'll have to visit that later."

"Stop," Mallory giggled. "We are respectable members of society. I am the daughter of the President of the United States after all. We don't go around having sex in every nook and cranny of a palace."

Reid brushed his arm casually against her breast. "You know you want to," he taunted as they stopped at the entrance of the ballroom.

Reid handed his card to the uniformed man and gave Mallory a wink.

"Mr. Reid Simpson and his wife, Mrs. Mallory Simpson," the man announced.

Mallory smiled as they walked down the small flight of stairs into the ballroom.

"Champagne?" Reid asked, steering them through the crowd.

"That would be lovely," Mallory said as she glanced around the crowded ballroom. The new King of Stromia would be making his appearance soon. Reid stopped a waiter and handed a glass to her.

"Mallory," a deep voice said from behind them.

Mallory turned around and smiled widely. "Ahmed!"

She leaned forward, and her old friend kissed both of her cheeks before introducing his wife, Bridget.

"And this is my husband, Reid Simpson."

"We're so sorry we couldn't make it to the wedding," Bridget told her. "We were occupied with that lead you gave us. There were some underworld negotiations we had to clear up."

"Well, since King Dirar just arrived with Prince Mohtadi, I assume you took care of it."

Ahmed simply raised an eyebrow in silent answer as the king and prince made their way over to them. "Your Highnesses, King Dirar Ali Rahman and his wife, the Queen, along with his brother, Prince Mohtadi Ali Rahman and his wife, Danielle," Ahmed presented, turning to the royal family. "And this is Mallory Simpson and her husband, Reid. They were instrumental in gathering the intelligence to stop a most unfortunate incident."

King Dirar leaned forward and placed a kiss on each of her cheeks before shaking hands with Reid. "We are most grateful for your assistance," the king said, smiling. "You are welcome in Rahmi as our guest at any time."

"Thank you," Mallory said as she smiled at them.

The king and queen left to make the rounds. Reid was trying to pry information about Mallory from Ahmed while Bridget laughed at them. The prince and his wife smiled at her and stepped closer.

"And I hear I have you to thank for saving my

husband," his wife said kindly.

"Your Highness . . ."

"Dani, please. And my husband prefers Mo."

"All right, Dani. It was my pleasure. Ahmed has told me how happy you have made your husband. I'm just glad you got your happily ever after."

Dani looked back and forth at her and Reid. "It looks like you did, too. It was a pleasure to meet you."

"Anytime you need my plane, it's yours," Mo said before sending her a wink. He held out his arm, and his wife slid her hand into it as Reid came to put his arm around Mallory's waist.

"They were nice," Reid said as they watched the royal family of Rahmi walk away.

"Yes, they are. I can't believe tonight is our last night here."

"I can't believe my mom is getting married next week," Reid said in mock dismay as he swept Mallory onto the dance floor.

"Troy is wonderful. They are so cute together. At least this wedding will be better than the last one we went to," Mallory shook her head remembering the nightmare.

"I still have nightmares of Aunt Flory wailing as Cousin Mary walked up the aisle. Not to mention the number of times she kissed Phillip. That man is a saint. However, have you noticed they've been hanging out at Mom's house more?"

"Thank goodness. It's good for them all. Mary has blossomed. I'm happy for her and Phillip."

"You know who I'm happy for?" Reid asked with a sly smile.

"Who?"

"Us. Now about that alcove . . ."

Mallory laughed as Reid grabbed her hand and hurried her from the room. She didn't need to meet any more royalty when she had her own prince ready to love her a little more every day.

The End

41782542R00164

Made in the USA
Lexington, KY
27 May 2015